Thirsty

A NOVEL

Thirsty

Kristin Bair O'Keeffe

SWALLOW PRESS ATHENS, OHIO

Swallow Press / Ohio University Press, Athens, Ohio 45701
www.ohioswallow.com

© 2009 by Kristin Bair O'Keeffe

This book is a work of fiction and, except in the case of historical fact,
   any resemblance to actual persons, living or dead, is purely coincidental.

To obtain permission to quote, reprint, or otherwise reproduce or
   distribute material from Swallow Press / Ohio University Press
   publications, please contact our rights and permissions department
   at (740) 593-1154 or (740) 593-4536 (fax).

Printed in the United States of America
Swallow Press / Ohio University Press books are printed on acid-free
   paper ⊗ ™

16 15 14 13 12 11 10 09   5 4 3 2 1

Library of Congress Cataloging-in-Publication Data

Bair O'Keeffe, Kristin, 1966–
  Thirsty : a novel / Kristin Bair O'Keeffe.
     p. cm.
  ISBN 978-0-8040-1123-5 (alk. paper)
  1. Croats—Pennsylvania—Fiction. 2. Women immigrants—
  Pennsylvania—Fiction. 3. Marital violence—Fiction. 4. Domestic
  fiction. I. Title.
  PS3602.A564T47 2009
  813'.6—dc22

                              2009024324

*F*or my mom

grandmothers

sisters

daughter

and

women all around the world

Life shrinks or expands in proportion to one's courage.

—Anaïs Nin

Acknowledgments

This book and I have traveled far together, and I am most grateful to everyone who accompanied us on the journey. A hearty thank you goes out to . . .

My grandfather, Steve Gecan, who worked in Pittsburgh's steel mills all his life, and my grandmother, Catherine Gecan, who made the best stuffed cabbage on either side of the Monongahela River. It was from their back porch that I watched the smokestacks flame and sputter and got inspired to write about the steelmaking milieu.

My parents, Peg and Jim Bair, for toting me to the library once a week as a kid, introducing me to Dr. Seuss, and listening to my crazy stories every night at dinner.

Traci, Nancy, and Amy, the three greatest sisters in the world who cheer me on, laugh at my tales of adventure, always believe, and would, without a doubt, push me from the path of a runaway train.

Christina Katz, dear friend and pillar of support, who has been chanting "go, go, go" since the day I wrote the very first scene.

Randy Albers, teacher and friend extraordinaire, who offered invaluable guidance on the early drafts.

Iva Jukic for her translation prowess, for chuckling at my affinity for "Marijana" and other old Croatian folk songs, and for keeping my Croatian connection alive.

The Fiction Writing Department at Columbia College Chicago.

David Sanders at Swallow Press for seeing, believing, and putting his keen eye to the manuscript.

My agent, Taryn Fagerness, for her support and enthusiasm.

My husband, Andrew, who rarely grumbles when I wake up in the morning, whisper "Sshhh, I'm in writer head," and disappear into my office.

My daughter, Tulliver, for being the world's most sparkly soul.

And finally, thanks to the big, beautiful universe for continuing to surprise and delight me.

1883

In the beginning, Drago smelled of dirt and bloom, the odor that would rise if you peeled the earth back at its seams. When he appeared on the doorstep of her father's farm-house in Croatia on the first anniversary of her mother's death, Klara was sixteen and grateful that the mourning period for her mother had finally ended. At sunrise that very day, for the first time in a year, she had put on the pale green skirt that lit her eyes instead of the black one that highlighted only her grief. But even so, she was still encumbered with the care of five little ones who clung like spiders to her, so that when Drago knocked and she opened the door, she looked more like the three-headed, seven-limbed monster that was fabled to live among the haystacks in the fields than an almost beautiful girl on a farm. The littlest child was wrapped around her neck, fingers clawed deep into the skin, and the eldest crawled up her back like a lizard. The remaining three hung at odd angles—upside-down and sideways—from her arms and legs. Only the littlest one was quiet; the rest cackled and shrieked and giggled.

At the sight of such frenzy, another stranger might have turned to run, but Klara had just baked a rhubarb pie and its scent kept Drago on the stoop. While he watched from the doorway, she pulled the pie from the stove, set it on the sill to cool, and stepped out to meet him, all with five little ones still dancing on her. The juices from the baked rhubarb ran down her arm, and as she looked at Drago for the first time, Klara licked her fingers clean. Close up, his full, rich odor blended with the scent of pie and filled her nostrils. Though he was dusty and road-worn, he had clear blue eyes, a strong jaw, and muscled shoulders. He carried a leather satchel and one small traveler's bag.

"Zdravo," she said. Though many travelers had stood in that very place, this man was surely the most handsome of all. Klara's stomach twisted into a funny knot, and a burning heat spread across her chest.

"Hello," Drago answered. He smiled and looked into her eyes. They were odd, but beautiful—green like the skin of a grape just before picking. Bright and luscious.

"Who are you?" Klara asked.

"Drago Bozic."

"Gdje ideš?" she asked, nodding to the traveler's bag.

"To America," he said. "Would you like to come?"

Klara's heart jumped, and although she didn't answer his question directly, she smiled. *Ameriku.* This man was going to *Ameriku.*

After a moment of silence that was thickened with more expectation and hope than she'd ever allowed herself, Klara looked past Drago to the rolling meadows beyond. A few houses were scattered in small clumps between the stoop and the horizon. Otherwise, she could see only apple orchards and fields of wheat and rye. She had lived in this village her entire life and had rarely traveled beyond its borders. Whenever she'd pointed to the road that led away from the village and asked, "Where does this go?" her father had said, "To trouble and back." And her mother had always agreed. Though Klara knew better than to answer back as a child, she'd never believed them. She'd let their answers drift far away and instead turned to her dreams for inspiration. In them, she saw that the world beyond was magnificent.

Klara looked at Drago again. "Would you like to come in?" she asked.

He nodded and stepped into the house.

After settling the children into their beds for a nap, Klara settled Drago at the table. Over a bowl of piping-hot potato soup and a slice of still-warm rhubarb pie, she invited him to rest with her family for a few days. As their home stood at a crossroads between the inland villages and the Adriatic Sea, her mother had often offered the same hospitality to passing travelers. It wasn't unusual to have a newlywed couple or even a family of four or five spend a few nights in the barn with the cows and horses for company. Once a family of fourteen had rested there for four days: a mother, a father, six children, three aunts, two uncles, and an ancient grandmother who had told Klara stories about traveling by boat. For many nights after, Klara had dreamed of waves.

Shortly after Drago agreed to stay, Klara boiled several buckets of water over the fire and poured a steaming bath for him. She stirred lavender into the water with a wooden paddle and then rubbed a few drops onto her wrists and neck. While she waited outside the door for him to undress, she thought about America. In that moment, she realized that all her life she had been waiting to leave this little village. Ever since she'd been old enough to read the letters that arrived from travelers who had stayed a few days on their farm, she had longed to follow them. She'd carried their letters to the swing under the apple tree or to a quiet corner in the barn and read each one over and over until the pages were worn through and tattered. This one told about the jungle-like forests and ferocious animals. That one told of fashionable cities, fancy shoe stores, silk stockings, and high tea. Though she'd never admitted it out loud, each letter had lured her farther and farther from her home, and the urge to go had been especially acute since her mother's death.

When Drago was appropriately submerged in the tub, Klara entered the room. The air was thick and foggy with lavender steam that gathered in small droplets on her lips and forehead. Her heart was pounding and her arms and legs felt as if they might give and fold. She looked at Drago's bare chest and smiled shyly. Though she had seen her older brothers naked from time to time, this was something different.

"*Bok,*" he said. This time his greeting was informal, almost intimate.

Klara smiled. "Hello," she answered, then she dipped a pitcher into the bath and poured the water slowly over his head.

"I haven't been bathed since I was a boy," he said.

Klara ran her fingers through his hair to push water to the roots. "And I have never bathed anyone but the children and me."

Drago stretched his arms out to let them float on the surface of the water, and Klara soaped them and rubbed them with her hands. The long sinews of muscle in his forearms loosened under her fingers.

She scrubbed his back and then wrapped her arms around him from behind to wash his chest. He made a quiet sound as she rubbed the soap in circles on his stomach, drifting for just a moment below the surface of the water. When she paused, enjoying the feel of his body, he let his head fall back against her chest. They stayed like that for a long minute, and when she finally stood and looked down, Klara saw that a wet spot in the shape of Drago's head was imprinted on her blouse.

Of course, she knew that bathing this man was a strange and premature adventure. If one of her older brothers had come in from the fields, she would have been chased from the room like a child, eternally chastised and bereft of this opportunity. If her father had come in for a cup of hot coffee, he would have beaten her silly. But despite her desire to venture out on her own and explore the world she had seen in her dreams, Klara knew that her only chance at escape from life in this village was a man. Otherwise, her father would never let her go.

So despite the danger of the encounter, Klara finished her task and left Drago to dry and dress. By the time company arrived, he was spit-shined and pressed, full of charm and stories.

When Klara woke the next morning, a raw wind was blowing through the village. It carried off everything that wasn't tacked down: wheat chaff, fallen leaves, Stjepan Levak's lost cap, a ball of fishing line from the river's edge, corks, school papers, and apple cores. It opened shutters and closed them again. It whipped Mrs. Rakovic's skirt above her head and moved a team of horses from one side of a field to the other. That mighty wind even lifted old Widow Zlata right off the ground as she walked down the path to milk the cows. The story later went that if her mind had been as withered as her body, she might not have thought quickly enough to grab onto a tree limb on her way up and might have traveled all the way to the moon.

Like a lost animal, the wind roared and whistled, and despite the fact that they didn't bring rain for a few days, thick gray clouds gathered overhead. Life was changing; Klara sensed it. God had knocked on her door and offered an answer to her prayers, and although she was surprised to discover he had dropped that answer at her doorstep in the shape of a man, she recognized it immediately. "Appreciate a good thing," she'd heard her mother say whenever one of the children complained. "God never delivers in the way we expect him to." So after washing her face and hands, Klara decided to heed her mother's words, and for emphasis, sprinkled lavender water in the space between her breasts and pinned her hair back so that long ringlets framed her face.

After breakfast, when Klara's father and older brothers had gone to the fields and the little ones were settled in the corner with blocks and dolls, Drago sat down with Klara in front of the fire. Weather darkened the room, and shadows played as if it were nighttime.

"Imam poklon za tebe," he said.

"A present?" Klara leaned forward. "For me?"

Drago reached into his pocket and pulled out a miniature horse that he had carved from a light, yellowy wood. It was shaped so that its mane and tail stretched far behind, as if the horse were caught in a swift gallop. He handed it to Klara, and immediately she saw that he had talented hands. The details were finely wrought.

"My youngest brother," he told her, "the one all the girls say was most handsome, was sliced in half last year by a piece of farm machinery. I found him in the field at dusk."

Klara glanced from the horse to Drago's face.

"We don't know how it happened," he continued. "He was alone. My mother was so distraught that she made us bury him in two sawed-off coffins—one for his upper half and one for his lower—set side by side in an extra-wide grave."

Klara didn't know what to make of this story. She felt Drago was telling her something important, something that spoke to the deepest part of his soul, but she didn't know what to do with it. She leaned across the table and covered his hands with hers. She had expected them to be rough, but instead found them to be rather soft, with raised scars here and there. Once again, that lovely heat spread across her chest.

The next morning, the wind had subsided a bit, and Klara asked Drago to walk with her through the pear orchard. They held hands under the gnarled, knotted limbs, and when they paused, Drago gave her another carving. This time, a wolf. It was made from a hard, dark wood, and the jaws and teeth were quite obviously over-pronounced. When she held it, a shiver shot up Klara's spine.

"My oldest brother, Josip, is a son of a bitch," Drago said.

Klara winced when he cursed. *Kurvin sin.* Son of a bitch. She'd heard such language from boys in town who gathered outside the general shop practicing their manhood, and from her father, who was rough and cruel and full of language she would like to forget. To ease the sting, she watched a fish leap from the river. His shiny back split the water.

"He's fleshy, my brother, covered with hair like a boar," Drago continued.

"Where is he now?" Klara asked, as the fish completed its flight and disappeared below the river's skin.

"He and his wife run the family farm. They have four boys and all the profits." As he spoke, Drago's voice grew thick with disdain and envy. His eyes darkened and his jaw clenched. Klara felt her stomach tighten and she wanted to run, but instead she leaned over and kissed him. The kiss was brief, but startling. When she pulled back, Klara covered her mouth with her hand and looked at the ground. Drago smiled. The darkness passed.

That night, the family gathered for dinner. At first, Klara's father was happy to have the stranger among them. He poured whiskey and offered a pipe. It wasn't until he saw Drago place a hand on the small of Klara's back that he realized it would be this man who took his daughter from him. And while his first reaction was anger, he remembered the widow from the next village over who had shown interest in becoming a wife. As long as he had someone to raise his children into farmhands, he was content. So he sat back in his chair, happy to be getting rid of a whiny, hungry mouth, and let fate run its course.

Finally, on the third day of Drago's visit, as a much-needed rainstorm burst overhead, Drago gave Klara an owl the color of dried cherries. "The owl has nothing to do with death as the gypsies would have you believe," he told her. "The owl is watchful and wise."

"It's my favorite," she said, turning it over in her hands. "Tell me about the brother you left out. You mentioned a third. What's his name?"

"Janko," Drago said. He smiled. "He is closest to me in age and friendship. When we were small, he protected me."

Klara relaxed. When Drago spoke of Janko, there was no sign of anger or darkness. He looked light and easy, as he had when she'd first opened the door of her home.

"Two years ago he went to America and settled in a town called Thirsty." Drago spoke slowly and pronounced the foreign names in English deliberately. He had worked hard to memorize each syllable. "Now he works in a mill where they make steel."

"*Čelik,*" Klara said. Steel.

"Hhhmm," Drago said. "Janko tells me in letters that the hills in this town are as steep and as lovely as those between your village and Zagreb." He turned in a complete circle, sweeping his arm in an upward arc. After a quick glance at Klara, who continued to study the fine details of the owl's awesome claws, he said, "Many of us," and he thumped his chest just once with a closed fist to indicate his fellow Croatians, "have already crossed and gathered in this town. Janko says there are many jobs."

Drago's lips twitched as he tried not to speak too ardently about America and a job on which Josip had no claim, but even so, Klara felt the urgency in him. His excitement was contagious, and once again, she felt that familiar longing to leave. She wasn't entirely comfortable with that urge, or any of the others she'd been feeling since Drago's arrival, so she was grateful that the owl gave her something to focus on.

The carvings and the stories were small presents. There were no jewels or fine dresses or bottles of perfume. But since the only significant gift Klara had ever received was the gold cross that hung around her neck—a present from her grandmother on the day she was born—Drago's earnest offerings quickly won whatever small places of her heart she had not already turned over to him on the stoop or in the bath. A few moments later, when he proposed marriage, Klara readily accepted.

They married the following Sunday in the village church and then crossed the ocean by ship. Though from the moment they climbed on board, Klara wanted to stand on the deck and watch the world change, she couldn't wait to get to their tiny cabin where she could be alone with Drago for the first time. The tension and heat that had begun to build during Drago's bath had mounted in the ensuing days, so when they'd finally stowed their luggage and retreated into privacy, Klara felt brave enough to peel off her clothes and stand naked in front of him. She didn't know what she expected, but what followed was even better. Drago smiled, tucked a loose curl behind her ear, and kissed her. They climbed into the berth and let the waves buoy them up and down for many days.

After the long journey at sea, they landed and traveled the new continent by horse and wagon driven by a man with one arm. When their journey was nearly over, they paused under a canopy of maple trees just a few miles from Thirsty. Here they unloaded from the hired man's wagon, rented a mule and hitch, piled their belongings high in the bed, and continued on. As soon as they were alone, Klara bowed her head and began to cry. She had expected to settle in a lovely place, like home, where gardens and green meadows and flowering orchards stretched as far as she could see.

A place where small villages were cast across the land like beans from a turned bowl. The letters that she'd read from travelers had described many lands just like that, but a mill town was something she hadn't foreseen in her dreams of a magnificent world.

The colors themselves were strange and unfamiliar—blacks, grays, and putrid yellow smeared like rancid butter across the sky. It was as if the entire town were in mourning. The tall stacks of the mills spit smoke so thick she couldn't see to the other side of the river. Along the muddy road, buggies, wagons, horses, cows, children, garbage, and chickens littered the path. As Drago prodded the mule forward, they passed boardinghouses and tenements, saloons and butcher shops. Drunks leaned against posts and slept against shop stoops; a man at the corner played a tambourine and sang while a small boy danced; a few beggars followed the wagon calling for coins; and women Klara knew to be prostitutes leaned their fat breasts on banisters and hollered out to passers-by. As she looked around, Klara thought about her brothers who had warned her against traveling so far from home. Then she remembered something her mother had said many times throughout her life. "We all die many deaths."

Though Drago looked as startled and out of place as Klara, he was determined to go on. "Wipe your tears," he said, then flicked the reins to move the mule. His voice was thick again, and Klara heard the same tension she'd sensed when he'd told her the story of Josip. A small bubble of fear burst in her.

"*Želim ići kući,*" she said.

"You are home, lady. This is your home now. There is no going back."

Klara closed her eyes. She tried to block out the scene and pretend that the one-armed man had delivered them to an exotic land where women were draped in silk and the trees hung heavy with fruit. But even before she could pull up the flavor of the fruit in her mouth, Drago slapped her hard on the knee with his knuckles. Her eyes flew open, and she pressed her hand against the sting.

"Why did you do that?" she asked. "It hurt."

"Lady, stop your whining and open your eyes," he said and gripped her wrist hard. The more she struggled, the tighter he gripped, until it felt as if her bone would snap.

He stopped the mule and stared at her. When she finally quieted, he loosened his grip, knuckle-slapped her again, and said, "Like I said, you are home. No use hiding from it now."

In the silence that followed, Klara stared into the folds of her skirt, feeling the bruise on her knee blossom into a deep purple peony. Though she'd often watched her father strike her mother and had even nursed her own wounds from his ready hand, she'd intended to leave all that behind. When she realized that she hadn't, anger swelled in her belly. But when it threatened to surge up and out of her, she swallowed it hard. Instead she listened to the sounds of the mill—rhythmic pounding, screeching, hollering, all of it echoing up and off the hills like thunder.

They climbed the road that wound its way up the steep hills to Thirsty, and when they reached the top, Klara breathed a small sigh of relief. Though it certainly didn't look anything like home, corn rose on the left and sunflowers stood tall on the right. Yes, all the greens and yellows had been dusted to a dull gray with soot from the mill, but it was something.

Thankfully, too, there was Katherine. Katherine Zupanovic. When Klara and Drago pulled up to their new home—one that Drago's brother had rented for them—she was sitting on her front porch, right next door, no more than spitting distance away. It was hot, and Katherine was wearing a knee-length cotton slip, with scallops of lace trimming the swollen top-curve of her breasts. Her legs were propped on the railing; she held a cigar in one hand and a bottle of beer in the other. After taking a look at Klara, who was layered in petticoats and ankle-length skirts, she let out a long, low whistle.

"Honey-girl," she said, "you best get on over here and let my Jake help your husband finish that work. You'll drop dead in this heat shrouded up like that, looking like a nun hiding from a priest in the abbey." Then she tossed back her head and laughed louder than Klara had ever heard a woman laugh. The sound of it reminded Klara of a sick horse her father had had years back. The old nag had snorted just like that for days, then died in the barn, legs poking straight up toward heaven.

From that moment on, Drago despised Katherine, and Klara loved her desperately.

In the middle of the nineteenth century, at a time when a stout rotten-egg stench billowed up out of the steel mills and coated the earth, sinking fingers and toes into skinny places between houses, Thirsty was carved into the steep slopes above the Monongahela River. It was just outside the city of Pittsburgh in the southwest corner of Pennsylvania, and although on the map, the town was called Pleasant Slopes, its residents—mostly immigrants from eastern and southern Europe—called it Thirsty.

While most mill towns were perched on sheer slopes, Thirsty was built on a terrace, with several hundred acres of scruffy farmland surrounding it. One precipitous, winding road connected it to the river valley below, but because gravel, mud, waste, and discarded odds and ends often washed down the hill during rainstorms and gathered in unmanageable piles in the crooks and coils of the snaking road, men heading to and from their shifts in the mills chose to trample footpaths through the dense forest of straight-backed pines and leafy maples.

Not many outsiders had cause to visit Thirsty back then, but every ten years a neatly pressed census-taker from the government bureau would climb the hill for a head count, trying to figure how many lost and how many gained. When he finally made it to Thirsty, sweat-soaked and panting, he always glimpsed a few pale-skinned, dark-browed Croat women huddled on a stoop, brooms gripped in raw-knuckled hands, babies cradled on their hips. He would stand there, on the edge of their lives, shifting his weight from one foot to the other while soot gathered in the folds of his shirt and smeared his spit-shined shoes. And the women, who rarely saw the cut of a man's face in the daylight unless he was crawling from bed for the next shift or stumbling from the chilled darkness of Penny's Saloon, would cock their heads and squint their eyes, trying to place him in their world. They would wonder over him, this short-winded, sugar-bellied man who bore no resemblance to their own lean-muscled, taut-jawed men who stood with their weight planted evenly on both feet. But even so, they always smiled and opened their circle to him. And he, mistakenly thinking them not so different from his own wife and her hen friends on the stoop of their cool valley home, missed the gravity lining their smiles. He missed the longing in their eyes, not knowing which had lost their husbands in mill accidents and which wished they had.

On the backs of these solid-footed men, steel magnates had built up their mills until they stretched like great fire-breathing dragons along the banks of the Allegheny and Monongahela rivers, all the way to the point where the two meet to form the Ohio, and beyond. The platforms and furnaces, ladders and ladles, railroad tracks, sheds, columns, and smokestacks were strung together like the bones of a massive metal skeleton. In these places, the air boiled, heavy with soot. Flames lapped, sparks skittered, and a single dissonant note was drawn out over space and time. It spread between the banks of the rivers—the clanging of metal on metal, the slur of shovel-heads into slag, the screech of train cars pulling in and out, the grind of wheelbarrows, saws, and chains—sound that shook the earth from water's edge to highest peak.

Intoxicated by the exchange of hot metal for money, mill owners ignored the filthy falling-down towns that littered the mountainside like abandoned bird nests. They settled their own families in the gently sloping valleys where water was easily pumped from fresh springs to fill their bathtubs and porcelains pitchers, while mill families had barely enough water to boil an egg. Back then, the City Council Water Commission laid pipe according to how much potential tax revenue the residents of any given town offered, so it wasn't until well after the turn of the twentieth century that ditches were dug for pipes and pumps in Thirsty. Each morning, until that time, as the sun crept unwillingly into the yellow marbled sky, the women trudged to the pump at the base of the steepest hill and lugged buckets of water, slung on yokes over their shoulders, back to their kitchens and alleyways.

The Bozics' house was plain. A squat, gray box in a line of squat, gray boxes, houses built out of necessity, not love. But despite its shape and color, Klara saw that the house had potential. There was a kitchen, a living and dining area with a large fireplace, and three small rooms upstairs for sleeping. There was even a cellar and a small crawlspace above the second floor for storage. Katherine and Jake's house was on one side, so close the women could pass a cup of polenta from kitchen window to kitchen window. On the other side and behind were a garden and a small copse of fruit trees. While Drago and Jake unpacked, Katherine pointed to the house across the way, a ramshackle shed with planks patched over holes and a leaning roofline.

"That's Tiny's house," she said. "He's been a bitter, coarse man since his wife died ten years back. Stay clear of him."

The new house was much larger than the one Klara had grown up in, but since the last tenants had packed their belongings and left the house clean and bare, it didn't have the markings of a home yet. That will come, Klara thought, and in spite of her trepidations, she considered her blessings. She would no longer have six brothers sleeping in the room next door; the garden offered promise with hard work; and already she'd made a friend.

As she walked up the stairs for the first time, Klara noted the creak on the third step. She thought about Drago's behavior in the wagon when she cried. Any tenderness he'd shown throughout their brief time together in Croatia and on the boat had nearly disappeared. She was looking out the window in the second bedroom when she realized she'd married a man just like her father, and just like her father, she'd have to watch Drago now. She would have to be on guard. Though she'd come into this marriage wide open, already she found herself closing slowly, like a honeysuckle bloom in the afternoon sun.

Despite Drago's protests, custom called for a welcome party the next day.

"I don't even have a job yet," Drago complained when he heard the news. "And the journey wore me out."

"I don't think it's up to us," Klara said. "Your brother will be there. I want to meet him."

"You can meet him quietly. We don't need a party for that." Drago's voice was thick again.

"It's not up to us," Klara repeated, and then she left him alone in the kitchen. Though she didn't like the fluctuations of his temperament, Klara was quickly becoming accustomed to them.

The night before, they had slept on a straw mattress on the floor of the bedroom. The fires of the smokestacks had lit the room so brightly it might have been noontime. Klara had wanted to fall into a heavy sleep and dream about home, but instead she had spent the entire night listening to the sounds of the mill and watching shadows move about on the walls. Drago had snored, and this surprised her. He hadn't snored on the boat or in the small rooming houses they'd stayed in along the way. She'd stared at him while he slept, studied his chin and the taut expression on his face. Even in sleep, he looked stern. Had she noticed this on the doorstep of her father's house? Had she missed it?

The next morning, Katherine overheard Drago's protests through her kitchen window, but she ignored them. She cooked all morning, and at noontime, Klara found her covered head to foot in flour and breadcrumbs.

"*Dozvolite da vam pomognem,*" she insisted, reaching for a pan, ready to help.

"*Ne, ti sjedi,*" Katherine said. "You sit." And she pointed to a soft-cushioned chair in the corner. "Long journeys call for rest, not work. You've got years ahead for that."

In a final attempt to put an end to the party plans, Drago stomped about on Katherine's porch and raised his fist. Katherine laughed, but Klara stood back and watched from behind a door. After a bit, Jake took charge. He grasped Drago by the arm and walked him down the road to the mill, with a promise to stop at Penny's Saloon for a beer and a hand of cards on the way home. Jake was a bear of a man—tall, broad, hairy, and strong. But he was gentle, too, and when he first met Klara, he had shaken her hand and leaned in to give her a light kiss on the cheek.

After they disappeared over the crest of the hill, Klara stood at the back door of Katherine's kitchen and stared at the smokestacks that rose up out of the river valley like tree trunks stripped of their leaves and life.

"Do they ever stop?" she asked.

Katherine was busy making custard. "Does what ever stop?" she said.

"The smokestacks."

"Do they ever stop what?"

"Do they ever stop steaming, smoking, spitting?"

"The stacks?" Katherine laughed. "Oh, every once in a while when the men go on strike, but usually they burn twenty-four hours a day, all year long. Not even a day off for Christmas or the Sabbath."

Klara looked beyond the smokestacks at the sky. It was mottled and yellowed. Repulsive.

"Even Sundays?" she said.

"Even Sundays," Katherine said.

No matter how long she considered people doing work on the Sabbath, Klara couldn't imagine it, even making steel, a material that seemed somehow sacred to these people. At home, with a never-ending haul of work to accomplish on the farm, most everyone was still and respectful on the Sabbath. Even the pigs. Klara lifted her nose like a hound seeking a scent and her eyes watered.

"What is that smell?" she asked. "All night it kept me awake."

"Rotten eggs," Katherine said. When Klara looked to the bowl of eggs on the table, Katherine caught herself and clarified. "The mill."

Klara shook her head and thought of home. There, ruddy apples weighed down the limbs of gnarled trees that had stood in the family orchard for centuries and thick-skinned grapes full of sweetness hung heavily on vines behind the house. Years before, her grandmother had tied a swing to the thickest branch of an apple tree, and if you pumped your legs hard enough, you could touch the leaves on the top of the tree with your toes. But Thirsty was different, separate, far away, farther away than she'd imagined. She wasn't sorry she'd left Croatia, but she wished she'd landed someplace other than this. She would be someone else in this place. She already was.

When things got too quiet, Katherine interrupted. "What is your mother like?" she asked.

"She died last year," Klara said. "She got sick on a Wednesday, a pain deep in her belly. Three Wednesdays later, my father dug a hole in the meadow behind our house, and we laid her in it."

Katherine wiped a bit of sugar from the rim of a bowl and licked her finger. "I'm sorry."

"Yes, it was hard. But even before that, my mother was busy with too many sons. I am the only girl, bound to service as soon as my closest brother was born. Second mother, he called me when he wanted to rile me. Because of the children, my mother was impatient, quick to anger. Once when Momma was feeding one of the little ones, I dropped a blue milk pitcher her mother had passed to her. Milk spilled, and the floor was covered with pale blue pieces of porcelain. When she heard the crash and saw what I had done, she came unraveled and slapped me in the face."

Katherine nodded. "And your father?"

"Oh, he's just a mean old man."

"Anything like your husband?"

"I didn't think so when I met Drago, but now I'm not so sure."

Katherine laughed. "You'll find out lots of things in these first few months. Some good. Some not so good."

"Is that how it worked for you and Jake?" Klara asked.

"Hhhmm. No, we've been married a long, long time now, and I still haven't found a not-so-good trait in Jake. But he's one of the rare ones. Most of them come troubled and rough."

Klara paused, wiped her finger along the edge of the sugared bowl like Katherine had, and licked it.

"Klara," Katherine said, "what did you dream about last night?"

The question stopped Klara short. She'd never thought of saying out loud the things she saw in her dreams. No one had ever asked.

At that moment, they heard voices. Drago's brother Janko, his wife Luisa, and their children arrived first. When they saw Klara, they hugged and kissed her. With Klara, Janko spoke Croatian, but because Luisa was a Spaniard, he spoke English with her and the children. The language was coarse against Klara's ears, and after a bit, she decided it sounded like the bumps and rattles of a wagon's wheels against a dirt road hardened by drought. She listened hard, knowing her survival in this place depended on her learning.

Soon after, Drago and Jake returned from the mill.

"Well?" Katherine asked.

"I begin working in three days," Drago said. He was high, giddy, already a little drunk, and his happiness was infectious. He picked up Klara at the waist and swung her like a bale of hay. Although his joy and attention seemed authentic, Klara resisted his touch. Something like fear pushed at her. Katherine, too, watched with caution. This man was no good, she believed. It was a deep feeling, and Katherine trusted deep feelings.

Then the party moved outside where it was cooler. The children raced through the cornstalks in Katherine's garden, and the grownups spoke of home. Luisa, whose black hair and olive skin shone bright under the fiery mill skies, sang a beautiful song in a language no one but she understood. The men drank heavily, and within a few hours, Drago was laughing at everything, even Katherine's stories. But his laughter wasn't light. It didn't float into the night sky with Klara's and Katherine's and Jake's. It buried itself in the ground, dug into the earth like a rat. When Klara touched his shoulder to bid him to come home, he turned on her. "Lady, leave me be. I'll be home when I'm home." He slapped her hand. When she stared and made a small sound of protest, he raised his hand to strike again. Janko turned away and toasted a friend, respecting the privacy of husband and wife, but Jake stood and shadowed Drago.

"I know you're new here, brother," he said, "and you're welcome. But you'll not strike your wife while I'm around."

"I don't know that it's any of your business what I do," Drago said.

"That's where you're wrong, friend. Now put your hand down."

Without answering, Drago lowered his hand, but not his eyes. Klara shivered. She pulled her shawl around her shoulders, nodded to Katherine and Luisa, then disappeared into the shadow of the great pine tree that separated the small yards.

It was with the first season of fruit that Klara would always equate the first time Drago struck her full in the face, taking her from whole to broken. The peach trees in their yard were stunted, long neglected by the previous tenant, and the peaches that year were small, hard knobs of pit that even the birds rejected. Unwilling to sacrifice a season of preserves, pies, and her favorite cobbler, Klara bought peaches from the shop in town owned and operated by BenJo, a Negro man. But this choice didn't come free of worry because from the beginning, Drago had forbidden her to even step into such a place.

"BenJo's a nigger," he said whenever the subject came up. "And we don't eat nigger fruit."

Before arriving in Thirsty, Klara didn't know any Negroes. She hadn't even seen a Negro until she landed in America. All she knew was what Drago told her about the ones who worked on his gang in the mill, *spooks* that talked in a language no good hunky understood. He called them all kinds of names that never felt quite right to Klara: *niggers, ghost-men, pickaninnies, slaves, jigaboos, jungle monkeys.* He said the women weren't any better than the men. "They're baby killers and thieves," he told her. "The daddies sell their own children for money and booze, and the womenfolk cast spells on anyone who wrongs them. Doers of evil," he said over and over, "and don't you forget it."

Klara didn't believe anyone could hand out such evil other than the devil himself so the temptation to disobey her husband was great. Even so, she was careful, and for days before stepping into the store, she made the journey to town to study BenJo. She hid behind wagon beds and passersby near his shop and poked her head up when she thought BenJo couldn't see her. From these vantage points, she watched him fill the bins in front of the store with plums and apples and oranges. She watched him sweep the stoop with a whisk broom. She even watched him bargain with a white man. Unknown to her was the fact that he was watching her, too, wondering why this pretty young white woman, with a husband already known to have Beelzebub's temper, was spying on him.

So while it might have been the need for peaches that got Klara to BenJo's stoop, it was curiosity that got her through the door. After all, he was the only black man in town who owned a store, and he was the only person anyone in Thirsty had ever known to be permanently bent over at the waist at a nearly perfect ninety-degree angle, as if someone had folded him over as a baby and gotten him stuck. Of course, Drago promised that such a frailty could only be the result of a spell cast by a wronged jigaboo woman, but because BenJo never told anyone but his wife how his curious angle came to be, no one knew for sure.

Once through the door, BenJo noted Klara's presence quietly and let her work be her own. For a good while, she stayed in the back, near the bins of vegetables lost in shadow. She wondered about the white women who talked so mightily to this bent-over Negro man, who took bundles of carrots out of his pink-palmed hands and shared stories as though they were old friends. It didn't make sense paired up with Drago's tales. That first time, Klara tried to keep her head low, but somewhere in the middle of filling her basket, BenJo walked right up to her. He lifted a peach from the bin, pushed it to his nose, and drew in a breath.

"This is how you pick a peach, Mrs. Bozic," he said.

She was surprised he knew her name. But she was even more surprised that his voice was so deep, so full of echo and shadow. It stopped her and made her listen.

"Fruit comes from the earth, like you and me," he said. He had a wide, flat nose, and his skin was black, black as the soot Drago carried home on his boots, but shinier, smoother, like a pleat of sky over her home village in Croatia. But as hard as she looked, she couldn't find a way into his face until he smiled and tapped a finger to the tip of his nose.

"This," he said, "this nose. My gift from the Almighty."

Klara shook her head, confused by the word *Almighty*. Her language skills were improving, but many words still brought her to a halt.

BenJo paused, then said, "My nose is a gift from God."

Klara smiled. She understood gifts from God, and in the years to come, she would become intimate with this particular one. She would depend on it for culling the finest produce from the stock when her own garden didn't provide. She would use it to help her figure out what was missing from yesterday's stew, carrying a few spoonfuls in a covered bowl all the way from her home to the shop. Over time, she and BenJo would share recipes for strudels and pies and homemade sausages, each one sending Drago into an angry roar. He made it clear that he would rather die than eat fruit or vegetables touched by BenJo's hands. Every time he bit into a pie, not knowing whether the fruit was from their garden or the shop, he would holler, "You best start getting your fruit at some other shop, lady! A spook can't be trusted."

When Klara left the store that first time, she obviously wasn't as comfortable with BenJo as the women who'd been shopping there for years, but their friendship had a definite beginning. She took the sack of peaches, shook BenJo's hand, and went home to make a pie.

News traveled fast in a mill town, and by the time Drago returned from his shift at the mill, he already knew about the origins of the pie. Without a word, he walked into the house, threw the pie out the back door into a mound of dirt, and punched Klara in the face like a first-class boxer taking down his opponent. There was no hesitation or restraint. His fist met her cheek clean on the bone, and she hit the floor hard.

"We're not eating nigger fruit," he said as he walked out the door.

A few minutes later, Katherine found Klara lying on the floor. "That son of a bitch," she said, tending to the cheek. "Jake will take care of this."

And as he would time and time again, Jake did. When he returned from the mill that night, he pinned Drago against the trunk of the pine tree until he confessed his crime, apologized, and promised not to hit his wife again. But like her mother's blue milk pitcher, Klara was already broken, and she knew her husband had made a promise he would never keep.

When the milkweed cottoned early that next year against Tiny's catawampus fence, caterpillars slumbering in their chrysalides woke too and got busy with their delicate transformation. Soon after, a swarm of yellow, red, and iridescent blue butterflies reigned over Thirsty. Numbed by the harsh winter, the people of Thirsty were dazzled by the dancing mosaic of color and the cadence of ten thousand pairs of wings. In fact, the drumfire caused such uproar in those devoted to the Christian faith, they decided that ten thousand angels had been sent by the Almighty to soothe their woes and brighten their landscape. It was a hopeful proposition, and when it was time for Sunday mass, so many parishioners flocked to St. Jude's that their weight fractured pews, and the magnificently carved wooden doors had to be removed from their hinges to allow the overflow to shift more easily. It was a mammoth church, worthy of such attention.

Father Tom, the keeper of St. Jude's, rejoiced at his good fortune. For years he had watched the gradual but steady diminishment of his congregation. More and more, folks were being drawn toward booze and carousing rather than to the word of God. As a learned man, he suspected the butterflies were merely a fluke of nature, but as a man of the cloth, he decided that he should treat the phenomenon as an act of God. In a gesture of his own faith, he threw away the collection of Latin prayers he had compiled over the years and recycled every few Sundays without the parishioners even noticing the repetition. Instead, he opened his Bible to the most poignant passages and spoke to the people from his heart in their common language—English.

On the first Sunday morning of the butterflies, Klara and Katherine sat in their regular pew near the back of the church and studied Father Tom. Before the arrival of the angels, he'd been rather subdued in his delivery of God's word. Boring, really. Each Sunday morning for the past year, Klara had watched him recite the Latin prayers quietly, with little emotion or expression. But now as he spoke, he waved his hands over his head and pounded the lectern with a clenched fist. With one eye, he watched the butterflies through the open doorway as they cut through rays of sunlight, and with the other, he watched his parishioners.

"I believe," he began that first Sunday morning, "that we, the people of this dreary town, have been blessed." He leaned forward and whispered, "Blessed, I say," then let out a whoop so vigorous it startled old Mrs. Babic and caused her to slip right out of the pew into the aisle on her bottom, and continued. "By sending these butterflies, these angels of mercy, God is saying out loud, out loud to you and me, take a look around you, people, see the beauty! Feel the beauty!" Father Tom's voice was hearty and full of spirit, much more characteristic of the black minister down the street whose church walls shook each Sunday morning with the blessing of the holy spirit than of the usual Catholic mass.

Every once in a while, Katherine leaned over and translated a few words for Klara. She was adamant that Klara learn to speak English. "You'll be even lonelier without the language," she promised.

Then halfway through the service, she nudged Klara in the ribs and rolled her eyes. "How did we ever live through those Latin prayers?" she said.

Klara laughed. Though mass was much more fun than usual, it seemed sacrilegious to be enjoying it so. She'd been taught to sit still—hands folded, head bowed—while listening to the Latin prayers she'd never understood, but this morning her heart lifted.

"Isn't God going to be mad?" she said, feeling guilt settle in her middle.

"God mad?" Katherine smoothed her hand over the Bible that lay in her lap. "No, God doesn't get mad, especially at things that bring people together."

While Klara moved that thought around in her head, she turned to watch the butterflies. In the sunlight, they looked like an undulating stained glass window, similar in color to the windows behind the altar, but ten thousand times more beautiful.

When the Vatican heard of the miracle taking place in Thirsty, a representative was sent from Rome to investigate the need for a papal visit. He was a small, buglike man with large ears and little hair who moved quickly and spasmodically. Right away he set to work recording the movements of the butterflies in a large, black book, sketching the shapes of their wings, listing the various color combinations, and attempting to count their actual number. For many days, he was seen running beneath the cloud of color with his head crooked at an uncomfortable angle, counting out loud and making small hatch marks in his book. It proved, of course, to be an impossible task, and after much agitation, he simply accepted the number offered by Father Tom— ten thousand.

When the representative boarded the train to begin his journey back to Rome, he gripped tightly to the black book full of angelic details and told the people of Thirsty that he had decided to recommend that the pope pay them a visit. The ladies of St. Jude's were so overwhelmed with excitement that they began preparations even before the train had pulled out of the station. In the coming weeks, houses were scrubbed from roof to stoop. Outhouses were torn down, filled in, and reconstructed on fresh ground. Children collected debris from street sides and alleyways. And in a desperate effort to protect Thirsty from the future effects of the mills' gaseous utterances, the ladies in the quilting bee set to work on an enormous tent that when completed would stretch over the entire town like a bubble. It was an absurd project at which both Klara and Katherine scoffed, but it was a noble one.

During the day, the butterflies whiffled around the milk-weed stalks and soared from one end of Thirsty to the other, never leaving the town limits, as if they recognized the boundaries set forth by city cartographers. At night, when the dew had set, all ten thousand returned to the great oak tree in the center of Thirsty. It was a massive, ancient tree with twisted limbs stretching in all directions. The butterflies settled along the branches, folded their wings together as if in prayer, and rested. It was only in these hours between dusk and dawn that the sky over Thirsty was still.

Few in town were unaffected by the tumult. The miraculous effects of the butterflies reached well beyond the church, and in fact, created such an overall flurry of goodwill that old grudges were forgiven and ancient rifts between families and friends were mended. The Korovcheks forgave the Hravics for cutting down the apple tree that had straddled their properties, and the Hravics forgave the Korovcheks for the ensuing twelve-year silence. Even Tiny gathered up his rusty tools and straightened his toppling fence posts for the first time in forty years.

As a girl, Klara had believed in all things invisible: witches, warlocks, fairies, trolls, goblins, ghosts, and spirits. On summer evenings, she had lingered at the lake near her home, hoping that the spirit of a child who had drowned there years before would appear and talk with her. She hadn't been afraid of anything. When her brothers hid in the barn and called to her in ghostly voices, she never ran or cried. She always waited, hoping that finally a true spirit had arrived to communicate with her. Instead, it was her father who taught her fear. He was rough and brash, and though he never struck the boys, he hit Klara's mother whenever dinner was a few minutes late or the weather damaged the crops. Klara was eleven when he turned his fist on her, and on that day, she'd stopped believing in most things other than God.

When the butterflies arrived, Klara was reminded of her girlhood and quickly opened herself to the possibility of marvel and miracle. Each morning after Drago left for the mill, she lay on her back under the cherry tree behind their house, waiting. Days passed, and one morning when she had nearly given up experiencing the power and angelic virtue of the butterflies, Klara went to the garden to work the clumps of dirt. It was a task she relished, one that returned her immediately to her home where, her mother had often told her, she had been carried in a basket as a baby from one row of greens to the next during the planting, growing, and harvesting seasons. "By the end of each day," her mother had often said, "you were blanketed by a layer of rich earth."

While Klara worked the dirt, she reminisced about that and other things. One moment, the sky stretched over her, gaseous and malodorous, and the sounds of the mill filled her ears. In the next moment, she heard the clamor of approaching drumbeats. She turned in that direction and saw the butterflies swarm around her, spinning and twirling like the colors and patterns of a kaleidoscope. As they passed overhead, she thought she heard them whisper, "Klara, look up! Klara, look up!" And when she did, their radiance against a rare spot of blue sky dizzied her. She flattened her palms against the earth to steady herself and then closed her eyes and stuck out her tongue to taste one of the creatures as if it were a snowflake. When she opened them again, she watched the butterflies dip and swoop, then round the corner of the house, and disappear. The drumfire of their beating wings softened until it was nothing more than a distant rumble.

Determined to finish the corner of the garden, Klara plunged her hands into the earth and separated the clumps of stiff dirt until her fingers ached. The butterflies left behind a peaceful calm that by evening turned into an oddly terrific drive for womanly things, something Klara found impossible to ignore and hadn't felt with such intensity since the boat trip from Croatia. Before Drago was due home from his shift, she bathed, washed her hair and pinned it up with ribbons, powdered and perfumed her breasts, danced a two-step while hanging out clean sheets on the line, and swished her hips when she walked until she caught sight of Katherine staring quizzically from her kitchen window. While the two women shared most secrets, Klara decided to keep this strange feeling to herself. She dove into a private chest of drawers in search of silky underthings, and not finding an appropriate camisole or slip, walked all the way to town for a pale blue nightgown and a jar of floral-scented cream.

When Drago walked into the house that evening, Klara called to him from the bedroom. Her voice was as low and gravelly as his had been when she'd poured a bath for him that first day they'd met. When he climbed the stairs and stood in the doorway, a little more than slightly drunk, Klara said, "I've been waiting for you." She stood, crooked a finger under his chin, and kissed him.

"What's this all about?" he said when she began to unbutton his shirt. "I haven't even cleaned up yet."

Klara continued working the buttons and said, "I want to make love," but really, she wanted to devour him. She wanted to take him in her mouth and roll her tongue over him, swallow him whole and hold him deep in her belly.

She removed her dress and petticoats, but forgot all about the new frilly nightgown hanging on the back of the chair in the corner. Without the layers of clothing, she looked much taller and thinner; her ribs poked out here and there, and her breasts were round and high. Without another word, she kissed Drago desperately without tenderness.

Each evening thereafter, until the death of the butterflies, Klara bathed and powdered. She met Drago after his shift at the peak of the hill and gripped his hand as she walked him home. If it were dark enough, she unbuttoned her blouse and slipped his hand onto her breasts. Once inside the house, she filled the tub with steaming water and herbs from the garden, fed him dinner spoon to mouth, then scrubbed the mill soot from him with a stiff brush. During these weeks, Klara's anger at having to live in such a dim, ugly town and at Drago for being so much like her father dissolved into the bath water. She smiled and reminisced about their beginnings. While his skin was still damp and fresh-smelling, they lay in bed—kissing, suckling, nibbling, and rubbing—then made love. Even Drago's fury subsided a bit during this time, and Klara went so far as to remove the three carved animals—horse, wolf, and owl—from a box in the back of a closet and set them on the windowsill.

As light was bending into dark on the final evening of this fragile truce, Klara followed Drago into the bedroom, sat down next to him on the bed, and leaned her head on his chest. She listened to his heartbeat blend with the faraway flutter of wings as the butterflies settled into the oak tree for the night. Drago leaned over and kissed her shoulder. His lips were rough.

"You are some woman, Klara Bozic," he said.

She leaned back into the pillow, spread her legs, and pulled him onto her. She could not believe that in these three weeks, the black bubble of anger and fear that had filled her belly had disappeared, and though she'd long ago lost her belief in fairies and goblins, she was delighted to discover that she still believed in angels. She wrapped her legs so tightly around her husband he could barely breathe, and by the time she fell asleep, the seed of their first child had been planted in her womb.

The next morning when Father Tom made his daily pilgrimage to the butterfly tree, he discovered nothing more than a dusty pile of colorful wings in the first stages of decay at the base of the great oak. Except for the customary rumblings of the mill, the sky was still and silent. For the next few days, until a brisk wind carried off the butterflies' remains, the people of Thirsty filed past the tree in sorrow. They recited rosaries and small prayers, lit candles, and left colorful bouquets of flowers nearby. Within a few weeks' time, the ladies of the quilting bee grew bored by the enormous tent project and returned to a more manageable bed cover. Klara was once again bitter toward her husband. Debris gathered in corners and along walkways. Attendance at St. Jude's fell off, though Father Tom continued to offer rousing sermons each Sunday, and the magnificently carved wooden doors were rehung on their hinges. And once word of the butterflies' passing reached Rome, the papal visit was, of course, canceled. The only remaining evidence of the angelic influence was Klara's belly, which continued to swell like a pumpkin on a vine until Halloween night.

It was too long since sunset for any of the afternoon's thin warmth to have lingered and much too cold to be naked in Klara's cellar, but it was Halloween. And despite the forces working against them—Klara's pregnancy and Drago's grumblings—the women were determined to retrieve a pumpkin from Old Man Rupert's field. They rubbed their gooseflesh and bent over the box of discarded clothes collected from friends and neighbors throughout the year, clothes that might otherwise have been dropped into the garbage bin or traded to the ragman.

Eight months pregnant, Klara had been feeling out of sorts all day. She was distracted and felt somewhat removed from the goings-on around her. Now as she stood in the cold cellar, she was suddenly dizzy and nauseated, lightheaded even. She straightened and pressed one hand against the wall, the other to her swollen middle. The belly was firm and round; her taut white skin gleamed in the candlelight and her navel poked out like a swollen lip. She let Katherine root through the box and listened to her exclaim over discovered treasures—a yellow-brimmed hat creased down the middle, a pair of overalls worn thin in the seat. The dizziness and the slow, pointed pain that accompanied it began to slip away as she took a few deep breaths. She caught her balance, and by the time Katherine stood, triumphantly holding two pairs of woolen long johns, two oddly shaped mill caps, and two long, black, moth-eaten capes, the discomfort had subsided. Instead of complaining, Klara smiled at her friend and the potential of the long johns to break the evening's chill. All this as Katherine studied the capes more closely and said, "I don't know who donated these to our cause, but thank you, Lord!" Then she looked up and noted the slight pinch of Klara's eyes and her hand pressed to her belly.

"You all right?" she said.

"Yes, I'm fine. Stop looking so worried. I'm just feeling the time pass is all." For months, Klara had been thinking about morning sickness, her expanding belly, and her swollen breasts, but now she thought of the child. Lost in her reverie, she imagined herself on a street corner in town, then in line at BenJo's shop, cradling the mite on her hip like she'd seen so many other mothers do. In her imaginings, she shifted her bags to accommodate the baby and smiled.

Struck by her friend's beauty in the candlelight, Katherine asked, "Has Drago ever told you how beautiful you look carrying a child?"

Klara stared at her. It took them both a moment to realize the absurdity of the question, and in that moment, the humor of it jerked Klara from her reverie. They laughed.

"Are we talking about the same Drago?" Klara whispered so that her voice wouldn't carry up the stairs. "*My* Drago?" She glanced down at herself, surprised as always by her swollen girth. She cupped a hand under each fat breast, bounced them up and down, and said, "But how could he not?"

That started them chuckling again, and their chuckles bubbled into raucous hoots until Drago thumped his boot on the ceiling to shush them. They smothered their laughter like schoolgirls.

"I believe these belonged the late Angelo Costello," Katherine said, pulling on the long johns. He'd been a heavy, gourd-shaped Italian butcher who had grown so fat at the end of his life, a special bed able to fit three times the normal-sized man had been constructed in his dining room, the only room in his house large enough to accommodate such an atrocity.

After they dressed, Klara and Katherine draped the capes around their shoulders and tied them at their necks. They smeared mud and soot on each other's faces. With their hair pulled tight and blackened mill caps set on their heads, they were nearly unrecognizable, even to each other, save for Klara's swollen belly. Without a word to Drago, they escaped up the steep, skinny flight of stairs that led directly from the cellar to the garden. Then they disappeared in the shadows.

The streets of Thirsty were busy with Halloween haunt-ings. Children in their parents' long, white nightshirts flitted from house to house, collecting cakes and apples in small sacks. Candles carried in hollowed-out pumpkins lit their faces. Older boys, dressed all in black, jumped from behind trees and buildings and wagon beds, hooting and hollering. The children and their mothers shrieked with fear and de-light. For over an hour, Klara and Katherine walked slowly through town, taking in the festivities. Then they climbed the great hill to Old Man Rupert's farm for a rest and a chance at his prize pumpkins.

"Hallelujah!" Katherine exclaimed, tilting her face to the night sky. She lifted her arms, palms up, as if delivering a sermon, and spoke in a voice loud enough for Klara to hear but not so loud as to draw the old man himself to the field, stinking of gin and raising hell. The October air was stiff, cool, and rich with the scent of decay, the pungency of roots and greens turning back into the earth.

"Heaven!" Katherine added. Her voice was rusty from making the steep climb.

"Heaven?" Klara said. She eased her belly to the ground and settled back against one of the largest pumpkins. "Nah, Katy, Heaven doesn't look anything like Thirsty, what with all this stink blowing around. Heaven must look exactly the opposite of Thirsty, everything Thirsty is not—a place where there are no smokestacks, no fires, and no soot."

"And no railroad cars clanging away all night!" Kather-ine added.

"No death whistle!"

"No mill widows!"

"No saloons!" Klara said, lifting her hand as if she were toasting with a jigger of whiskey. She pretended to swill it back, then wiped the back of her hand across her mouth.

"And no Drago!" Katherine added, and the two women hooted with laughter. From up there on Rupert's hill, they could see all the way down to the river, which wound through the valley like a black snake making its way through a furrow in the garden. It was sprinkled with the lights of boats and barges as they crawled through the water. The sky was orangish-black with streaks of green and gray, and a head of flames shot up from each smokestack. When they finished laughing, Katherine kneeled next to Klara and said, "You know, I still recall the sky over home as clear as I recall taking a piss this morning. Stretched out like a soft blanket, big enough to cover the whole earth and soft enough to curl up in, the sounds of cows telling stories after dark on nights when the moon was just a sliver of a penny." She paused and listened as a horse and cart trundled past on the road below, the rhythmic beat of hooves disappearing around the bend. "You know how my Jake says that those flames coming out of the stacks are our moon and stars?"

"Yeah," Klara said, "that man of yours is as crazy as you, Katy. He'll tell you anything to get you into bed."

"He doesn't have to tell me anything," Katherine said. "I'm already between the sheets waiting on him." They laughed again, and their laughs boiled into howls that echoed off the surrounding hills. Up there, so close to the sky, they could say anything. Their words lifted like clouds and drifted away before they had time to reach Drago's ears. Up there, Klara didn't have to fear his wrath.

"Ssshh!" Katherine whispered, holding a finger to her lips. "If we startle Old Man Rupert, he's going to head out here and have target practice with us before we make off with one of his pumpkins."

Klara turned and looked behind her at the house, set back away from the pumpkin patch. Like all the houses in Thirsty, it was constructed of plank-board, but it was much grander—three stories high with the roof coming to a sharp point in the middle and a stone chimney on each of three sides. "There's not a lamp lit anywhere in the house," she said. "All the windows are black." She turned to Katherine. "He's probably passed out in bed with a bottle in his hand."

"A bed? You think Old Man Rupert sleeps in a bed?" Katherine laughed, then leaned over and pressed her palm to Klara's swollen belly, waiting for the youngster to kick.

"What do you mean? If he doesn't sleep on a bed, where does he sleep?"

"On the floor, right on top of all the money he's got hidden under there. I imagine he lies down flat on his back with his rifle on one side and his shotgun on the other, just like they're his favorite ladies."

The women laughed again.

"What happened to his wives?" Klara asked. "I never saw the first one. She must have died before me and Drago moved here, but I remember seeing the second one down at BenJo's buying cucumbers or lettuce or something close to that. Leastways, I was told she was the second one. It's going on half a year now, and I haven't seen her since."

"Most likely she's buried in there with all his money. Bones and bills tucked up under the floorboards."

"You really think he's got money in there?"

"Oh, yes," Katherine said. "Everybody around here knows it. Lots of it, too. You don't know all the years he's been hoarding money from the poor folks in this town. People like us. Even Drago, who doesn't borrow anything from anyone, owed him a bit after that last bet got tarnished. And you know Rupert didn't share any with his first wife. Pennied her in life, then let her dry up and die, lonely as a sheep lost from its herd. And who knows where the second wife is. Hopefully back with her own people. Even money isn't worth that kind of living."

Klara looked down and saw that her long underwear was covered with bits of dirt and vine. The air was closer now to chilled with a light damp fog filling in the spaces around them, obscuring the mill just enough so that it took on a mystical quality. Its sounds seeped through like faraway music, not taking Klara's attention but floating somewhere on the periphery. The night air cracked against her teeth; she ran her tongue across to warm them. The women moved closer together until they were side by side, so that whispering was enough.

"Honey-girl," Katherine said, rubbing her hand on Klara's lower back, in that place that always hurt when carrying a load as big as a baby, "did I ever tell you about Amen?"

"Amen?"

"Yes, Amen."

"No, not that I recall."

Katherine smiled, laced her fingers together, and blew on her hands. She was the kind of storyteller that demanded an attentive audience, one she was sure wouldn't drift off somewhere in the middle. "Well, I have to tell you about Amen. Should have told you before but I guess there's a right time for everything."

Klara closed her eyes and let her mind follow Katherine's voice.

"You see, Klara, this is a story of creation. You know all about the book of Genesis, so I don't have to explain all the details, but after God got done creating land, seas, sunrise, sunset, moonbeams, dinosaurs, and coyote howls, she set to work on man and woman."

"She?" Klara said without opening her eyes. "You think God is a *she?*"

"Well, why not? Do you think God would have sent angels in the form of ten thousand butterflies to Thirsty if he were a man? No, a male God would have sent dogs or deer. Only a female God could have thought of butterflies."

"Hhmm," Klara said. It made sense put like that.

"Now, hush, and listen. Most of God's creations worked out well on earth. There was a little problem with dinosaurs, but She took care of that early on. Eventually, She got to thinking about men. She knew that men and women were on earth to stay; one couldn't get by very long without the other. But from what She saw from up there," Katherine paused and pointed to the sky, "men were causing a ruckus of trouble. Every time She looked down, some man was walloping a woman on the head or getting sly with somebody or, as in Old Man Rupert's case, hoarding hard-earned money from the poor folks. She decided the only way to fix it was to include men in every prayer Her angels offered up. And it was a good thought, too, because you and I both know how much men need to be prayed for. So God went to Her angels and asked for suggestions. It was a stumper, being that the angels weren't so pleased to begin with that God created a species so mixed up with trouble that it needed to be included in *every* prayer. But God is God, so the angels gave in and rubbed the tips of their wings together in thought."

Katherine paused. Klara was leaning on her, head tilted with her ear close, quiet in the way someone gets when what's being told matters to them and what's being told next matters even more. She continued.

"Finally, one angel said, 'We could just add *And this includes men!* at the end of every prayer.' God thought for a moment, slowly considering in the way God must, but after a few minutes, She shook her head. 'Right idea,' She told them, 'but too easy.' Besides, She didn't necessarily want men to know how much help from above they really needed.

"Then a second angel said, 'How about *Men, too?*' This was shorter, sweeter, and closer to what God had in mind, but still not quite right.

"Finally, God decided to let the angels sleep on it."

"Angels sleep?" Klara interrupted. She turned to look at Katherine.

"Well, sure, angels sleep. All that praying is exhausting work. Now hush, child, and listen. And tell that baby of yours to listen, too."

Klara leaned back in the field, one hand to her belly, until her head rested on a small pumpkin.

"Now the next morning, all the angels gathered around the sun, basking in its warmth, while God led the morning prayer. Their wings were smooth and soft; their halos glimmered in the sunlight. When the sky lit up as brightly as it possibly could, lots of pinks and yellows, like we used to see over home, God began. 'Let there be ample food and drink for all on earth!' She said. The angels bowed their heads, eyes closed, but God kept Her golden eyes open, one eye on Her angels and one eye on earth. 'Let there be joy,' She continued. She heard laughter and smiled. 'Let there be peace,' She said. But just as the words left Her mouth, She saw a man dragging a woman through a forest by the hair. The woman was bleeding from the mouth and crying up a storm. For a moment, God thought She was going to have to summon Noah again, all those tears. But as you know, God feels everything, and as that woman cried, God felt her pain. It was huge. And without thinking, God uttered out loud in despair, 'Aahh, Men,' and the angels, with their eyes still closed and believing Her utterance to be the new part of the prayer, repeated God's words . . . 'Aahh, Men.' It was quiet for a moment, and then God smiled. Another surprise discovery. It worked. 'Aahh, Men.' It was quick, didn't add much time or stress to the angels' toil, and men, if the utterance was given quickly enough, would never guess it was special for them."

Klara smiled.

"So thereafter, each and every prayer—whether said for giraffes to have longer necks or for the growing season to produce juicy peaches—ended with the simple 'Ah, Men.' Over time it got shortened to Amen, and ever since, men have been receiving special prayers they know nothing about. The good ones even say it themselves."

When Katherine finished her story, she laughed so hard her belly ached. Klara laughed, too, imagining Drago kneeling at Sunday mass, listening to the priest's prayer, and ending it, like all the other men in church, with *Amen.*

"Ahh, Men," she said out loud. She was having such a time, she didn't want it to end. After she dried the laughter tears from her cheeks, she rubbed the chill from her arms and said, "Do you have any more of that custard at the house?" She knew how much easier her night would be if she, and the baby, could listen a while longer to Katherine's stories. She looked at her friend, this heavy-thighed, wide-hipped woman with the strength and know-how to look Drago Bozic in the eye and tell him to mind his business.

"Ah, Klara-girl. You know I have more custard, but before we go, let's get one of these big pumpkins. I'll carry it home."

They moved to their knees and surveyed the pumpkins that lay closest to them. Klara tucked her hands under her belly to take some of the weight, and Katherine set a hand on her back to steady her. They were so deep in thought and story, repeating *Amen* over and over, chuckling, and trying to choose the pumpkin that would serve up the most delicious Halloween pie, they didn't even hear Old Man Rupert at first. He hollered for them to get out of his field, off his land. When she finally turned, Katherine's eyes popped wide. Old Man Rupert was running full speed in their direction with a rifle pumping up and down beside him. "You good-for-nothing hoodlums! I told you I'm going to shoot the first one I see!" He was screaming something awful, and every couple of yards, he came to a teetering halt and attempted to wedge the rifle against his shoulder. Klara and Katherine scrambled as best they could to get themselves on their feet and get moving. Once upright, they tried to balance

Klara's belly so they could race off down the hill, but it was just too big. They stumbled as the first shot cut through the fog and whizzed over their heads.

"Don't shoot, Mr. Rupert!" Klara screamed. Katherine lodged herself in front of Klara's belly and waved her arms wildly.

But Old Man Rupert was already in the pumpkin patch, and the only thing that Klara could figure was that he'd been sitting on the porch, just inside the shadows. He'd been silent, perhaps asleep or passed out for a while, and he must have come to when they rose to go.

A second shot whizzed by, closer this time, and Klara felt a sharp pain in her abdomen. She felt prickly and faint, and as the third shot cut the air, she grunted and fell back against the crackling vines. She stumbled on the pumpkins, knowing that she hadn't been hit, but that her water had broken and was spilling down her legs. The seat of the late Angelo Costello's long johns was soaked with it.

"Katy, the baby," she said. The crisp air was suddenly thick with soot, and Klara could taste the bitter burn of each individual flake as it landed on her tongue.

Katherine was angry now. She stood over Klara—legs spread, hands on her hips—and faced Old Man Rupert's attack head-on. "You stop there, old man, or I'll kill you myself!" she screamed.

Klara was already lying flat when Old Man Rupert got close enough to realize his error.

"Mrs. Zupanovic?" he said, slurring his words. "What are you doing in my field?" He leaned close, squinted his eyes, lowered the rifle, and teetered from the effects of liquor. He was a short man with a shaggy beard and trembling hands. Katherine could smell him five feet away, like a loaf of rum-sopped bread.

"Mr. Rupert, get yourself together and drop that gun. We've got to get Mrs. Bozic to your house. Then you have to go for a doctor. Do you hear me? Mrs. Bozic is on her way to giving birth."

Klara, though previously unacquainted with the pain of babies, knew instinctively that this one wasn't going to travel from the field to Mr. Rupert's house, then to her house to wait on a doctor, not while it was in her belly. She groaned and grabbed Katherine's hand. "Katy, we don't have time. The little one's coming now."

The next few minutes laced together like the silky strands of a spider's web. Katherine spread both capes beneath Klara and removed her long johns. Mr. Rupert removed his coat, which Katherine tucked under Klara's head, and his shirt, which Katherine draped over her. It was soft and warm, and smelled strongly of his sweat and the bottle. Katherine rolled up her sleeves and kneeled. When she realized that Mr. Rupert was still standing there gawking, she hollered at him to get help, but even before the moment when she could no longer hear his footsteps in the dried pumpkin vines, she was holding the head of Klara's baby girl in her hand.

"That's it, honey," she told Klara. "That's it."

A moment later the baby slid into the night and began crying without even a finger to clear her lungs of fluid. Though Klara begged to stop pushing, Katherine urged her on until the baby wrappings slid free, too. Such heat was coming from between Klara's legs that steam rose into the crisp night. Katherine held the baby there, warming it, and murmured Croatian lullabies, while they waited on Old Man Rupert to return with the doctor.

"Klara, are you all right?" Katherine asked.

Klara looked up and squeezed her knees together until she felt the baby's tiny fist flutter against her thigh. The sky spread behind Katherine like a variegated quilt, and all Klara could think was that if she felt stronger, she would reach right up and grab hold of its corners, which stretched out somewhere in faraway lands where other women of other colors and beliefs were lying on their backs in fields with babies warming between their legs, vines rustling, pumpkins looking on. If she felt just the slightest bit stronger, she could pull that sky down to cover all the women of the world, cover all that hurting, like a tent, a blanket, a second skin. Of all the moments she would someday forget, those too painful to study closely in the light of day, those that would just disintegrate into the folds of her mind, this would not be one of them. This she would remember forever.

"Sky," she said suddenly.

"What about it?" Katherine asked, lost in her own thoughts of motherhood many years before.

"Sky," Klara repeated. "My baby. I'm going to call my baby Sky."

In the years to come, Klara would enjoy the scent of dirt and bloom only on the days that Old Man Rupert came to wonder over Sky, this little being who had been birthed in his field, or when she visited BenJo's shop at the hour the farmers delivered fresh goods, when the scent was just strong enough to overthrow that of the mill. While she smelled of peach meat and yeast, blackberry jam and talcum, Drago now smelled of fire. The flames of the furnace had already tarnished his natural odor and devoured any others that had gathered about him during his youth. Folks might argue it was just the stench of the mill carried home with him, like a slip of steel in the sole of his boot or a hammerhead tucked in his pocket for fixing, but she knew that the white-hot smell of fire came from within. His original smell, the one that had drawn her to him when she'd opened the door of her father's house and discovered him on the stoop, had been seared from his soul. Even his sweat reeked of fire, and on occasions of sex when Klara buried her head into his chest and under his arms, she was so overwhelmed by the scent of flames that when it was done, she often felt she'd been singed.

1892

When the mill workers went on strike, Klara got a job. Like many women in Thirsty whose husbands were now temporarily unemployed and underfoot, she took cleaning work in a big house in the valley below. While the men stood fast and refused to cross picket lines, the women crossed mahogany thresholds into kitchens and dining rooms, Spanish-tiled bathrooms and carpeted verandahs.

On her first day of work, Klara left home just before first light, leaving Sky in Katherine's care for the day. The air was humid, but because the mills were quiet, the sky was strangely clear. At the bottom of the hill, she stopped at the well for a swallow of water, and then she took the path through the woods to Quill Street where the Stoughton family lived. Although she didn't know quite what to expect, Katherine had warned her that the Stoughtons were one of the wealthiest families in Pittsburgh, dining at night with the Mellons and the Carnegies. Along Quill Street, the houses were at least ten times larger than Klara's, twenty times larger than BenJo's. As Klara walked, she thought about possibility, about how easily, given the right dream or circumstance, it could have been she who lived in this blue house or that red brick one instead of in her own.

When she saw the address of the house where she was to work, Klara took a deep breath. As Katherine had predicted, the house was enormous, the largest on the block.

Windows lined the front like a hundred eyes, and nine chimneys rose from the roof in a line. The house was made of stone, light gray and dark gray stones fitted together in an intricate puzzle, and it reminded Klara of a cobblestone walk near her home in Croatia. Although it seemed impossible given its proximity to the mills, there was not a speck of soot to be seen. A Negro man in a gray uniform similar to the one Klara had been given by the service that hired her was already at work in the yard.

"Howdy," he called when Klara stopped and turned to face the stone house. "It's a little early in the morning to be lost down here. Might you be looking for something?"

Klara smiled. "Just looking for this house, I think. The service told me I'm due to begin working here today."

The man set the bucket and ladder he was carrying on the ground and walked to meet her. "Welcome," he said, holding out his hand. "I'm Jonah."

"Klara Bozic," Klara said, and she took his hand. "What are you doing out here before dawn?"

"I'm the stone man," he said. "I keep this house clean."

Klara looked at him quizzically.

He smiled and gestured with a broad sweep of his hand.

"I begin in the front," he told her, pulling a soft-bristled brush from his back pocket and holding it up. "I scrub the front, top to bottom, 'til it shines like a polished rock, not a spot of soot anywhere. Then I move my scaffolding to the side of the house, the side with bushes because that's the way Ma'am likes it, and I scrub some more. I do the same in the back and along the other side. By the time I find my way to the front again, soot has covered it like a funeral veil. Right off, I start cleaning. Been circling this house like that for ten years. Think I'd be dizzy by now."

Klara smiled and thought how odd it would be to have a hired man circling her house from morning 'til night, scrubbing the endless rain of soot from the cracks and crannies.

When she turned and began moving up the front walk to the house, Jonah called, "Missus Bozic?"

Klara paused and turned. "Yes?"

"You'll want to head around back. Help in the back . . . guests in the front. Way of the world, I suppose." He smiled as he gestured with the brush, then bent to return to his work.

Klara shook her head, but changed her direction. She'd never been asked to enter a home through the back door, and she felt suddenly hideous. After turning the corner and walking under an intricate trellis grown thick with vines and white flowers, she saw that the back entrance was much less grand than the front. Though the door was made of a deep red wood, there were no trees or flowers carved into it. The pillars that stood on either side were thick and sturdy, but plain. Even the bushes that grew around the base of the pillars seemed less green, more fragile. For a moment, the feeling of hideousness threatened to swallow her whole, but after catching a bit of blue sky between a chimney and the roofline, Klara forgave herself the feeling. She knocked, and after a moment, a black woman with stubby legs and a hump on the crest of her back opened the door and led her to the servants' receiving area. While she waited, Klara tied up her shoes.

After a few long minutes, Mrs. Stoughton came to meet her. She was a tall woman, with legs that seemed to stretch on forever, and she wore heeled shoes that sparkled. Her voice was high and thin, and the sound of it made Klara cringe.

"First," she began after eyeing Klara from top to bottom, "you will call me *Ma'am*. Second, you'll have to do a much better job of ironing that uniform before coming to work. But for now, come along." She moved through the doorway and down the hall toward the front of the house. She continued to talk as she gestured for Klara to follow. "You'll be responsible for keeping the great room and a good portion of the first-floor rooms spotless."

Despite the fact that Mrs. Stoughton clipped along at a brisk pace she never would have marked herself, Klara followed closely. She was awed by what she saw. In the front room, nearly everything was blue. Blue vases were lined up on the mantel, and blue flowers filled each vase. Blue velvet curtains hung from each window and draped like ball gowns. The carpet, thick and plush, was blue with speckles of gold here and there. Even the silk throw on the back of the blue couch was blue.

All Klara could think was that although it seemed like that much blue in one room should be nauseating, it was the most soothing thing she'd ever experienced. She would have stood there all day, just taking in the blue, but Ma'am put her to work immediately.

For the next few weeks while the mill sat quietly on the riverbank, Klara polished vases, wiped mahogany tables, beat dust from rugs in the backyard, and wiped fingerprints from fancy mirrors.

In addition, she quickly noticed the obvious: Ma'am and her husband treated Klara and the other servants as poorly as Drago treated blacks. To each other, the Stoughtons were kind and respectful; they spoke in hushed, formal tones. But when speaking to her, their tone turned dismissive and rude. Unless they were instructing, reprimanding, or lecturing her, Klara discovered, she was invisible to them. It was a new feeling for her. Anywhere she'd gone in her life, she'd been quite visible, even if it had been in a negative light. But here she could move about like a ghost. When Ma'am or her husband walked past her on the stairs, their eyes were on her, but she quickly learned that they saw right through her, as if she were made of glass.

When she arrived to work each morning, she hung her coat and her kerchief on a hook in the servants' room, and as expected, the servants saw her just fine. Jonah always smiled, waved, and called a cheery greeting from the ladder;

Constantine did the same from her post in the kitchen; even Bellows, who didn't greet anyone but who saw everything, took a fair liking to her and nodded ever so subtly when she walked by. But once she moved from the back rooms to the front rooms, Klara disappeared.

The first time she realized this, she was a week into the job and was walking slowly through the hallway that connected the living area to the dining area. It was a long skinny hall lined with paintings of fruit: bright lemons on a crimson tablecloth, blueberries in a bowl, apples scattered under a tree. Though she knew she shouldn't linger, she couldn't stop looking, and at the moment Ma'am entered the hallway, she was leaning quite close to the lemons, her nose nearly touching the canvas as if she might be able to smell them.

She heard Ma'am's footsteps just before Ma'am plowed into her. Klara hit the ground like a sack of potatoes.

"Klara?" Ma'am said, leaning to the floor to investigate what it was that had gotten in her way. "Where in the world did you come from?"

"Right here, Ma'am," Klara said, rubbing her elbow.

"Well, get on up from there and get to work. We don't have time for such folly," Ma'am said, and she was gone, sparkly heels tip-tapping in her wake.

The ability to disappear was a miraculous realization that gave Klara more freedom than she'd ever imagined. She learned to listen for the click of Ma'am's shoes, and until she heard the shoes, she often did as she pleased.

It was a feeling she began to enjoy. "I could be naked," she told Katherine one evening after returning from the Stoughton house. "I could walk through that house naked, and the only people who would pay heed would be the other servants. Ma'am and that man she calls a husband wouldn't even notice."

At night, after a long bloody battle with Drago, she'd lie in bed and imagine what it would be like if she could be invisible at home as well. She imagined Drago heading home from the pub at night, stumbling up the stairs for a go at her, but finding nothing in the bed, despite the fact that she was there, sleeping peacefully on her pillow. Her only fear then was that he would turn on Sky.

But becoming invisible was not the only strange occurrence brought on by the strike. There was the field of sunflowers that suddenly blossomed; the rumor of a love affair between Sam Turner and Rosa Willow; the unusual sight of falling stars in the night sky; and unfortunately, Jake's hiccups.

A few days after the mill went on strike, Jake got the hiccups. Not light, easy, hiccups that were bothersome but endurable, but hiccups that shook his body from toenail to hair follicle, earlobe to heel; and with each spasm, bones slammed against bones, vertebrae slid and crashed one against the other, and even his collarbone—broken as a child during a warned-against leap over a haystack—ached and throbbed. His ribcage swelled and bruised; his muscles seared with pain. Jake got hiccups the likes of which Thirsty had never seen.

The first hiccup erupted like a chortle, so close to laughter that Katherine, baking in the kitchen, mistook it for such. She glanced in the direction of the front stoop where through the doorframe she could see that her husband was indeed alone, without company or reading material. Odd, she thought, for although Jake enjoyed a solid joke and a well-told tale, and although his laughter came easily and often, he was not prone to private musings. She looked away, then glanced again, thinking for a moment that he might be going out of his head, then deciding that whatever was entertaining to him was his own. It was only after the fourth or fifth hiccup that she became curious enough to step from the kitchen to the stoop to find out more.

"What's this?" she asked, indicating her throat with her hand.

"Hm, don't know," he said. "Hiccups, I suppose."

"Hold your breath. You sound like an animal gone wrong."

Katherine turned and walked inside, but before the door settled in its frame, Jake hiccupped again, this time so aggressively that it jerked him into an upright position and made his eyes water. Katherine paused, returned to the doorway, and watched her husband struggle to regain his composure. The hiccups continued in this way; each great intake of breath and dramatic exhale of the same accompanied by a pig's squeak or a cat's cry. One hiccup sounded much like the warning bark of a cornered bear, and another reminded Katherine of the chittering call of chipmunks in the garden. With each hiccup Jake and Katherine believed that this must indeed be the last, as they knew of no cases that lasted longer than an hour or so. Throughout that first day, they kept to their usual routine, except for the fact that like all the men in Thirsty, Jake was not at the mill when it was time for his shift to begin.

On the second day, Jake and Katherine were truly confounded. Although Jake might have preferred to keep his condition private, Katherine was so concerned that neither her husband nor she would sleep peacefully again that she was quite pleased when the community got involved. Since the mill was closed, men who were not needed on the picket line had little to do. They spent their morning treading on their wives' clean floors and looking on with wonder as their children, who seemed so calm and well-behaved in the late evening, raced like heathens through and around their houses. When word spread that Jake had been halted by a critical case of the hiccups, his friends and co-workers, thankful for the diversion, bid good-bye to their wives—who were also thankful—and hurried to the Zupanovic house to offer much-needed assistance. Their tactics were not unique. A few hid behind trees and attempted to startle Jake into stillness when he walked outside to smoke a cigarette or look toward the smokestacks with curiosity. Fred Bartlett drew a knife to his throat; Frank Grskovic jumped him from behind and wrestled him to the ground; Brian O'Malley ran straight at him on a good-sized horse and only eased up and off to the right just before contact. Jake was dutifully startled by each of these events, but despite all efforts, he continued to convulse with hiccups. Throughout the afternoon, men brought home remedies mixed up by their wives and offered on plates, in bowls and bottles, under neatly pressed checkered napkins, and with specific directions—salt under the tongue, garlic and onions eaten in three massive bites, liver and onions consumed over an hour's time, a dollop of peppered lard in the left nostril, homebrewed moonshine chugged not sipped, an apple peel soaked in sugar and sucked on like hard candy, and so on, to no avail.

On the third day, Jake and Katherine at last believed the hiccups might go on forever and began to face the fact that they might even be the malady destined to remove Jake from the natural world. He looked horrid. With no sleep for two nights and three days, his body had conceded to exhaustion even deeper than the exhaustion he felt after a mill shift, which Jake had previously believed impossible. His skin thinned and sagged off his ribs, under his eyes and chin, from his thighs and calves, from his belly and buttocks, though Katherine was the sole witness to this final disgrace. Three upper teeth had cracked with the convulsions, and twice he'd bitten his tongue so hard it bled and swelled. His eyes, normally brown, were gray, and depending on whether he was in the middle of a hiccup or between one and the next, either crossed or rolling about in his head. His skin was the color of blanched wheat, and the hiccups had become so violent that his body had tensed in an effort to counteract itself, so it looked as if he were made of wood. He sat upright in a hard-backed dining chair, unable to participate in daily life.

The hiccups, coupled with the silence created by the strike, made for an unsettling atmosphere. Katherine and Klara summoned Father Tom to pray for Jake's recovery. The priest arrived quickly and said a few prayers, but after an hour was so overcome by sympathetic hiccups that he feared for his own existence and left the Zupanovics to homemade remedies. Katherine and Klara asked the librarian to read up on the history of hiccups. Mrs. Neddle was a nosy old woman who was happy to receive the assignment; it wasn't often that anyone asked anything of her, besides schoolchildren looking for simple readers or a teacher seeking the correct spelling of a seldom-used word. After scrounging through some ancient texts in the off-limits reading room near the back of the building, she discovered a book that made reference to a case in which the gentleman in question maintained the hiccups until his death, five years from the onset. As this was an ancient text, there were no accompanying pictures, but Jake and Katherine could well imagine the ravages five years of hiccups could exert on a man. This was not what they wanted to hear, so they chose to call the tale fiction and turned a closed ear to the anxious librarian.

Friends and neighbors continued to call, toting remedies from their home countries—poultices, nasty concoctions, and scare tactics that did little more than startle Jake from his hard-backed dining chair to the floor. But it wasn't until eight-year-old Sky pounded on the Zupanovics' door in the middle of the third night that Jake neared the end of his journey. Eight-year-old Sky tearing across the patch of dirt between her home and the Zupanovics', her feet bare, her head tied in a rose-colored kerchief, the tails of her nightgown flying behind her like bat wings, small fists pounding on the door, and the feeling of relief searing her body as she felt Jake lift her into the air at the same time they were moving, running, flying, door then steps, and the great jerk of his body as a hiccup, one of the last, cut through him.

The candles in Sky's house burned bright and showed clearly Drago bent over Klara in the living room, a foot buried in her gut, blood gathering at her left temple, an ankle twisted queerly beneath her. The sight was enough to make any child close her eyes, but Sky kept hers open, and as soon as Jake stepped through the door, Sky felt him still, from the inside out—and she knew his hiccups had ended.

Sky watched the scene unfold from behind the coatrack in the small hallway between the front door and the kitchen, the same hallway through which her father walked at least ten times a day and through which her mother walked at least a hundred. She found it curious, even at eight, that so many things could happen in a hallway, the emptiest room—if you could even call it a room; she found it curious that for long periods of time the hallway could be a peaceful place, a place to sit and look at a book, and then, in the middle of the night, when everything else seemed right, when a candle was blown out and her mother kissed her good night at the same time—that the hallway became a hiding place.

When Sky went to bed on the third night of Jake's hiccups, tension in the Bozic house had risen like heat in the kitchen on baking day. She knew, as she always did, that within an hour or two she would break through the front door, cover the ground between her house and the Zupanovics', and beg for help. So she didn't sleep. She lay awake in the middle of her bed, limbs splayed like the points of a star, listening with her whole body—attuned to the movement, location, voice, and rhythm of her mother.

And as always, when she heard the first strike by her father, Sky went flying.

Klara believed in the word of God. When she opened the door of her childhood home and found Drago on her stoop, smiling at her, she took that as God's word. When Drago guided her to the sea, led her onto a ship, and told her never to look back, she took it as God's word. When they arrived in port after a seasick but passionate journey, she swallowed her nausea and remembered God's word. When she first witnessed Thirsty, she shook her head and cried, but promised herself that somewhere in all that mess—God's word. Her first child, and those to come, shined as God's word—whispers from above. Katherine—God's word, loud and clear. The melons and carrots and snap beans that flourished in her garden—God's word. The rare but always welcome spots of blue sky over Thirsty were sure to be God's word—couldn't be anything else. Her friendship with BenJo—God's word. The brilliant orange pumpkins in Old Man Rupert's field—God's word. Blackberries and blueberries growing wild along the railroad tracks, the fragrance of honeysuckle squeezing in around the rotten-egg stench, the moon in the sky—God's word. Sometimes Klara could taste God's word in the beef stew she simmered over the fire for a full afternoon. Sometimes she could smell it in rising bread. Sometimes she heard His word so clearly it was like the slam of a door or the kick of a mule against a board. Other times, she heard it gentle and easy, like church bells or a Sunday morning hymn or even the buzz of the nighttime crickets. In the beginning, even in the early years before her mother died, she listened for it, the small snap— God's word. But over time her attention to it diminished and often she was surprised, as opposed to expectant. So when the strike occurred and the mill shut down and she had to go to work cleaning houses for the rich folk in the valley, she said okay, and again promised herself—God's word. She took God's word into her mouth like a stone, one from the water's edge where it had been rolled smooth in the river surf, and held it under her tongue. She held it there each day as she worked—polishing vases, wiping tables, washing out more sheets than she thought possible to own—and throughout each day, she rolled that stone in her mouth, tasting it, reminding herself—God's word.

Then one day, Ma'am asked, "Klara, have you cleaned the pantry?"

She had not.

"No, Ma'am." The word *Ma'am* clicked against the stone, and the stone felt suddenly large, as if it were expanding in Klara's mouth. "I'll do it next."

Mrs. Stoughton looked at her watch and tapped one heel against the floor. "It should be finished by now."

Humiliation was not God's word. And when Mrs. Stoughton moved on to address other household woes, Klara looked around the big stone house in the great green valley. The floors were made of tile that Mrs. Stoughton had warned her not to crack because they'd been shipped in all the way from Spain. The tables, carved from mahogany, had feet the shape of lions' paws. The blue porcelain water pitchers had no chips on the edges or spouts. The crystal vase in the center of the dining table glittered like a jewel. And most astonishingly, water was pumped directly into the kitchen. No one had to trek nearly a half mile down a steep hill for a single sip of water.

Suddenly struck by this reality, more than anything Klara wanted to stand over the pump in the kitchen and let cool water cascade over her hands and splash on her face. She wanted to let the basin fill and overflow. On that day, she even found herself wanting to remove her blouse and dip her breasts into the basin. Water was God's word. Clear.

Full. Powerful. Crisp. She wanted to crawl into the basin and drown.

But the silver was tarnished and the pantry was disorganized and the bedroom rugs needed to be hung over the clothesline and beaten before the rain moved in.

When Klara left the Stoughton house that day, she never went back.

1896

Georgie and Ivo arrived more traditionally than Sky, pushing into the world only after hours of contractions and great effort on Klara's part. First Georgie in 1893, then Ivo three years later, each boy growing like a funny little weed. Arms and legs and fingers, ears and toes, penises and noses, all sprouting and growing like it was the most natural thing in the world. And Klara supposed it was, though it seemed like magic to her. She was in awe of those little ones, and for long hours at a time, she would sit out of her work, squeezing and stroking them, figuring what would make them smile, long before they were sure enough in the world to crawl away and run into their own lives. She did what she could to grow them well, but knew from the beginning that Drago's temper darkened each of their days. From the time they were big enough to poke their heads over the edges of their cradles, she could tell they knew something wasn't right. As soon as Drago started ranting, they'd pull their heads back quicker than a frightened turtle's into its shell. From early on, those little ones were more full of fear than joy. The worst part was watching Sky turn from a lovely, giving little girl to a smaller, but equally pained, replica of her. But isn't that what daughters do? Become their mothers? Isn't that what she had done?

One morning Katherine came by to wrap Klara's sprained wrist and deliver freshly baked bread since it was obvious Klara wouldn't be kneading dough for a few days. As she folded the clean cut of sheet into a rectangle large enough to keep the wrist stable, she asked as easily as if she were asking about the weather, "Do you love him?"

Klara eased back into her chair and gauged the ripeness of the apples that lined the windowsill. There were six, and each one was a little redder than the next. Sky had put them there herself, studying each closely before climbing up on the chair, reaching over the breadboard, and placing it on the sill. Beyond the window, Klara could see the smokestacks, clouds of steam and smoke, and a hazy glimpse of the houses that filled the slopes on the other side of the Monongahela.

"Do I love Drago?" she said after she was sure Sky had lined up the apples in the right order.

"Yes, Drago," Katherine said. She placed her hands flat on the table and waited.

"That's a hard question," Klara answered. She held up her wrist. "I don't love this. And I don't love that my children are frightened half the time. But the way I see it, I have to accept my fate. God says the union of marriage is forever."

"Hogwash," Katherine replied, and she slapped her hands on the table. "God didn't mean for us to be tortured by our husbands. If I'm sure of anything, I'm sure of that. Remember the story I told you on the night Sky was born, the one about dinosaurs and amen?"

"Of course I do."

"Then you should know that God would forgive you if you left Drago behind and moved on to safety."

The house seemed to swell with those words out in the open like that. And though she knew Drago was at work, Klara glanced behind her to reassure herself that he wasn't standing in the doorway listening.

"And just where would I go?" she finally asked when she was sure she could hold back the tears. "Back to Croatia to a father not much different than my husband? To New York City with three children and no skills other than those

I use to run this house? Or maybe just downtown to one of the whorehouses? Maybe I'd be good at that."

Her words stung, but Katherine stood and walked around the table to Klara's side. "I know," she said. "I don't mean to push. I just don't like having to guess whether I'm going to find you dead or alive in the morning. And Jake worries even more. After nights when Sky's been at the door, he keeps watch on your place at the window, always making sure Drago holds true to his promise of no more that night."

"Ah, don't you worry about me," Klara said. "I'll surely be the death of Drago before he is the death of me."

Katherine looked at her, but kept silent. Klara couldn't see her way to different, and talking until the river ran dry wouldn't change that.

About that time Old Man Rupert started coming round with strawberries or ribbons or snubs of wildflowers for Sky, intended, in his words, "as an offering to the little one born on my land." Ever since he'd seen her lying in that pond of dirt between her momma's legs, blood darkening the dirt, he couldn't stop thinking about miracles. And despite his weekly drunks, he plotted each day to see her again, to watch her grow. He'd never had children, never wanted any, but now, as an old man, he saw the blessing in them. It had taken nearly thirteen years for him to walk from his farm to Klara's house, but when he finally did, he felt better than he had since before his father passed on. His hair was combed, his clothes—though stained with last night's dinner—were pressed, and he carried his hat in his hand. It was a suspicious sight, one that had folks talking for weeks, but his intentions were genuine.

The first time he presented himself, Klara didn't know what to make of the sight and kept him standing on the porch longer than she would any other guest.

"I brought these for Sky," he told her, holding out a bunch of yellow flowers. "Just want you both to know I didn't mean any harm that night."

"That night?" she said, confused.

"The night you birthed her in my field."

Klara looked at him funny. Nearly thirteen years had passed without a word, and now this?

"I've been meaning to come," he added when she didn't respond, "but I've been scared and, uh, under the weather."

Klara waited.

"Anyway," Old Man Rupert continued, "I talked with BenJo, and he assured me you'd let Sky accept my offering."

When Old Man Rupert mentioned BenJo's name, Klara looked from his shoes to his face. He wasn't smiling or frowning, just looking. "BenJo told you that, did he?" she said.

"Yes, ma'am."

"BenJo decided what I'd do before I was even told what the option was?"

"Yes, ma'am, he did. Very kindly, he did."

Klara leaned against the frame of the door and looked at Tiny's house behind the tangle of weeds and brush. When she looked back at Old Man Rupert, she saw no malice in his face, only softness. "Well, then," she answered, "I suppose you should come on into the kitchen and have a cup of coffee. I'll call Sky in."

"Thank you, Mrs. Bozic, but coffee isn't necessary. I just need to give these to Sky."

A few minutes later when Sky came into the room, Old Man Rupert stood for a long moment, looking as awkward and as uncomfortable in the clean sunny kitchen as an elephant might have. Though Klara, and then Sky, repeatedly invited him to sit, he chose to stand with his hat and the flowers held in both hands at his belt buckle. Together they watched him take a deep breath, and then, seemingly ready for anything, he handed the flowers to Sky and told her the story of her birth in his pumpkin field on Hal-loween night. He told how he had polished off a bottle of whiskey on his own and how when he had woken on the porch, he'd seen two shadows packing pumpkins to go.

"Without question," he said, "I grabbed my gun and ran at them like an angry goose." He grinned nervously and looked at the floor. "Truth is, I almost killed your momma. I tried to, anyway. I shot as close to her as I could. Lucky for me, I was drunk as a thirsty skunk and my aim went awry. And lucky for me, Mrs. Zupanovic didn't turn the gun in my direction when she finally got me stopped. I've never seen a woman madder or stronger than Mrs. Z that night. But instead of killing me, she sent me for the doctor, and when I returned, there you were, lying in my field, all covered in dirt and blood. Pretty little thing you were. Still are."

Sky smiled at Old Man Rupert. Though she'd heard the story many times before from both her mother and Katherine, and though it usually embarrassed her to the point where she'd walk out of the room or hide her face in her hands, she wel-comed his version. It was funnier, wilder, but equally reverent.

"Thank you, Mr. Rupert," she said when it was obvious that he was done. "I appreciate you stopping by to tell me that." And as she passed him to leave the kitchen, Sky set her arm on the sleeve of his shirt and smiled. It was the first time someone had touched him in a long time, and that moment changed him even more.

From then on, Klara knew that every few months Old Man Rupert would appear at the door with some small gift for his girl, and although no one would have thought it possible, he would be mostly sober, brushed and combed, and in awe.

"You told Old Man Rupert he should come by to visit my Sky," Klara said when she walked into BenJo's shop on the morning after Old Man Rupert's initial visit.

BenJo was bent even lower than normal with his hands buried in a bin of cherries. When he heard Klara's voice, he shifted his head and swung around to face her. "I did," he said, and he smiled.

"Why's that?" Klara asked. She didn't feel like wasting time today with friendly talk about pies or strudels; her wrist was throbbing, and she wanted to know that her instincts about the old man were right.

"Because that man needs a friend, someone to believe in. He needs something to think about other than liquor or his falling-down house."

"I accept that, BenJo, but with a husband like Drago, do you think I need some old drunk coming around to make trouble? If Drago had been there, he would have lifted the old man by his belt loops and thrown him clear to the next country. And then he would have started in on me, assuming that I'd invited such a visit."

"I know, Mrs. Bozic. I told Rupert to wait until he saw Drago head for work before knocking on your door. And he did, didn't he?"

"Yes, but I still don't want any more trouble than I've got."

"He won't make trouble."

"How do you know?"

"He's past trouble. Sky changed him."

"What are you telling me? Sky was born almost thirteen years ago. We haven't heard a word from Old Man Rupert since the night he nearly shot me down cold."

"Well," BenJo said slowly, "thirteen years isn't so long in the scheme of things, is it?"

Klara grunted. Sometimes conversations with BenJo were nothing but frustrating. She turned for a moment and watched people pass by the front window. "No, I suppose not if you're referring to the life of the mill or the life of this earth," she finally answered, "but, yes, in the life of people, thirteen years is a very long time."

"Not so much," BenJo said. "Some people just take longer to think things through. Some people take time to gather courage. They have to ripen, like an apple or a pear. No use trying to eat an apple or a pear before it's ready, right?"

Klara knew he would put this question to her until she talked back, so to satisfy his need for an answer, she said right away, "Yes, I suppose that's true."

"Well, Mrs. Bozic, the same is true for people. Rupert's just one of those folks who takes time to ripen. But he's a good man with a good heart. I've known him a long time."

"You feel that's the truth, huh?" Klara looked skeptical.

"Whiskey's made him mean, for sure," BenJo admitted. "But whiskey's not who he is."

Klara let that sit awhile and walked around the store adding a few pieces of fruit to her basket. BenJo waited on Mrs. Kendall, and while he did, Klara watched. She wondered how many years it had been since he'd stood upright. That position, bent at the waist like that, had to hurt, especially his neck, which in order to meet folks eye to eye had to be cricked up sharp. Sometimes at home in order to get his view of things, she imitated his posture. It always felt strange to be so much lower than most, and even though she never did it in front of people, she suspected there was something humiliating about always having to look up.

When BenJo finished, he returned to Klara's side. "Take these to the boys," he said, handing her two plums, "and this to Sky." He handed her a lemon. Sky liked to squeeze them into tea with sugar.

"I will," Klara said. "Thank you, BenJo."

"Rupert won't harm her, if that's what you're worried about," BenJo said. "In fact, just the opposite. He may just be the one to protect her."

Klara nodded. "I'll trust you on this, BenJo, and if Mr. Rupert asks, you tell him he's welcome back any time, as long as Drago isn't close."

BenJo smiled. Klara paid for her goods and closed the door behind her.

Purposefully Klara took the long way home, past the pond that was once full of trout and turtles, but where now you would have little chance of catching even a frog, past the cemetery where many of the mill workers were done and buried, past the patch of blackberry bushes that could be depended upon to produce no matter what the winter handed them, and up the great hill so steep that when you reached the top, you were sure heaven was just a few more steps away. She wasn't sure where public land ended and Old Man Rupert's land began, but she was pretty sure it was somewhere around the ancient pine tree that towered like a sentry just before the spot where his fields were marked. Once she passed that pine, she was careful to stay on the road, not knowing if the old man was perched in the crook of a tree or hiding behind a flowering bush, waiting for trespassers to take a single step in the wrong direction. She hadn't been up there since the night of Sky's birth and strangely enough, it felt rather peaceful. Despite the fact that his fields hadn't been dug up in years and that they were choked with weeds and vines, she could imagine how beautiful it all must have been when Old Man Rupert's father was alive. After scanning the porch and scouring the windows for signs of trouble, Klara dared to take a seat on the mighty boulder that sat in the field across from his house.

Over the past thirteen years, the house, if it were possible, had sagged deeper into disrepair, and now it looked as if a giant had sat on it to rest and nearly squashed the structure back into the earth. All windows but one in the front were broken. The third-floor balcony was lying on the ground in what used to be a much-talked-about rose garden. And the roof, instead of being flat and even from one eve of the house to the next, was high in some places and low in others so that it looked like the scalloped hem of a fancy dress. Klara closed her eyes and tried to imagine the house at its best, the wraparound porch brightly painted and full of happy folks. It was hard, but she could see it. And when she considered the fact that Old Man Rupert looked much the same as the house, sat upon and squashed, it was not disgust that she felt, but sympathy. Everyone has a story, she thought.

A few hundred yards beyond the boulder, in the direction opposite the house, the land began its steep descent down to the mill and then, the river. The mill sounds—shrieks and wails and thumps and rattles—all blended into one so that, as usual, Klara couldn't distinguish the clatter of a passing railroad car from a barge's horn. But up there, the constancy of the sound that often made her want to drive a poker through her own eye wasn't so torturous. It seemed distant, far away, manageable. So, enjoying the feeling, she sat on the rock and studied Old Man Rupert's house until the light began to go and she knew Drago would be looking for his supper.

1898

But what was heard as a single note from Old Man Rupert's perch was an intricate collection of individual sounds to those within the mill. Sounds heard close up, next to the ear—a bit of metal whizzing past, the syncopated thump of your neighbor's sledgehammer, the screech of a ladle being shifted over an ingot mold—and sounds heard from a distance, sounds from work being done that you couldn't see but could imagine because a thousand times you had passed by those places, those machines, those men, bent at the waist, bent at the knees, heads bowed, heads cocked, arms raised and lowered.

So when the deep-throated howl sliced through the mill yard, breaking one sound from another in the way that only human sound could, Drago turned and watched Jake fireball from a flaming third-story tar roof. He watched him arc, like a falling star, a tail of fire streaking the rotten sky behind him. For a moment, Drago couldn't stop watching, but as Jake landed not more than fifty feet away, he closed his eyes. The thud of Jake's body against the ground was absorbed by hiss and rattle, but imagining that he could feel the vibration of the landing through the bottoms of his feet, Drago lost the rhythm of the line, loosened his muscles so that the shovel he gripped in his hands, blade full of dolomite, dropped and swayed. His knees folded. He locked them and pulled hard to straighten his back.

Eighth in line, readying to cast his load into the craning mouth of the furnace, Drago steadied himself, wiped sweat from his jaw with a raised shoulder, and stared as the flames rose three feet high from Jake's body. He watched as bare-chested men smeared with soot snapped their shirts over him and hollered in all directions for water, until a young black boy ran up with a bucket, cocked as if ready to swing and pour. But struck in mid-swing by the stench of seared flesh, burnt hair, and crisp fingernails, the boy stumbled and spilled most of his holding behind him, then crumpled and vomited into his hands. Another boy, this one white, followed, stepped close to the fiery pyre, raised his bucket, then poured slowly, up and down the body, as if watering a patch of snap beans. After he pulled back, he rested the bucket on his hip and surveyed the results of his work. Then only a pillar of steam rose from that place. Drago stepped closer to the furnace, felt the bite of heat on his cheeks and forearms. The urge to run to his fallen neighbor, to look down at what remained, was great, but resistance to the urge came just as strong. He couldn't relinquish his place in line for anyone, not even Jake; as quickly as he'd step out, someone new—a Dago or a German or some Irishman watching from behind a pillar or crate—would step in, filling that spot, like water filling a well hole, leaving him to return to the pit, which he would never do. No man would. Down there, scraping slag all night and all day, got a man ready for his grave quicker than digging it himself.

Each man before Drago easily slung his own shovelful into the mouth of the furnace, muscles tense beneath the damp cloth of their shirts, then cheered as the dolomite cut through the flames, striking square at the back of the furnace's belly. A few men gathered Jake's remains onto a stretcher, using hands and spades to lift him evenly so as not to lose the fragile, queerly twisted limbs. Then they covered him with their shirts and carted him off. The white boy with the bucket still resting on his hip followed a few feet behind. The black boy on the ground, sure that expectations of him were finished, scoured his hands with cinders, wiped them against the thighs of his trousers, eased into a squat, then rose, spit, and circled in place three or four times, as if he didn't know quite where he was or where he belonged. For the remainder of the day's shift, he would suffer the shameful tongue-lashes of *yellow-belly* and *sissy-nigger,* and the next morning, his mother would have to shove him down the stairs and out the door, hollering in a voice strained with despair, that if he didn't get his shiny ass to work, he shouldn't bother toting it home.

Drago watched the stretcher disappear behind a shed. Only the odor of singed flesh lingered, reminding him not of one particular memory, but of many: the burned hull of a horse chestnut at the bottom of a woodpile when its sweetness had gone up with the smoke, the fresh bones of an old hound he'd accidentally dug up in a new field when he was a boy, the sullied rot at the bottom of a fruit barrel. All of these at one time or another had made him struggle not to lose the contents of his stomach as the black boy with the bucket had; he fought hard in this instance as well, but in the end it was only the surprise of a hand on his shoulder that kept him from such disgrace.

"Jake's gone," a heavy voice said in his ear.

"I saw." Drago looked up into Janko's eyes; they were round and brown, but sunk back into his skull, overshadowed by a bulbous nose and jutting forehead.

"You watched him fall?" Janko asked.

"Yes, I heard him holler. When I turned, I saw him leave the roof."

"Are you going home to help Katherine see to things?" Like a good brother, Janko kept his hand on Drago's shoulder.

"No. The rest are woman things." When fear or anger overtook him, Drago could easily become the ugliest man in the world. His face, normally long and thin, contorted into a tight mask, which he loosened after a moment with a shake of his head. In the mill there was no mistaking him for someone else—not so much for the exact features, eyes nose lips, but for the rigid pole-like stance he kept, no matter how heavy the burden. Fifteen years before, on his first day in the yard, a stream of hot metal from a tapped ladle had spilled down like a waterfall close enough to drown him. Janko had collared and pulled him to safety even before he himself had realized any danger. "Heeooww!" Janko had hollered, slapping his brother on the head, then went on his way, rocking back and forth on wide feet, looking back over his shoulder at the young man who stood solid, straight-backed, staring at the place he'd been standing moments before as it filled with hot metal.

"The women come down yet?" Drago asked. He checked his place. Two more in front of him. The line at the furnace was like most lines . . . waiting as long as it took to reach the front, but always having to keep moving so that the rhythm wasn't broken. Much of the workings of the mill centered around rhythm, doing exactly what was expected of you at each precise moment, and never improving or taking a new turn with things. Men's lives depended on it.

"Naw, the whistle hasn't even gone yet."

Drago looked up again. "It hasn't?" He couldn't remember having heard it or not.

"Maybe those white shirts are hoping they can save him."

"No one's going to salvage anything from that mess. I could have told them that when he was in the air."

"They're always hoping."

"They ought to know better than to wait to sound it."

"Yeah, they ought to."

"Makes three this month."

"Yeah, and four fingers gone on Murphy." Janko held up his right hand and wiggled his fingers.

When Drago stepped up to the furnace, Jake's voice echoed in his head. *At the end of the arc, throw your left*

arm . . . throw it high! Keep your eyeballs from burning up."
Drago planted his feet, swung the shovel back, pitched it
forward, let the load fly, all while keeping his eyes on the
flaming hearth. He threw his arm high, just like Jake had
taught him, then cried out as the dolomite hit square on
the back wall.

Then the whistle went. The death knell. Its unbroken hollow
bleat summoning the women, feeling its way through white
breaths of steam shooting up from the furnaces and ribbons
of colorful gas layering the sky, riding up the sheer hillsides
on rifts of wind, wings of butterflies, backs of beetles. It clung
to the hindquarters of stray skin-and-bone hounds and
flea-bitten rumps of mules and nags and spread through
thick patches of maple trunks and junipers. It tripped over
chestnuts and pinecones, red berries and clumps of moss,
crawled along branches and stems, was swallowed by the
drooping heads of violet buds and viburnum blooms, then
spewed out again. It skimmed ponds and creek water, seeped
into stalks of milkweed, cattails, and sidled into Thirsty and
all of the surrounding mill towns, settling over gardens, creep-
ing into houses and stores, schools and shops, until all the
women scrubbing work shirts in metal basins in their back
alleys froze in their work and turned their eyes toward the
billowing smokestacks.

In her kitchen, Klara lifted her hands from a ball of
sweet bread dough, wiped them on the apron tied around
her waist, then moved to the back doorway. In the small
room she could cross in five strides, she seemed large, over-
grown. Her head, shaped like a heart, was full of thoughts
she didn't have words for, and as she looked out at the
sky smudged with oranges, grays, and yellows, she found
herself surprised, as always, that nothing she saw through
the frame of the door looked different during the whistle.

In the alleyway, she saw the button man's cart with its bells and chimes hung on worn leather straps from the handle. She saw the reddish roofs of the houses clinging to the hillside below, and beyond that, the jagged line of smokestacks carved into the horizon and the autumn-colored sky that pressed down on the town like an insistent pair of hands. She didn't know what she expected during the whistle, perhaps a spot of blue sky or a black flag raised on a post, but every time it was the same. Life moving on, moving past, never slowing, even for the loss of a man. Sometimes the whistle went once a week, sometimes only once a month, depending on the output of the mill—how much steel was being poured, how many hours the men were logging, how many shifts they'd worked without resting. Those were the times when men died, when they were heat-drawn, bleary-eyed, slow-footed.

She returned to the table, set the dough in a bowl, covered it with a clean rag, and placed it on the windowsill with the others to rise. She rinsed her hands and shook them dry. This house was so familiar to her that she barely remembered any other. At night, after the children fell asleep, she extinguished the lamps and moved like a blind person through the pitch dark, lifting her foot instinctively at the top of the stairs where one board had swelled and buckled, swinging wide at the place where the toy box jutted from the wall, and gliding easily past the rocking chair in the living room. On nights when the moon miraculously found its way into the sky above Thirsty, she lay awake in bed and imagined each individual patch of light the moon carved throughout the house—the triangle against the baseboard near the front door, the half-moon at the foot of Georgie's bed, and the skinny rectangle crisscrossed with hatchings just below the dining table. And on many nights, after waiting for hours for Drago to return from his shift or from a night down at Penny's Saloon, she listened curiously as he collided with first one piece of furniture, then another, all the way from the front door to the bedroom, cursing and bellowing, waking the boys and Sky from their slumber, as if he'd never before moved through the house.

Now, early evening, she listened past the whistle for the footsteps of the women moving down the road. When she heard the familiar shuffle, feet not lifting but sliding and scraping in the dry dust and gravel, she gathered the boys and Sky by her side and moved onto the front porch, holding her breath somewhere between lungs and belly, not letting go of it until she spied Katherine waiting on the stoop. Katherine, who smiled over the whistle, stood and spit the cigarette from between her lips onto the ground.

"Calling out the hogs again," Katherine said as she and Klara stepped in front of the gaggle of women and led them—wives and mothers, daughters and sisters—through the pool of summer heat that had settled in around them, drowning the gray cardboard town in damp humidity. The women's heads were wrapped in soiled dull babushkas; their hands were raw and caked with bread dough and garden dirt. At each house they passed, a door opened and one or two women joined them, three or four children, a few mutts looking for a handout, until the group stretched full across the road's width and a quarter of a mile behind. Even Lillian Wilcox, who was unpaired and not right in the head, followed in the rear, swishing back and forth across the road like the tail of a horse swatting flies.

"Who do you figure it got now?" Klara asked. She let all but Ivo walk ahead. She kept him on her hip until they reached the Hravics' place, then set him on the ground and held his fingers in her own. He was small for his age, and she didn't know if she'd ever be ready to let this one grow up.

"If I knew that," Katherine said, "I'd get more than my share in this world."

Klara nodded. "Did you see that dress Miss April is wearing back there?" she asked.

Katherine turned to look. Miss April was wearing a freshly
pressed pink dress with a bow at the neck. "Looks like she's
heading for a wedding, not somebody's death," Katherine
said. "I guess she figures she might meet a man down there.
Doesn't have the sense yet to know that the fence keeps us
apart, doesn't bring us together."

Unlike the men who traveled the paths through the woods
when walking to the mill, the women took the road, slipping
on loose gravel and stepping over old wheel mounts and
empty bottles. As they moved under the canopy of leaves,
Klara felt the temperature plunge. Her skin cooled. The
scent of damp earth and pine needles blended with the
light fragrance of lilac pushing up from the bushes lining
the edge of the road. Nestled by the arc of trees overhead,
sound shifted so that Klara could hear the odd nibblings
of conversation of birds and insects. She wanted to pause,
sit down on a stone or a fallen tree and rest, but she could
feel the movement of the women behind her, like a hot
breath, pressing her forward, so she continued, letting the
urge pass.

The women herded their children like sheep, prodding
them along and calling to them in familiar mewing sounds.
Most kept their eyes on the ground, lips moving in silent
prayer. When they finally pulled around the last curve in
the road and arrived at the fence that separated the mill
from its surroundings, the women gathered in tight groups:
Croats with Croats, Germans with Germans, Slavs with
Slavs, Italians with Italians, Serbs with Serbs, and so on,
bowing their heads, whispering to one another in foreign
tongues, praying a bit more, as if prayer might undo what
had already been done. Klara and Katherine were still in
front, pressed so tightly against the iron fence, Klara could
feel the knuckles of the woman behind her gouge the small

of her back. As she caught her breath, she was consoled by the thought that if the woman pressed hard enough, she would slip through the tiny openings of the fence until she was safely on the other side. Then she would be one of them. For a moment, she wondered about Ivo, squeezed his fingers with her left hand, and looked down to locate the top of his blond head. She always expected him to panic in the throng of women, the way Georgie and Sky used to, hollering in high-pitched squeals until she pushed them through the suffocating crowd into open space. But not Ivo; her eyes found him nestled against the curve of the women's legs, wrapped in their skirts. Instinctively he looked up when she looked down and he smiled, holding out a handful of shiny cinders he'd plucked from the ground.

She didn't bother to search out Georgie or Sky. She knew they'd be where they always were during the whistle—Georgie in the bend of the road rolling marbles with the other boys and Sky chatting and giggling with her girlfriends.

Like a stone statue, Katherine stood and waited, her shoulders pulled back and her boxy chin jutting out. She'd come to the fence so often she knew the spots where it had been eaten away by curds of rust. She knew it was better to breathe through the nose than to swallow the rotten-egg stench. She knew each woman's name, even those she rarely passed in the street or shared news with at the market. Emilia stood behind Klara. Martha stood next to her. Beatrice wore the purple scarf around her neck. Evonne, the Irish lass, had the reddest hair and the most alluring smile. She knew that Clarice, who'd lost her husband, a crane man, only two months before, now came to the fence to support her sister Blanche, who was married to a foreman. She knew the fear that gripped Klara, freezing her in the moment. She used to feel it herself in the beginning. And she knew that John, the manager whose job it was to deliver the women their news, had to walk 252 long-legged strides between the gray office building beyond and the clump of women on the opposite side of the fence. Still, it was impossible for her to know the excruciating pain moving into her life, to know that within minutes she would be mourning a loss so great her world would never feel wholly blessed again.

"Klara," she said, raising her voice above the sounds of the mill, "set your worry aside. I've told you this over and over again. Drago's a lout. You and me, we know this well. Everybody in this town knows it. But that man, he's got luck. All these years in the mill and not one accident. No one's ever heard of such a thing. Saint Drago. That's what Jake always calls him. Saint Drago. All these years and not one broken bone. Not one smashed finger. Not even a knock on the head, which wouldn't do him any harm if you ask me. Saint Drago, Klara. He's got luck."

Klara glanced at her and then turned away. She measured the empty space between her and the office, a low gray building set apart from the furnaces, safe from the dangers of stray sparks, and wished she could run to it, instead of waiting for John to come to her.

"I know, Katy," she finally said, "but how long is luck like that going to last?"

A few yards from the women, near the gate, a hand-painted sign leaned sideways against the fence. In crooked, black letters, it read *No Injuries in _____ Days*. No one at the mill remembered who painted it, or when, and no one ever filled in the blank; it just leaned in the same spot near the entrance, the letters fading a little more at each turn of the seasons. Klara thought about all the men who'd been lost and broken here, and she felt a twinge of guilt that she sometimes had to wrestle the urge to kill Drago herself, drag him down to this river and hold his head under until he went limp; but she knew the mill taking him would be something different, a passing she wouldn't wish on anybody.

Finally, John appeared in his crisp shirt and thick tie. He trudged across the mill yard, dodging the wheelbarrows and stamping out stray sparks with his feet. Only the women stopped for the whistle. The men kept working, moving, stirring, cooking the steel, waiting for word of the latest victim as news traveled barrow to barrow, ladle to ladle, furnace to furnace. Those who weren't scheduled—the ones who were home sleeping or drinking at Penny's or another of the pool halls or whiskey clubs—couldn't sacrifice their few hours of rest, so when the whistle sounded, they waited for the women to return with the news, poking their heads out of doors and open windows, quizzical looks on their faces.

As kind as any messenger of death could be, John had a soft voice and soft belly that pushed up over the top of his trousers. A widower with eleven mouths to feed. And although Klara pitied him, even fixed him up a basket of fresh bread and vegetables from the garden every couple of weeks in the summertime and passed him canned goods in the winter months, each time she stood at the fence, she imagined a pair of black wings sprouting from his shoulder blades. Great ebony wings with tips stretching high above his head and tail feathers dragging behind him in the dust, the face of each man lost in the mill tattooed on the crow-black plumage. She imagined him soaring overhead, flapping those wings, stirring the puffs of steam and clouds of colorful gases into a thick black soup.

"Here he comes," Katherine said. She took Klara's hand.

A murmur of *amens* and *lord almightys* slipped through the crowd.

Looking across the expanse of land between himself and the fence, John eyed the flock of women on the other side and the gaseous eggplant-colored sky that stretched out behind them reflecting the burning fires in the furnaces.

Silently the women moved as one, surging toward him, the fence buckling out, then sinking back, giving and receding, like the measured wake that followed barges as they cut wide swaths in the river. Never once, in all his years on the job, had John witnessed a woman cross into the mill yard. He imagined that was what the bosses had intended when they constructed the fence: keep the men in and the women out. Each time he crossed the yard, the distance seemed to grow, to stretch farther and farther until it seemed the women were unreachable, and then suddenly he'd be up close, so close he could kiss them. And although from far away they looked beautiful and full of promise, up close they looked worn, cheerless, and incurably sad, with dark skirts frayed at the hems, soiled from the procession down the soot-covered road, their wild hair tamed beneath babushkas. As he drew closer, he saw the faces of the smaller children, knee-high, peering at him from behind the skirts, and in their regular places at the head of the group, he spotted Klara and Katherine standing shoulder to shoulder. In that moment, he remembered when his own wife had passed and he'd applied himself to the exhausting task of cleaning out her closet, delivering her shoes and clothes to the charity house run by the parish, and writing the letter telling the news to her parents in Croatia. He swallowed at the knot tangled up in his throat, tightened his grip on the box he carried, and lowered his head.

"Dammit," he said.

Like Katherine, John knew every woman by name—how many children each had borne, the name of the street where each family lived, what language they spoke around the dinner table in the evenings. He'd been meeting them at the fence for years now, looking into their pleading eyes, confessing their fates. If he happened to meet one of them on the street, passing on the way to church or the market, they would nod, exchange formalities, but nothing more.

To be seen talking with John was a sign of bad luck, and he knew that no matter how much he prayed, he would never find another wife in these whereabouts.

When he finally stood at the fence with his feet planted shoulder-width apart and the bottom edge of the box resting on his belly, the hum of voices grew louder. Word passed from front to back that he'd arrived. But once even the newest wives, who gathered at the tail of the crowd away from easy view, knew of his presence, there was a hush. He stood for a moment, his head bowed, letting the sounds of the mill evaporate and the women's silence wash over him. It was nearly nightfall. He raised his head and took two wide sidesteps until he stood directly in front of Klara and Katherine. A chill rose up under Klara's skirt. She let her gaze wander from his boots to the patches on his knees to the shiny buckle of his belt. She counted the black buttons on his shirt, then let her eyes graze his face. It was skinny and bright red, and each time he swallowed, which was often, his sharp-edged Adam's apple jerked up and down in his throat. She licked her lips again and raised her eyes to meet his. But instead she found that he was looking at Katherine.

"It's Jake, Katherine," she heard him say. She watched as he turned to face the crowd, and in a louder voice repeated, "Jake, Jake Zupanovic."

His words were short, clipped, and the gaggle of women let out its breath as Katherine shoved back from the fence and fell to her knees. The women backed away in relief, then despair, muttering prayers in Katherine's direction. On mornings or evenings when their own men's names had been called, many had felt the same blow. Klara stood still, scraping the palms of her hands against the fence. She watched John's knuckles whiten on the corners of the box and his lips continue to move as he closed his eyes. A sob rolled up from her belly. She felt Ivo's fingers grab at her calves. It was Jake? Their Jake? Without so much as a warning, her life, as well as Katherine's, changed forever.

"It can't be," she said to him, but John nodded without opening his eyes. Then she knew. Bending at the waist, she half-dragged, half-pulled Katherine closer to the gate where John now waited, holding the box awkwardly in front of him like a gift. She thought Katherine would rise to her feet and pull up the strength she had shown so often in their lives, but she didn't. Instead she curled on the ground, becoming tinier and tinier, shrinking until she was the size of a cinder, and to keep her from disappearing altogether, Klara folded over her like a quilt. Together they rocked, making a bundle on the ground.

But despite Klara's comfort and warmth, Katherine's bones went cold, toes and ankles, knees and elbows, jaw and spine, cold. This was sorrow—the kind of sorrow that snaps you at the stem. Jake had planned only four more years in the mill, then he and Katherine were going to spend their time on the porch, watching the kids play stick ball in the street or race down the hill in their wagons, wheeling to a halt at the edge of the cliff. Katherine bucked under Klara's weight, leaned back on her heels, then dove forward and ground her cheek into the gravel. She retched, buried her face in the pool of bile that filled her mouth and nostrils, and prayed that she would drown.

John stepped through the gate and hovered. While Klara cooed into Katherine's ear, he turned to watch the rest of the women wander back up the road, now in a thin scattered line, spread out in their prayers, joined in Katherine's agony. He knew that after his shift ended, he would lie down alone in his bed and dream about the faces of the women, blending all of them into Katherine's. In his dream the women would crawl over the fence to capture him. They would cross the border between the men's lives and their own. They would be naked, their breasts bare with the nipples dripping sweet sorrowful milk onto their swollen pregnant bellies. He would see Katherine on the ground, creased at the waist, her mouth opening and closing for air, and before he could turn to run from the women, he would feel her tears crack like glass against his chest and wake to find his own sweat gathering beneath his nightshirt.

With a nod of his head, he broke up a circle of boys still squatted on the ground rolling marbles and motioned for Sky to take Georgie and Ivo home. Sky stood still for a moment, looking not at Katherine and her mother, but at the mill itself, and though John could tell she was struggling not to cry, she turned, gathered the boys without shedding a tear, and followed the rest of the women up the road.

Alone now with Klara and Katherine, John stood, clutching the box that held Jake's personal items: a black iron lunch pail; a blue-and-tan checked cap; the clunky pocket watch Katherine had saved for and given him on their twentieth wedding anniversary. Though someone had obviously tried to wipe it clean after the accident, the watch was still tarnished with smoke and ash from the fire.

"I'm sorry," John said. "It was fire. Crawled up a wall and caught Jake on the roof. He was tarring a leak. He jumped, but he was too high. Burned up on the way down. It happened fast." He leaned and offered the box to Katherine.

In that moment Klara remembered her first visit to the fence. The whistle, the trail of women and children, the sound of the mill drawing closer and closer as they moved through town until she could feel its vibrations in her teeth. Maggie O'Flanagan's husband had been crushed by a rail car, a slip in the lock, crushed so flat that afterward rumor told that the only bones not shattered were those in his head. Accompanied by Katherine, Klara had been at the front against the fence as far back as that, and on that morning she'd watched Maggie O'Flanagan—a girl not far past puberty, not too much older than Sky—faint cold into the arms of her womenfolk. Not a sound. Some went quiet like that. Odd, she thought as the images gathered and passed—the flash of red hair, the gray dress with yellow buttons down the front—how thoughts find you when you're not looking. She looked from John to Katherine. The box hung between them as if suspended by an invisible wire, and then she felt Katherine yank her body from her embrace.

"Katy . . . ," she began.

"I don't want this!" Katherine screamed. She pulled her arms free and flailed them over her head, knocking the box from John's arms. As it fell, the pail spilled onto the ground next to her. She watched the apple she'd washed and packed eight hours earlier roll out over its lip. Her eyes followed it, until it stopped, striking the edge of the fence. It was green, bright green, sour the way Jake liked. In one place he had taken a large bite out of it, probably during his walk to work, and the white meat in that place had browned. Katherine threw herself toward it. Growled. White spittle gathered at the corners of her mouth. She flattened her belly against the gravel, grasped the apple in her hands and wrestled with it, banging it off her forehead again and again until a dark bruise began to form. Klara crouched a few feet away, holding the gold cross that hung on a chain around her neck in a closed fist. After a few minutes, Katherine held the apple away from her and rubbed her thumb over its smooth skin. She drew it close and pressed her lips against the spot where Jake's teeth had dug in.

There was hardly anything left of Jake's burnt-up body— not his clothes, nor his whiskers, nor his firm round belly—so the parishioners of St. Jude's Church shut his charred bones in a pine box, whispered a prayer, and hammered a couple of sturdy nails through the lid, just in case Katherine grew desperate or the local children curious. Not far from anyone's thoughts was Widow Aberdeen, who just a few months before in her funereal despair had pried open her husband's casket, removed his body, and dressed him in the set of work clothes she'd washed and ironed the morning of his death. Sometime during the night, she set him at his regular place at the head of the breakfast table with a bowl of polenta in front of him, frightening the children half to death when they awoke the next morning. Women got like that when the mill took their men, touched in the head and bereft of reason, so steeped in sorrow they'd get lost heading home from the market and have to be steered in the right direction by do-gooders who kept a close eye. Some had been seen wandering the fields at dawn, naked and frenzied, pulling at their hair and muttering to themselves; others returned to the fence day after day until a loved one locked them in their home and broke the ritual. All of the widows who ever spoke publicly about their loss said they'd spent so many years listening to the relentless clamor of the mill that the silence that blanketed them during the hours surrounding the deaths of their husbands delivered them to a place they couldn't navigate. It wasn't so much the loss of the men themselves that cracked the women in two, but the freedom the mill had to reach into the grit-stained houses and take whatever it wanted, without so much as a change in rhythm. You couldn't even call it stealing, because the mill owned them, everything around them, inside and out, hearts and mountains, rivers and veins; and regardless of how final each death seemed, there always existed the promise of another.

So on the first dry day following Jake's death, the parishioners crossed Thirsty on foot, carrying him at the head of the procession, three red blossoms set on top of the casket. They buried him in the side of a steep hill, set a couple of smooth, rounded stones to mark his grave, and planned to go on with the rest of their lives. The men he'd worked with at the mill wouldn't miss him for long; even before his body struck the ground at the end of its sizzling flight, an ambitious third helper from the pit—a brawny Dago who'd been shoveling slag for a couple of months—stepped up and grabbed Jake's toolbox where he'd set it before climbing to the roof to patch the leak. He picked up where Jake had left off. Only Katherine, who lost all of the hair on her body forever after, from the top of her head to the knuckles of her toes, so that even her pubic bone was as smooth as the skin of a ripe plum, and the Bozic family, anticipated feeling his absence for long.

But the wake tricked everyone. During the three days between the whistle and the funeral, with Katherine's grief-stricken face and John's fallen one etched in her mind, Klara ordered everyone from the kitchen and cooked with such vigor that friends and family, stiff in their Sunday best, could have closed their eyes at the burial site and followed their noses all the way to the Bozics' house. A sweet, pungent odor cut through the sulfuric stench of the mill and floated over Thirsty, close to the ground, like a low-flying sparrow. In a flurry of spices, dry goods, and other ingredients, she prepared two pots of stuffed cabbage bedded in sauerkraut, five ropes of nadiv, warm loaves of sweet bread cracked with real butter, fried chicken, pickled beets, fresh-cut beans, apple pies, custard pies, even a chocolate pie with whipped cream on top. When she ran out of sugar, she traipsed from house to house collecting half a cup here, a third of a cup there, until she gathered enough for a three-tiered lemon cake that sat in the center of the table. Someone brought a tamburitza, and the music pulled the old people onto their feet. Children danced in pairs under the tallest cherry tree. Men smoked. Bottles of whiskey and slivovitz were passed hand to hand. Even Katherine, who refused to paint eyebrows over her eyes or to cover her smooth, bald head with a scarf or cap, sat on a padded chair near the music and tapped her foot.

But it was the woman with the wavering voice who brought this gathering to tears with a love song so moving that shirttails and skirt hems became saturated. As she sang, parishioners were suddenly reminded that the celebration was in remembrance of Jake, a burnt husk of bones left in the side of a hill to rot, and in sorrow, they filtered out of the yard under the first dark of night, in ones and twos, heads bowed, slowly realizing that nothing would ever be the same again. They realized that in the morning, over peppered eggs, Katherine would face an empty chair, and in the evening, that same chair, the one with a snapped rung where Jake had leaned all his weight one day, would be sitting in its place, unmoved. It would not be pushed back against the wall as Jake always left it when he finished a meal; it would be tucked under the table where Katherine preferred it to be. All that singing and dancing, eating and drinking. All that high-spirited laughter. Even Klara felt tricked. For a little while, right in the middle of the day, her urge to weep had drifted. The thin air that had covered her face like a silk veil for nearly seventy-two hours, making her light-headed and blue-skinned, thickened. Now, in the shadows of late evening, left alone for the first time since Jake's death, with Katherine tucked safely into bed next door, she swelled with rage, feeling as full and close to bursting as she imagined a cloud to feel just before a downpour. It came on her like it always did, slow, one thought leading to another, loss and disappointment building, until all thoughts led to the fact that this was not the life she had longed for. And now, with Jake gone, so was her safety.

Then thoughts let go and feelings presided and everything ached and blurred, like the constant rumble of trains passing in the night. The impulse to strike out didn't surprise her at all, but she was so caught up in the reverie, she didn't even hear Drago approach. She didn't know how long he'd been standing there, watching her, with that flat-brimmed hat of his tilted off to one side, pulled tight over his eyes. She looked right at him—something she rarely did anymore—saw the smooth plane of his chest rise and fall beneath the blue dress shirt she'd pressed earlier in the day and his eyes squint, as if the sun were blinding him. Most of the time, he was just an object in her peripheral vision—a pot bubbling on the stove, a dark windowpane behind her children, a jar of jam teetering on the edge of a table. She watched him raise one closed hand to his face and scratch at his whiskers with his knuckles. The dry, brittle sound crawled up her back.

Alone now, at the edge of the garden, a small light shone from the kitchen window where Sky had lit a lamp, and the scent of damp earth floated up as night-drawn dew gathered. Klara breathed in and leaned against the edge of the table. When she saw Drago flinch under her gaze, she almost smiled. She was full-bodied, strong, curved in the face with a lean jaw and wide cheekbones. Her skin and hair were soft, but over the years, she'd learned to fight hard.

"Where are you going?" she asked when he turned his back to walk down the road to Penny's Saloon. It seemed to her that anytime he had a few moments to spare or extra nickels in his pocket, he was off to that saloon where all the men from neighboring villages in Croatia gathered and the home language was spoken in heavy, grumbling voices. There, slivovitz was downed by the bottle, not the glass, and wives and children were set aside and forgotten like rusty tools.

Drago stopped, but didn't turn. Just stood like a straight-up post in the ground. "Don't give me a time about this, lady," he said and slid his hands into his pockets. Unlike many men in town, the only time Drago ever visited the church was to celebrate a wedding or carry the pine box for a fellow's funeral. Klara knew that acting proper in church where the air was so quiet it turned crisp wasn't Drago's way. He was more comfortable in the saloon with splintered tables, a layer of cigarette haze between him and God, Tiny picking away at the piano keys, and girls from down the way sitting on his lap for a penny. But Klara didn't care. She never stopped wanting him to be different, wanting her life to be different, wanting to disappear from this town and reappear in a peaceful, quiet place where the knot that gripped her middle, tying her up and making the rage swell, unwound and slipped away.

"You have any money for me?" she asked in a louder voice, reaching up to loosen the bun of hair at the nape of her neck. After so many hours, it nagged her. Two wisps of dark curls escaped and framed her face. Somewhere an owl called. A train blasted its whistle. She looked across the tops of the makeshift tables splayed in the yard between her and Katherine's houses, spotted a large, metal serving spoon, and moved toward it. She picked it up and held it in front of her like a sword, then faced Drago again. She always began a fight with a weapon.

"Klara, I gave you proper money last pay."

"If you are going down to Penny's, you better split what-ever's in your pocket with me first. I spent my last dimes on goods for this wake. Sweet lemons don't come cheap."

"I bet they come cheap from that nigger-man you go to visit for them. I've told you not to shop at his place, and again and again you defy me."

"And I've told you I shop where the goods are fresh. BenJo's got the best in town, and he's a decent man. You're always judging what you don't know."

"I know enough. Heard all the stories I need to hear down at the mill."

"You men and your stories. Worse gossips than women, then telling us we talk too much."

"Now you've got it. You talk too much."

"Are you giving me any money?"

"I haven't got but a couple of pennies in my pocket, and I'll be damned if I'm giving them to you tonight."

"Then sell me three and spend three on your goods."

"I'm not giving you anything more. Nobody ordered you to spend everything you had on eats for the whole town, filling up all these tables with enough nourishment for the disciples at the last supper. Lordy, woman!"

"Better on eats for the whole town than liquor for your dry gullet. And how many times have I got to remind you not to take the Lord's name in vain?"

Sometimes, in the beginning of a battle, Klara got the urge to reach out and run her fingers along the lean muscle on Drago's arm until she reached the soft spot where the tuft of hair grew wild in his pit, finding that spot just below that would make him moan low and tender, but by now, her jaw taut and her fingers itching for hard contact, she couldn't back down.

"Jake hasn't been gone a week and already you're acting foolish," she said.

"What are you bringing a dead man into this for?" Drago stepped toward her. In the light she couldn't tell if he was watching her or not, but she heard the jangle of coins when he pulled his hands from his pockets.

"Jake being dead doesn't have anything to do with you not taking proper care of your family. You're just like that brother you got back home, hard headed and full of spite." Her voice sharpened, and in the empty space that followed, she heard Sky shuffle across the porch and slip behind the trunk of the cherry tree, where a few hours before pairs of children had danced. The dishes were washed and put away; the boys were in bed. She figured Sky wanted to try to stop the forward motion of this fight, but there wasn't anything to stop it now, and the thought of her daughter stepping in angered Klara even more. She stiffened her back and set one hand on her hip, felt the heat of the spoon in the palm of the other.

"Sky, what are you doing out here? Haven't I taught you not to go where you're not needed?"

Sky followed her shadow from behind the tree. "Mum, can't you come inside now and let Pap go? We've got left-overs that will last us for days."

"This doesn't have anything to do with you! Get in the house!" Klara said. As she did, the rage swelled until it over-flowed, and she turned, raised the spoon high, and struck Drago in the head. The shallow hull fit neatly in the curve of his temple, making a solid thud. He stood still, just a slight rocking of his head as it absorbed the blow. Klara lowered the spoon, readying for his pounce. She locked her knees and stiffened her muscles.

At the moment Sky stepped between them, Klara remem-bered standing between her own mother and father. She remembered looking up at their faces, jaws set, knowing that if she stood there a moment longer, she was going to get smacked, and standing there anyway. She remembered feeling her head loll back and forth on her neck and seeing tiny droplets of white light mixed with streaks of red rain down in front of her eyes, a slice of pain reaching around her shoulder and into her neck. She remembered, in a memory not wholly her own but one passed down through blood and gene, her grandmomma and her great-grandmomma standing in this very spot. Women in this family had been standing in this place, in this battle position, for as long as the tree stretched back in time. She knew she was the one doing the striking now and she wondered how that had happened so fast when it seemed like yesterday she was the one looking up. But it was too much to filter, and instead of saying the soft words that wanted to come out of her mouth, *Come closer,* she cracked Sky across the face with the back of one hand and brought the spoon down on Drago's skull for a second time with the other, listening to the crack of metal on bone. Then she felt herself being dragged by the waist to the ground and again it was too late to change the path of things so she bent into the fight.

"I'm going to kill you!" she spit with a mouthful of blood.

"Klara, I am not playing tonight!" Drago said into her hair, then raised up his fist and knocked her cold. He stood, stepped over her body, picked his hat from the dust, and moved on down the road.

"Sky," he called back without turning, "get your momma in the house."

Before Jake's death, whenever her parents took to tangling, Sky would race out of her house and over to the Zupanovics' where she would pound on the door with the flat of her hand. She would stand there, the tail of her nightgown caught in the breeze, sometimes drenched by a rainstorm, sometimes knee deep in a snowdrift, always panting and wild eyed. As she waited for Jake or Katherine to open the door, she would stare up at the sky and talk out loud to God in a voice that seemed separate from her being. However futile her effort, she would beg, plead, and pray for peace and stillness. When Jake finally opened the door, she never had to say a word; the pounding and the stricken look of terror were more than sufficient. When she was still small enough to be carried, Jake would hoist her into his arms and tote her with him on his mission, setting her on the staircase of the Bozic house before pulling Klara to safety or Drago to a messing up. When she grew too big to be carried, Jake would grab her hand and stomp across the patch of dirt between their houses, up the porch steps, and through the door. He always wanted her close, fearing that if he left her behind, she would simply disappear.

Once Klara got free, Katherine, who was never far behind, would ease her into the cubbyhole behind the kitchen and clean her wounds or rock her until the crying ceased.

Sky would watch all of this from the doorway, holding her breath, stopping her heart, keeping the blood from pumping through her veins, pretending she was already dead.

Now with Jake's passing, Sky realized there wasn't anything she could do to stop her father and mother, so she took to spending time down at the end of the street with that loose-lipped hussy girl Constance, smearing ruby-red lipstick onto her cheeks and following the older boys into the cornfields for a bit of fooling around. She was incurably sad from all those years of watching her parents battle, and she knew that no matter how much she begged or cried or took the blows for her mother, she couldn't stop it. But more importantly, she discovered that when she was being stroked or sucked on or whispered to in the cornfields, all that sadness drifted far enough away so that she could forget for a while. It was like discovering sugar. When she was on her back or straddling the waist of some local boy, that sadness floated up like a cloud, letting her be to enjoy the tremors that traveled up and down her body—the quivers and starbursts. Of course, the sadness always hovered nearby, waiting, like a spirit, to return to her. But even that she could forget. Those evenings in the cornfields might have been something else—romantic even—had they taken place on the crest of a hill far from Thirsty where the moon was fat and full, lighting the way up Sky's silky spread-open-wide legs. They might have been different if the rotten-egg stink had disappeared and puffs of unspoiled air had billowed up into her nostrils, filling her head with wonder, making her dizzy, making colors dance before her eyes. But the cornfields—full of hungry rats and nests of bees and scratchy dried-up stalks—were better than the cow pastures where the prospect of rolling into a fresh cow patty, or worse, was more likely than not—which Sky discovered the first time Chuckie McGuire led her over the wooden fence into the Scotts' pasture. She'd never been down that far and had heard rumors of a black-faced bull with a brass ring pierced through his nose, but it wasn't until her dress was peeled away and Chuckie's trousers flung off that either of them heard the bull's steamy breath or the swipe of his hoof against the dry August grass. Then, in the light of the furnaces over the hill, they saw his silhouette. His chest was broad, his legs stocky, his balls low and tight. When he took a few slow steps toward them, Sky saw that his eyes were black and hard, without the hint of heat or anger or fire.

"Come on," Chuckie whispered, one hand protecting his privates, the other gripping Sky's upper arm.

"You think he'll charge?" Sky asked, crawling onto her knees, then leaning back onto her haunches, her dress draped over her shoulders like a cape.

The fence—ten or so feet behind them—didn't look like it would hold a charging bull.

"Sure he will. Haven't you ever been on a farm?"

They inched backward on their heels, until their shoulders bumped the lowest rail on the fence. The bull stood still, huffing, taking in their scent, watching, pawing at the ground, and as Chuckie and Sky scaled the fence, splinters biting into their palms, he turned and sauntered away, snorting. Once on the other side, Chuckie bent Sky over the fence, took her from behind, finished what he had started, and she, with her eyes on the bull, rubbed hard on that place at the top of her legs that she'd discovered years before until she shuddered, emptied, groaned, and again filled with that overwhelming sadness.

Even Georgie found a way to relieve his grief after Jake's death. With ten or so of his neighborhood pals, he invented a game called "Belt Him In." They played on the dirt road in front of the Bozics' house, gathering within the four corners that marked the boundaries around the playing field: one corner where a stack of scrap metal was piled, another where the alleyway met the main thoroughfare, the third where an old wagon bed lay on its side, and the final corner at the end of Tiny's crooked fence.

Later in their lives, the boys would reminisce, remember the game, the power it instilled in them, the laughter, the frivolity, but like most people, they would forget all about the pain they inflicted on one another and the joy, the rush of ecstasy, as they did.

Once inside the playing field, the boys removed their belts and twisted a stick into the loops of their trousers to keep them from falling down. They chose who was first to be "it," usually the smallest and youngest of the gang—the runt, somebody's little buck-toothed tag-along brother. Then "it" hopped on one leg, holding the other behind him with one hand and flailing the other hand in the air, trying to tag the boys as they raced around within the boundaries. The boys didn't make it easy; they dodged and taunted, poked fun at his mother and his patched-up clothes, called him *nigger, dago, spick, redneck, spook, wop, potato-digger, ditch-digger, injun, cheapskate, bastard,* and *mill hunky.* They leaned in close, then peeled away when he reached out to tag them; they sniggered and laughed and chuckled and chortled; they said that his two-fingered father had to feel up his mother with his pinky and that she had to get her thrills from the dairy man whose dick hung down to his knees; they pulled up their eyes, waggled their tongues, hockered on his cheeks, farted downwind; they hollered and yelled and grunted, calling him *shit-ass* and *nose-picker* and *chicken* and *momma's boy.* They ran laps around the lame, hopping runt, and "it" hopped and hopped, from the scrap metal to Tiny's fence, to the alleyway, and back, his leg tiring and his face growing red. All this until "it" lost his balance and in a moment of weakness, surrendered and dropped his second foot to the ground. Then the other boys whooped and cheered and hollered, "Belt him in! Belt him in!" at the tops of their voices, like some kind of war cry, so that even the echoing clank of railroad cars at the mill was drowned out for a millisecond. Then they unfurled their leather belts, raised them high over their heads, and proceeded to whip and wallop "it"—drawing blood and raising crimson welts—until "it" managed to crawl or stumble or crabwalk or belly-slide outside the boundaries of the playing field, where he curled on his side, tried not to bawl, nursed his wounds.

1903

After Klara told him about her dream and fixed up his foot, Drago thought of Ana, the only woman, girl really, who had come before his wife. Frail-boned Ana back in his home village who had worn her pale hair—yellow as hay but soft as corn silk—in a single braid that tickled her spindly calves. At the swimming hole one summer, he had let his eyes wander to the tail of that braid where the taut cords along the backs of her knees framed a shallow indentation which he'd imagined would taste as sweet as nectar from a honeysuckle bloom. For a full year thereafter, he'd secretly followed her from school, across fields and creek beds, silent as the flap of an owl's wing, and had formulated in his mind the words that he would someday speak, playing out their sounds of admiration and devotion. But never once had he gathered the courage to profess his love. On hot days, he'd surprised her by leaving wisteria blooms, a fish from the river, or a bundle of sweet-smelling clover on her stoop; in wintertime, he'd collected smooth stones from beneath drifts of snow and left them on her windowsill. But he was not her only suitor, and on the day he'd vowed to discover his voice, the priest of the local parish had announced her engagement just after the sermon at Sunday mass. Three months later, she'd married his brother Josip.

But as quickly as Ana entered his thoughts, Drago banished her to that place in his mind where he stored special things. Although he didn't believe for a moment that she, especially the image of her on the bank of the swimming hole, was gone for good, he forced her out of the everyday thick of things. He knew better than to consider what could have been, had he, and not Josip, discovered his voice. And he knew that if he allowed that pale sliver of light to penetrate Thirsty, he would find himself unable to look at his own children, though he rarely did anyway.

He thought of all this during his walk to the mill, after Klara's kindness on the porch had startled him into a thin guilt—for what he couldn't set a finger on for sure. But first that morning he'd sat hunched on the porch steps, pulling smoke from a rolled cigarette in the sharp January freeze. He watched the smoke roll off the tip of the fag and listened to the jangle of the button man's cart come around the corner, followed by his song. "I got buttons, blue and gold. I got buttons, nothing sold. Wear 'em on your coat! Sew 'em to your cap! Trousers and blouses and short pants and that! Thread to pull. Needles to pierce. Yarn for your afghans. Get it all here!" There was a short pause, another jangle of bells, all before the button man came into sight, and, "I got buttons, yellow and red. I got . . ." Once a week or so he worked his way through Thirsty, hawking his wares, pushing his cart up and down the steep hills, a short, dark Italian with blotchy skin and a bushy white mustache, thin legs and a swollen stomach. The bells and song announced him, and even on winter days like this on ice-slick roads, he carried news and letters from one family to another, taking his payment however the women offered it: coins, apples, cuts of pork, lard, flour, promises of next week, or a quick fuck in the pantry.

Then the button man passed the house, slowly, his steps becoming smaller and smaller until it seemed as if he weren't moving at all. He paused in his song and looked Drago's way, but Drago only lifted his hand in greeting and nodded, dismissing him. The button man moved on, and Drago awkwardly cradled his foot in his lap. The sole of his boot had given way during his last shift and a sprat of steel had seared into the thick of his heel. The pain reminded him of that raw-eyed dog his father had kept chained in the barn, the one that had buried its teeth into Drago's calf when he had accidentally moved into range while cleaning the stalls as a boy. It was the kind of pain that curled his lip and drew tears to his eyes no matter how hard he wrestled the urge. He'd slept with a slab of lard smoothed across the burn, but overnight it had bubbled up, and by three o'clock that morning, when Klara shook him out of sleep to ready for his next shift, his heel looked like the crusty top of a pan of baked polenta.

Then Klara was in front of him. She kneeled and said, "Give me that foot." And with a quick, hot needle, she pierced the bubbles, then held an old teacup underneath to collect the poison, which she would later mix with a bit of water and pour out the kitchen window into a snowdrift. Afterward she lifted his foot into a pail of cool water. "Nurse this a while, and don't move off until I come back with salve. Last thing we need is infection taking on."

"All right, *stara baba*," Drago answered, thankful, if for nothing else, for her efficiency. He stared into the lean morning light that spread a pale lavender shadow over the small collection of houses, mill colors bled between, flecks of soot floating down like a fine rain. Across the way in Tiny's nest of pine trees, a woodpecker kept time to the blackbird's call. The morning was crisp. There was so much snow already on the ground, then yesterday's rain, and now ice, with more snow to come from the look of the clouds hanging low and full in the sky. Drago flicked the smoldering butt of his cigarette into the snow, smoothed his hands over his rough-spun shirt, and arched his back to stretch the muscles on his shoveling side.

The house that stood behind him was painted white, coated gray with soot, square, solid, like a strong man squatting on his haunches. Although he had not built the original frame, he had strengthened it over the years. He'd added a new staircase with a sturdy railing, a front porch, a back stoop, new window frames, and a tiny room on the second floor that would someday be a bathroom, but not until water was finally pumped up the hill and not until it was someone else's home. When Klara asked, he added shutters that opened and closed. When Sky complained that she needed more storage space for her dresses, he built an extra closet in her bedroom. He made much of the furniture in the house: the kitchen table, three dressers, a canning cupboard, three bedside stands, and a pair of bookshelves. In the cellar, he kept his tools, clean and organized, on a workbench. No one was allowed to touch them, especially not the children. In a drawer he stored the treasury of small, thin-bladed knives with which he had carved the tiny animals he'd carried in his satchel on the day he'd appeared on Klara's doorstep back home. He didn't carve anymore. Whenever Klara asked why, he said he didn't have time with so much work to do. Really he meant that when he'd arrived in Thirsty, he'd believed it was a place where people came to live, but after so many years in the mill, he knew it was a city where people came to die. As the years passed, he watched slag piles grow into mountains, while people shrank into pebbles. He didn't tell this to anyone, just thought it to himself as he walked to work or when he had to fold during a poker game at Penny's. He thought it along with a trail of other thoughts, but had not had time to seek out answers.

Klara returned with a jar of salve. She set it on the top step and moved around in front of him. She reached behind her and untied the strings of her apron, then knelt with the apron spread across one palm. Without looking up, she lifted his foot in her hand from the pail of water that was close to developing a frozen skin and wrapped the apron over it. Wisps of hair fluttered around her face in the breeze. She patted his foot dry.

"That hurt?" she asked, setting the apron aside.

When she spoke low like that, her voice sounded like dry autumn leaves rustling against each other in a wind. "Nah," he said.

She opened the salve, eased a bit onto her palm, and spread it on his heel. Drago closed his eyes.

"I fixed your boot," she said. "I got a square of cheap leather from Mr. Ragonelli last week. I sewed it into place before I woke you. You shouldn't feel a bite today."

"Thank you."

"I stitched you a new pair of gloves, too. Those cheap ones you got from the mill store cost half a day's labor and don't last any more than a couple of turns on the furnace. Don't go buying them again."

He leaned forward as she folded the damp apron in half, then quarters. She smelled sweet, like milk and salt, and he knew she'd been fixing butter.

"You know," he said, "I would've liked to meet your ma before she passed."

Drago's statement was so sudden it nearly knocked Klara clean off the stoop. She had been lost in thought, trying to decide whether to cook up a chicken or vegetable soup for dinner, calculating how many potatoes she had left in the cellar, and wondering if Sky would be home to help with Georgie and Ivo or if she would run off as she usually did, chasing some boy or skulking around with that Constance girl down the road, leaving Klara with too many burdens. She half-stood, teetered, and then grabbed hold of Drago's shoulder for balance. He set a hand on her hip to steady her.

"You might not think so had she lived," she said. "My ma would have taken a strap to you long ago."

Drago threw back his head and laughed. Again, Klara was caught off guard. She looked at him, not knowing exactly what she expected, but knowing it wasn't this. She thought maybe he was mocking her and waited for him to reach out to thump her on the head. But he just kept laughing, looking at her and shaking his head. Like the rest of him, his face was narrow, but the crown of his head ballooned out slightly, like an upside-down pear. Three deep wrinkles lay under each blue eye, and tiny lines were carved into his upper lip beneath his mustache. His teeth—yellow from smoking—were square, with a small space between the top front two. When she realized nothing was coming but laughter, Klara let go and laughed with him. Her eyes filled with tears, and when she looked from his face to the apron she still held in her hand, the red embroidered flowers blurred into a hum of color.

"Klara," he said, "sometimes what I expect to come from your mouth never does and what I don't even imagine is there pops out instead." He squeezed her hip, then let his hand fall away. He looked around at the small square of yard, down toward the buckeye tree he had planted a few years back that was finally filling in, set his hands over the bony caps of his knees that poked out through his worn trousers, and rubbed. "Feels like they're going to crack easy as dry timber."

Klara smiled and sat down next to him. An uneasy quiet settled between them.

"You would have been surprised at my ma, too," he said after a bit. The lavender light was turning a tender blue, reflecting off the snow and the flames in the smokestack over the hill. "She was a strong lady. Kept the farm running even when my pa got too liquored to plow. Our house is built on stilts, you know, and Ma kept the pigs and cows underneath, even the mule. At night I used to listen to the animals shuffling around, like they were nudging each other before settling down to rest. The chickens got to wander all over the house, even into the room where me and my brothers slept. Ma cured the meat in the smokehouse on top. That was my favorite place in the world." He paused. He might have been talking to himself because he'd told her these same stories over and over again throughout the years. "Ah, but you know all that," he said, then leaned over and kissed her on the forehead, then the mouth. "I remember the first time I saw you, standing at your pa's door looking at me like I was crazy to come knocking. You were all points and bends, sharp in most places."

"Yeah, well, I'm not sharp anymore, not after giving birth to those three hellions we've got." She reached down and turned his bad foot so she could see it. With her thumb against the carved-in space below his ankle bone, she thought she could feel the thrum of his pulse, and she remembered the beginning, when she'd been too afraid to ask for anything. She hadn't even known what to ask for. She just did as she was told, first by her father, then by Drago. For a long time after they were married, she'd even been too afraid to say his name out loud, just repeated it over and over in her head.

They heard the crunch of ice and snow and saw Sacko Gekic turn the bend. He waved a hand and paused in front of the house.

"You go on," Drago hollered. "I'll be coming along."

Once Sacko was out of earshot, Klara said, "Has he said anything to you about marrying Stella Jevic?"

"Just that he's been thinking on it. Nothing for sure."

"You might want to let him know that Andy Pavelic's been sniffing around, and Stella says she's not much interested in going on alone. I saw her pass him a slice of pie on his way from work a few days back. And you know that once Stella's apple pies start changing hands, marriage isn't far off."

"I'll tell him, but it's not been long since he dug the grave for Alice."

"If it's long enough for the ground to settle and long enough for him to be courting, it's long enough to marry." Klara stood and pointed to the boots in the corner. "Get them on. I'll get your lunch pail."

When she returned a few minutes later, he unfolded the cover napkin and peeked in. Three pieces of boiled chicken, a slice of apple pie, and a thick roll of bread already speckled with soot.

With his cap pulled tight to his head, leather gloves tucked into his back pocket, and lunch pail in hand, Drago kissed Klara's cheek. He made for the garden, cut through the alleyway, and then pitched himself down the steep grade into the woods, ignoring the gripe in his left foot. His boots rattled against the icy stones and slid along the sheerest grades. Finally he cut through the stout line of trees onto the road that ran along the Monongahela to the mill.

The sun hadn't yet bared itself completely, but the fiery sky lit the thin line of men filing along the road in the worn trenches between snow drifts, all headed in the same direction with their heads sunk against their chests, still sleeping, taking an easy walk for extra shuteye. The rare quiet moment with Klara drifted away, and as he walked, Drago wondered if Ana was still wearing that braid.

After Drago disappeared from the alleyway, Klara sat alone, wondering over her husband's unexpected kindness and letting last night's dream percolate in her mind. She sat just long enough for the town to shake off sleep and stretch before going inside and removing a few emergency dollars from the coffee tin behind the bread box in the kitchen. She tucked the money into her pocket and, with little more than a nod, left the boys under Sky's care. She walked through Thirsty to the downtown area, playing the dream she'd had the night before over and over in her mind. In it, she drove a caravan of camels from the land of Ophir to that of King Solomon, great stinking beasts packed with precious gems and stones. Despite the fact that it was early January, she could feel the heat rise from the desert floor and envelop her like a fog. An earthy-sweet odor gathered under her arms and behind her knees, the kind that gathered in summertime when she worked in the garden. She felt the hard leather saddle stiff between her legs, chafing her thighs in a pleasurable way, and as the camel rose from its knees, tipping forward, then rising and leveling out, she grew dizzy. While the camel moved, she was entranced by the silkiness of the white gauze that enmeshed her body, leaving only her eyes visible, and the jangle of a thousand bracelets on her arms. It wasn't often that any woman in Thirsty enjoyed such a delirium, so Klara eased into it and walked past the butcher shop where men rested their feet on the railing, smoked and gawked, the scent of fresh blood spilling from the doorway. She floated along the cindered avenue, letting the call of the muezzin pull at her ears, and she didn't even glance into the frosted windows of the five-and-dime. There was nothing so delicious as forgetting where she was and how she came to be there; even the crisp winter air could not crack the spell.

At the railroad crossing, a train snapped its whistle. Klara paused, leaned on a post, and waited with three others for the load of scrap metal to rumble past. Flat cars were piled high with parcels of salvaged steel, corroded pipe, and old castings scrounged up from scrapyards throughout the country. People's junk to be melted down, stirred, and cooked into steel. A thousand lives per car rode into the mill yard on that rail line, the vein that pierced the heart, slipped past the furnaces, and snuck out the other side.

The snow was knee deep, so Klara walked in a path flattened by the morning's foot traffic, tucked her head from the wind, and blinked icy flakes from her lashes. In the snow, all curves and colors disappeared. Everything cut a straight line, blocks and rectangles stacked one on top of another. Shades of gray. Gray like flint, a mouse's back, the outer rim of a bruise. In the street, people trudged along, heads down, hands dug into pockets. Thickly woven caps and heavy coats slowed their movements. Klara's mittens were bulky, black, homemade. In her nightgown drawer at home, she kept the sleek, red, store-bought gloves that Katherine had given her as a Christmas gift the year before. She didn't believe she would ever own another pair as beautiful, so only took them out to admire before bed on nights when the sky pressed down too hard.

Usually the snow and wind irritated her until she spoke out loud to them, but today she barely took note. Instead she listened to the throaty, rolling commands of the camel drivers, sold her ear to their music. The more intently she listened, the further she retreated from the city. Blindly she passed Millie's Millinery, the Stop-n-Go Diner, Ted's Pool Hall, a drug store, a tobacco shop, and a bakery. It wasn't until she heard the bells of St. Jude's ringing out that she realized that she'd walked too far and had to retrace her steps for a block or two in order to reach the door of Lucy Giller's High-Style Beauty Salon. It was the bottom floor of Lucy's home with three steps leading to a verandah that stretched the full length of the house and even turned the corner along one side. In summertime, ladies congregated here. They lounged in rocking chairs and sipped mint tea served up in frosty beer mugs. They shared news, complained about prices and men, and waited their turn under Lucy's miraculous hands. Beneath the layer of grit and snow, the house was painted canary yellow, one of Lucy's many attempts to brighten and colorize the dreary town.

When Klara pushed through the door, Lucy sang out in delight. She had a smooth, seductive voice that could lure a jackdaw from a chimney nook and hips that had been heading in opposite directions for fifty years. Her nest of crabapple-red hair was tied up in a satiny blue scarf. Her lips were painted orange.

After unwrapping Klara from her cloaks, she sat her in a tilt-back swivel chair ordered straight from a New York City catalog, spun her to face the mirror, and plucked hair-pins from the bun at the base of Klara's neck until locks of hair tumbled down around her face. She smiled and said, "Honey, when I finish with you, that man of yours is going to sweeten your coffee with three lumps of white sugar and two drops of nectar!" While she clucked and cooed and fluttered about, lifting and examining locks of hair, Klara watched herself in the glass. Her dark brown hair was springy, like peels of carrot skin curled up in a pile from a knife's edge. It was long and wild, and fell far below her waist. As a girl, she'd despised it. She'd wanted straight, flat hair like all her friends at school, hair that glistened under the sun's rays. To achieve this, she'd tried everything. She'd waxed it, ironed it, slept on it flat, steamed it, and even smeared it with lard. Whenever possible, she'd made wishes on four-leaf clovers and falling stars, but no matter how she'd tried to tame it, her hair had grown like wild flowers. When her mother was still living, she'd promised that curly hair was a sign of fertility, something a girl could boast of, but Klara had just shaken her head and cried. When she was eleven, Klara had stolen the razor-sharp shears from her mother's sewing basket and knicked off her hair close to her scalp, letting it fall around her feet in tight, scratchy piles. It hadn't been cut since.

Lucy's shop was homey and bright, and it smelled of lilac water and hair tonic. As Klara's frozen face began to thaw, her cheeks brightened and the tip of her chin stung. She reached a hand from under the cape and rubbed her face with her palm. When she looked around, she realized she was the only customer and said, "Guess I'm the only woman crazy enough to come for a hairdo in weather like this." Lucy laughed and patted her shoulder, then announced, "Honey, I'm not setting my scissors to all these beautiful curls, but I will change the color. Brighten you up a bit. I've got a new process I've been meaning to try out. Won't charge you but a few extra pennies for the practice." And as Klara sat under Lucy's easy hands, she underwent a miraculous transformation: She began to see her own beauty. Of course, it wasn't hard with Lucy highlighting every positive characteristic.

"Sweet pea, you got a nose to ogle at! There aren't going to be any crows roosting on that petite little thing. Couldn't get a foothold for trying. Just a nub of dough shaped just right!"

And, "Pumpkin, with skin like that, you could ship off to New York City and be a model in one of those high-falluting magazines. Not a blemish to be found. Skin like cream, baby-doll. Sweet, sweet cream!"

And, "Them eyes, sugar dumpling, cut them emerald eyes at some high-moneyed man and you'll be strolling in fine mink furs and diamond-stacked heels! You won't have time to look poor Lucy's way."

By the time the proper concoction was blended into her hair, sucking away the chestnut hues, Lucy had convinced Klara that when Drago saw her golden tresses, he would sweep her into his arms, turn her in a quick waltz across the living room floor, and stay home from Penny's for good. He would call her *sweetheart* instead of *stara baba* and buy her two cream puffs from the bakery each evening. It was a fantasy Klara began to enjoy. She spun in the swivel chair and turned the pages of a fashion magazine. The strength of the peroxide pulled tears to her eyes, and the models swam in a watery rainbow.

But somewhere beyond last night's dream and Lucy Giller's fantasies, Klara knew the anger that would rip through Drago when he saw her new hairstyle for the first time. He didn't like her wearing anything extra, especially jewelry. "Take them goddamn baubles off!" he'd holler if she came down the stairs with a bracelet on her wrist or a pair of earrings for church. But she wanted the new hairdo anyway, and as she spun in the chair, slowly now, her own rage began to tangle and knot. It was often this way for her; she would begin a day feeling light and open, and by the end of that same day, she would be closed and full of rage.

"You know," she told Lucy, leaning back for the final rinse, "Drago might head down here after dark for a slice at your throat once he finds out you're the one who's done this to me. Better lock up those razors good and tight tonight."

Lucy laughed louder than Klara had ever heard a woman laugh, even Katherine. "Aw," she said, "I'm not afraid of a little old husband. They're as harmless as most spiders once you get them on your side."

When Lucy spun her once again to face the mirror, Klara's hair was wild like white flames around her head, full of light and fire and sun. Her skin was bright. Her green eyes shined. She smiled and forgot all about that nasty spider of hers.

Three steps into the walk home, the snow stopped. Klara paused in front of Trillman's Hat Shop, looked in at the small-nosed mannequin posed in a sleek black dress, velvet-brimmed hat, and red silk stockings, and then primped at her own reflection in the plate-glass window. The winter air smelled like a bright shaft of light. She began to climb the hill—the steepest in Thirsty—the kind that shot straight up to heaven for a mile, settled into a sharp peak, then zipped back down the other side. It was the kind of hill you didn't want to face too often in your day because the only way to accomplish it was to keep your eyes on your feet, counting steps or making a list in your mind of things you didn't want to forget. But the urge to look up and see how far you still had to go was like the urge to urinate, hard to ignore. And once you looked, especially on a winter day, and saw that the hill stretched on and up forever, touching the bottom of the sky, you'd likely decide that whatever it was you were needing from the store or the butchery wasn't all that important, something you could surely do without or borrow from a neighbor. And you would turn around and head for home. But since Klara had already climbed the hill once that morning to come into town, she had no choice but to climb it again to get home. Halfway up, she gave in to the urge to look and saw BenJo crossing the street on the crest of the hill.

As Klara neared, she waved until BenJo recognized her. From the look of surprise on his face, she realized her shock of hair could melt the snow and bring an early spring. He nodded his approval without saying a word—for talking to a white woman in the street was altogether different than conducting business in his store—but as he tilted his whole body to catch her eye, the crate of oranges he'd carried from the train station tipped and the oranges sprang free. They rolled and spun joyously down the hill, sliding over ice piles and bouncing over mounds of snow. BenJo spun with the empty crate swinging by his side, his head crooked up at a painful angle, and he chased the fleeing oranges with his cries. "Stop my babies! Stop my beautiful babies!" Using her cloak as a sack, Klara collected as many as she could, carried them the rest of the way up the hill, then dropped them into the crate one by one.

"Thank you, Mrs. Bozic," BenJo said when the crate was once again nearly full. "Take two for the boys."

She buried the oranges in the deep pockets of her cloak, then turned and looked down the hill. The remaining oranges, now still, were scattered at intervals along the street, bright balls of color embedded in the white snow. Lucy should see this, Klara thought.

At nineteen, Sky was both weedlike and sexy. She had what her mother missed, a flat stomach and full breasts, and also a few things Klara was happy to do without, including a heart so open to love it was bound to get broken. She had the same curly hair Klara had, lighter though, nearly blond, and emerald eyes, too. In the moments that the pain of her life quit riding her, Sky was downright pretty, but anger at her father ate at her from the inside out.

Every six months or so, Sky dreamt that a child disappeared from Thirsty—silently, without a trace, no bits of clothing left behind, no clues—nothing but a neat pile of chalk-white bones on a cliff overlooking the Monongahela River. In the dream, she always saw the man who took and killed the child—a lean, yellow-haired man leaning into the bed of a wagon, a red patch on the backside of his tattered gray pants.

Knowing she was next, Sky always turned and ran through her mother's garden, between tall rows of tomato plants and corn stalks, and into the cellar. Swallowed by the kind of dark you can swim through, she would trip on boxes and barrels. But despite the cover of darkness, the yellow-haired man always caught her. Grabbed her from behind and swung her around to face him. With one arm, he held her; with the other, he reached up into the wooden rafters where her father stored his ladders and oversized tools, deftly grabbed a pair of giant pruning shears, and opened them wide. Though for a moment she was free from the man's grip, Sky always stood still and waited. Just waited. Until he raised the shears up over his head, lowered them around her, and locked her into the space between the handles. "At least he's not going to cut me with them," she thought every time, then closed her eyes.

In the final moments of the dream, the man would bend and put his mouth to the shallow space between Sky's breasts as if he might kiss her there. As if something tender might actually unfold. She screamed then, but always the house remained silent. No one ran to save her. No one even cocked an ear to listen. After this, the man would open his mouth and gnaw, gently at first. Then she would hear him chewing on her sternum, a low crunching sound, like footsteps in winter snow that has already crusted over. And he would chew, as if there were no skin to chew through, as if she were already just bone.

When Sky saw Klara coming up the stairs with a new head of flaming hair, she thought *beautiful,* but knowing how her father would steam and blow, she dropped the plate she was drying and folded into ugly. The plate shattered. She felt herself stiffen and fought an urge to crack her mother across the face. "Oh, Mum!" she cried. "Daddy's going to kill you." Then she wondered why her mother didn't do everything she could to keep the peace in their home, why she instigated anger, why she couldn't just behave like other mothers, nodding and agreeing when necessary. "You better tie on a scarf before he gets home," she said, then grabbed a coat from the rack in the hallway and ducked out the back door to Constance's, leaving the pieces of the plate where they had settled on the floor.

Klara fed and sent the boys to bed, then tucked the ends of her hair under a babushka so that not a strand was visible. She was standing at the window washing dishes in the basin when Drago's whistle sifted through the front door and along the short hallway and slid into the kitchen.

"Klara? You here?"

Klara turned toward the door as he moved through it. Like always, he had scrubbed up at the mill before walking home, the skin on his hands ground crimson-raw from the stiff wire-bristled brush, gleaming cheeks, but a pitchy smear slept along his chin, under his jaw.

"Evening," she said. "Give me that pail. I'll wash it quick while the water's hot." She reached a hand toward him, swiped the rag under his jaw, and then turned back to the basin of water. "Are you ready to eat?"

"No, come on out to the stoop. I'm going to have a smoke," he said and rubbed his hands together. "The air's warmed a bit. Must be getting ready to snow again." He opened the back door, pushed through, and cocked his head around until he saw her out of the corner of his eye. "And get that goddamn rag off your head. You're not the town chimney sweep."

Klara reached up with both hands, pulled the babushka tighter over her ears, and watched her husband move down the yard. The nighttime air slipped under her skirt like a pair of icy hands, and she felt her resolve settling into place. No matter what happened, she decided, she was not changing her hair back to the way it was. She stood still, letting her anger solidify into something she could use. Drago struck a match, then lit the end of a cigarette. He leaned, his back to her, against the trunk of a peach tree. His shoulders were straight and strong, and despite what was coming, Klara remembered the day she birthed Georgie, an afternoon so still and hot that even the birds quit singing. Left alone for a few minutes with her and the baby, Drago had whistled for a while, then smiled—one of his rare, deep-down smiles that unfolded the lines on his forehead—and fanned her with a newspaper. Later that evening, she listened as he settled on the porch to sleep, banished from the house by Katherine, the planks creaking and giving under his weight. Halfway to dawn, when he considered her sleeping, he'd called to her in a raspy voice, "I love you, girl." She hadn't answered, but grabbed at the moment as if it were a butterfly to lock in a jar.

From the back stoop of the Bozics' house, you could see the smokestacks jutting up from the valley floor, and from their tops, flame-heads danced out orange and red. If you'd never seen a night sky, velvety black with bright spots of stars and faraway planets making intricate pictures, you'd have thought this was the loveliest sky in the world—layers of light, ribbons of bright, gaseous colors smeared with giant clouds of white steam.

Finally, Klara stepped through the door onto the porch and slid the babushka from her head. She unpinned the curls, letting them fall loose across her shoulders, over her breasts, and down her back. She tucked the pins and scarf into her pocket. The cold breeze slipped through the buttonholes of her dress, and the pillows of snowy quiet cushioned the nighttime sounds coming from the mill.

When Drago turned, he flicked the butt of his cigarette into the garden, then looked up at her. He leapt from leaning to standing and stamped his feet. She cringed, quivered inside, swelled, that dizzying mixture of rage and fear, one always trying to outdo the other.

"Klara?" he grunted.

"Mmm?"

"What in God's name have you done to yourself?" He stumbled over the words through twisted lips, not needing anything more than the tone of his voice to let her know what was coming.

"Drago . . . Drago, wait!" Her voice was even. She felt the hard wood of the doorframe at her back.

"You better tell me that hussy-blonde mop you've got on your head is one those wigs from one of those goddamn magazines you've got stored in your underthings drawer!"

Klara didn't move, just hung her head and tangled her hands in her hair. She glanced next door. Not even a lamp in Katherine's window. Jake buried and gone.

"It's not a wig," she said, standing straighter, combing her hair back with her fingers.

"Don't tell me that."

"It's my hair."

"What the hell have you done? It's Katherine, isn't it? She's done this to you!" He shoved his hands into his trouser pockets and kept his eyes on his wife.

"No, Katherine didn't do anything. She hasn't even seen it yet. I went down to Lucy Giller's place this morning after you left and got it done . . . by myself . . . all by myself." Klara tipped her head left and right, shaking out the curls. Her daydreams about him surprising her with an "I like it just fine. Makes you even prettier than you were before" were shattered right then, and her eyes filled with glimmering shards of light. It hurt to look at her husband. "I like it, though," she said. "Look closer." Her voice softened, but she might as well have been talking to herself. "It looks fine, Drago, just fine. I get tired of nothing ever changing around here, and sooner or later my brown hair will grow back. Just let me enjoy this one thing." It was too dark to see for sure, but even from the stoop Klara felt Drago's chest muscles tensing, the muscles on his shoveling side quivering taut.

"Like it?" he said. "You look like one of those broads down at the saloon, winking and hanging out their breasts, smacking their painted lips together like they're always hungry for something!" Under the bare branches of the peach tree, Drago began to strut on his tiptoes, swirling his hips awkwardly back and forth, left and right, and poking his chest out toward Klara, pretending he was one of those hussy broads at the bar. "Hey, mister, how about a beer?" he tittered, jumping his rough voice up an octave. Then he stopped quick and shuffled his body back into place. He paused. "No wife of mine . . ."

"Then how come you got to go there if the women are like that?"

"Don't you start on me, Klara. Me or the saloon. I stop now and then for a beer after work and it doesn't have anything to do with your head of hair looking like someone set you on fire!"

Drago wrenched his hands from his pockets and strode up the yard toward the stoop, slow, but steady, arms hanging at his sides, fingers and thumbs fisting up tight. When he got within a few yards, Klara saw the hard, black pupils of his eyes and the set jaw.

"You keep back, Drago Bozic!" She screamed this time, then pitched forward, out of the slice of mill light that had been cradling her. "I'm keeping my hair!" Fear filled her up, like hot tea in a teacup, splashing over her edges. She turned as fast as she could, yanked open the door, and raced into the house, but Drago caught the door before it slammed shut.

"I'm cutting it off, Klara! And tomorrow you'll go back down to that damn city woman and get what's left colored back the way it was!"

The Bozics' kitchen was a large, yellow-walled room that ran the full length of the house in the back half with a window looking out over the garden and a long, oblong wooden table taking up the middle space. Next to the wash basin under the window hung a cabinet Klara used to store odd and ends, and from a cup of sharpened pencils in the cabinet, Drago pulled a pair of scissors and held them over his head, opening and closing them.

As he moved slowly around the kitchen table, Klara positioned herself on the opposite side and planted her hands on her hips. By now there was nothing kind or wistful remaining on her face. Her mane stood on end, electrified. Her lips pressed down in a snarl.

"My hair is staying on my head, Drago Bozic. It hasn't been cut since I was eleven, and you aren't cutting it now."

Drago stretched his torso across the table, then his scissors arm, but the table was too wide; he couldn't reach her and he growled. He took a few steps around one end of the table; Klara headed in the same direction. Drago stepped the other way; Klara shifted with him, keeping the distance between them equal.

"Klara, get over here!" Drago grunted, waving the scissors above his head. She bunched up the pleats of her skirt in her fists and hiked the skirt so high her bare knees stuck out. Though she suspected that in the end he would win, she wasn't going to make his struggle easy. She was prepared to race around that table until morning, back and forth, until he was worn out or until he just gave up and stomped away, but then the boys' cries rushed down the stairs. Klara stopped, turned her head.

"Drago, calm down. You're frightening the boys!"

"No wife of mine is going to strut around town looking like somebody's hussy. Come here. I'm taking that hair."

He chased her in circles, slapping his free hand on the table, until an oval of sweat gathered at the neck of his undershirt and his tongue lolled out of the side of his mouth like a dog's. The boys moved from their bedroom halfway down the staircase and hollered something awful. They were too old to cry and too young to fight back. Finally out of breath, Klara banged her fists against her breasts, letting her skirt fall into place, and sobbed. She dropped into the corner like a rag doll, curling against her knees and letting her head crack against the wall. Drago stopped. He was panting. His face was coated with sweat. Klara remembered Lucy's words: "Aw, I'm not afraid of a little old husband. They're as harmless as spiders once you get them on your side."

But Drago was never harmless, so when Lucy Giller's voice faded, Klara screamed, "Come on, Drago Bozic, come on and get me!" She leapt up again, this time coming at him, fear replaced by rage. She grabbed at the ends of her hair and yanked them to arms' length from her head. "Come on, take my hair!" she panted. The boys whimpered, then grew quiet.

Slowly Drago rounded the table, shoved Klara to her knees, and hovered over her. He lifted the scissors and in quick strokes, sliced close to her head until her lap and the bare wooden floor around her swirled with flaming locks. Klara wailed and wailed. She wailed until she screeched and then screeched until Katherine pounded up the back stairs and into the kitchen. From the doorway, she could see the boys standing in the hallway half-hidden by the coatrack. She held up her hand, signaling them to stand still, not to move.

"Drago!" Katherine said. She remembered how even Jake's voice had always been when he'd talked Drago down. "Easy. Take it easy." Though she wanted to leap on him, strangle him, stab him with the scissors, she restrained herself, knowing that if provoked, he might take the scissors to Klara's neck.

For a long moment, it was silent, then Klara began to laugh, hysterical laughter that poured from her mouth. It was suddenly funny to her—her husband, heaving and sweating with a pair of scissors wagging at her over his head.

"What are you laughing at, Klara?" Drago said. He butted his face close to hers, long strands of her hair glittering on his chest.

"You!" Klara said.

"Drago," Katherine said, moving in from the doorway until she stood across the table from them, "it's time you go. Get on out of here and don't show your face back here tonight. Find a resting place elsewhere. You've done enough trouble."

His eyes darkened, narrowed. "This is your fault, Katherine. I've got nothing to do with this. You're the one always feeding her thoughts about changing things around here. And nothing needs changing except you!"

Klara laughed again, so hard her nose began to bleed. Blood smeared over her lips and chin, filling her lap. She crawled away from Drago on her hands and knees, sprigs of hair poking up from her head like the first spring crocuses. What remained was tangled around her like the vines in the grape arbor, no longer connected to her, no longer rooted.

Drago stared at her for a moment. There was no remorse . . . just a brief thought that his wife had finally driven herself mad. He turned, threw the scissors into the dishwater, and slammed out the back door.

The boys rushed in, knelt close by. Now that their father was gone, they expected to be drawn into the circle of warmth and protection, but when Klara looked up, eyes full of love and hatred, she said, "Go to bed," in a voice that sent them farther away than they'd ever been.

Katherine lightly touched their shoulders. "Get on, you two," she said. "Don't worry. I'll take care of your mum."

Nigger Heaven was almost full by the time Klara stepped from the dimly lit stairwell into the dark balcony. The usher boy who escorted her, perplexed by this white woman's insistence on sitting in the place where black people were relegated, held the door open far enough for the light from his lantern to mark her path, distracting the audience from the dancers on stage.

"Ah, mister, shut down that light!" a voice called from the back.

"Close the door!"

"We paid like everyone else."

But the appeals, to a deaf white ear, only made the usher boy open the door wider so that faces were lit and the woman shaking herself from one end of the stage to the other glanced up and hollered, "Shut up, up there. Can't you see I'm trying to dance?" The usher grinned and laughed out loud. He was a short, stocky boy with clipped brown hair and bluish eyes. For that moment he was bold, but then he remembered that he was alone with thirty or so black men, all older and bigger, and he obliged his fear by easing the door closed a crack. He hated having to come up the stairs at all and usually he didn't have to. "I just keep it the way they leave it," he told people who asked, and that wasn't very nice, with rotting wooden seats, mildewed walls, and a sour stench where men pissed in the corner when outside seemed too far away. But because this white woman insisted on climbing the stairs, he was obligated to accompany her and see her safely to a seat. If he hadn't and his boss had found out, he would have lost his job for sure.

Finally, two men near the front rose and stepped into the aisle.

"Ma'am," one of them said, "there's a seat here you're welcome to."

The usher boy felt obligated to interrupt one more time. "Ma'am, we've got plenty of seats downstairs."

Klara turned to face him. A pale green scarf was tied over her freshly shorn hair. Light and shadows cut her face in half. "This will be fine. Thank you."

She smiled, passed close to the two men, and seated herself in the second row. After a few long moments, the usher boy closed the door and darkness caved in around her. She had never sat in the balcony before and was surprised to find that the view was much better than from the seats below. The white people down there had to strain their necks to see the whole stage, but here she could look straight ahead and see everything. It seemed to her that all people carried secrets.

When her eyes adjusted to the dark, she glanced around. On her left was a man so lean he could have been strummed like the string of a guitar. On her right was a small man with a roundish head and sloping shoulders. Neither looked at her, although both could feel her eyes on them. No one knew exactly what to make of her presence, whether she was there to start trouble or to escape it. So while the men usually laughed and joked during the show, talking back and forth to one another, all were silent. Only Toby-Toby made note of her presence.

"White woman coming up the stairs. What to make of that?" he said.

No one responded. Klara thought to, but couldn't find the words to explain that she believed this would be the only place where she didn't stand out, where her pain was just a part of a whole. Most in the balcony wouldn't have been happy to hear that, believing no white woman could imagine their pain, and maybe she couldn't, but she knew her own. Here, no one would recognize her, and even if they had, they wouldn't have anyone to tell. No black man in his right mind would walk up to Drago Bozic and tell him his wife had not only been to the show house, an entertainment of which he did not approve for women, but that she had climbed the stairs to Nigger Heaven and sat between two black men, close enough to touch knee to knee.

She recognized many of the men from the back door of BenJo's shop where he sold the wilteds cheap to his own. Kentucky Wonder was seated behind her. A man as big as a riverboat and so black, she sometimes thought he was blue, the most mysterious shade of blue, one she'd never seen on anything in Thirsty but that somewhat reminded her of a deep spot of ocean halfway between Croatia and the States, sinkable blue, blue that absorbed and held. His eyes were large and red, and whenever he exhaled after a long sip of bourbon from the bottle he kept in his pocket, she could breathe in the liquor and feel as if she'd been sipping it herself.

Toby-Toby leaned against the far wall with his eyes already shut. When he wasn't talking, he was sleeping. Slept anywhere. In doorways, on corners, against tree trunks. He couldn't stay awake longer than an hour or two on most days, so over the years he just learned to settle in wherever he was.

Klara relaxed in the seat and let the sounds of the theater settle into her ears—the tapping of the dancers' shoes on the wooden stage and the organ music as the organist picked up the tempo, some twinkling tune that filtered through the air like stardust. Someone threw a candy ball at Toby-Toby when he began to snore, but without waking him, it bounced into Klara's lap. She lifted it to her nose in the dark, smelled its sweet sugar, and tucked it into her pocket. She hadn't known what to expect from this new place, but as she sat, she realized how much it reminded her of being in church on Sunday mornings. The warm, close air, the shadowy darkness, the whispers—all were rounded in the same way that they were rounded in church. Edgeless things. Easy to run your hand over. Sitting so close was the same as well, knee to knee, shoulder to shoulder, touching without flinching or pulling away. Here she found a kind of peace that she hadn't even known she'd been seeking. At church she could disappear into the prayers, and here she could fall into Toby-Toby's rumbling snores with one ear and in the open space, consider the past day, the loss of her hair, and the news that Widow Toussant's last baby had died, trampled in town by an unruly horse. Early that morning, before dawn, the widow's cries had reached Klara's door and seeped through the cracks until Klara could no longer bear it. Then later in the day, the small coffin had rolled by on a wagon bed drawn by the button man's mule, Widow Toussant following behind.

No one ever figured out how the fire got started, whether it began on the floor and rose to Nigger Heaven, or whether a lost cigarette in the balcony had burned through the floor and devoured the show house for good. All Klara could remember was that Kentucky Wonder had lifted her in his great arms and carried her down the stairs to safety, then returned to the fire and done the same for three others before giving in to the smoke and flames. Once outside, Klara waited with the others while the water wagon arrived and was dragged into place.

"Looks like death is going to follow us everywhere we go," she said to a woman dressed in blue, one of the dancers perhaps, who had propped herself against a pole. "I've been walking around this town for years trying to get away," Klara continued. "Somehow I just haven't been allowed. It's like God's up there looking down, making sure I got enough misery to count on."

"Miss, you know the Lord doesn't give you more than you can handle. You must be a strong woman for God to count on you like that."

"Well, he's not paying close attention, because I'm about at my limit. Carrying death is harder than hoisting water from the well. Rather do that a hundred times a day."

"It's God's will, Miss."

"I used to believe that."

"Got to believe it. You don't have a choice."

"None at all?"

"None at all."

"Every day I wake up, first thing I think is who is he going to take today."

"Be thankful it's not you."

"Be better if it was."

"Naw, Miss, think of all those who'd miss you, all those who depend on you."

"So God takes them, and I get to do all the missing."

"If that's His plan."

The fire roared up again, turning the wooden planks of the walls into ash, and all the men fighting it, trying to keep it from jumping to the sewing shop next door and the lumberyard down the way, leapt out of its path.

"How many have you lost?" Klara asked.

"Too high to count," the woman said. "Just keep praying He lets me keep one of my babies until I'm old. Got to have somebody to care for me when my legs won't hold me up anymore."

An explosion made the women jump back a couple of feet. Klara rocked from one foot to the other, waiting for the firefighters to carry Kentucky Wonder out. She didn't know how they'd manage his girth, with him being four times the size of most men and dead weight being so much heavier than live. His wife waited under a tree, crying so much water into the bark that Klara believed that tree would grow three feet the very next day.

"You know anything about how this fire got burning?" the woman asked.

Klara tried to remember something, anything, but even the images from the stage were blurred in her memory now. A woman. An organ. Toby-Toby's rolling snore. She remembered smelling smoke, then that drowsy feeling that covered her and put her to sleep, and finally Kentucky Wonder's arms lifting her as if she might be going to heaven after all.

"No."

"Where were you sitting?"

Klara paused, thought about the usher boy who seated her. "On the floor," she said slowly, "in the middle."

"Probably one of those niggers getting careless in heaven."

"Mmm," Klara said. It was easier this way. Not right, she knew, but easier. Then three men burst from the building carrying Kentucky Wonder between them as if he were a lopsided piece of furniture. They tilted and maneuvered him until they fit through the doorway, set him on the ground away from the flames, then walked away. He was long dead.

"Those niggers don't have any respect," the woman said, turning away. "Careless with Wonder like that."

Klara was silent. She looked at Kentucky Wonder's wife staring down at the body on the ground and decided to leave before she had to watch her kneel over her husband and wail. She turned down the road and let it lead her into the dark tunnel of leafless trees, up the hill with wind and smoke at her back. When she set a hand on top of her head, she realized the pale green scarf was gone and that she'd been standing on the street with bits of white hair of all lengths poking up from her head. No one had even noticed.

Though she hadn't seen him in a dark corner near the back of the balcony, BenJo had witnessed Klara's visit to Nigger Heaven, and on the day following the tragic fire when she walked into his store, instead of looking at her with disgust for her presumptuousness, he instead looked at her more deeply and with more understanding than anyone had since her mother's death. His look was so piercing and so palpable in her heart that she had to lean against a bin of apples with a hip and both hands to prevent herself from falling over, but the warm, vibrating sensation that remained after the initial shock of pain subsided proved to be a most pleasant and everlasting one. His was not a reaction shared by many who survived the fire's wrath; even Kentucky Wonder's wife, who in her deepest moments of grief had glanced up from her husband's body to wonder just who that white woman thought she was, looking on like that, as if she belonged. There was a thick wall between the races that few dared to even approach, let alone scale, and those who did paid dearly in one way or another.

As Klara leaned, trying to catch her breath, BenJo moved through the narrow aisle toward her. His shop was small, with bins of fresh produce lining each side of the aisle, floor-to-ceiling shelves stocked with the necessary dry goods, and an entire countertop of homemade pastries and cobblers his wife had prepared with love the day before.

"Mrs. Bozic?" BenJo said as he neared her, the question implying both an inquisition of her well-being and permission to help her steady herself on her feet.

"Yes, BenJo. I'm all right," she said and accepted his hand under her elbow. For a moment, the world look cockeyed, but after a bit, she could see her way clearly once again. Beneath her babushka, she could feel the short stubs of hair, and she recalled at once Drago's order to see Lucy Giller first thing this morning to get them cared for properly. And though her rage had once again been replaced by fear, instead she'd come to see BenJo.

"BenJo, I saw a terrible thing last night."

"I know. I was in the back row watching on."

"You were? Why didn't you come forward when we made it outside?"

He didn't answer.

"Then you know that Kentucky Wonder died?"

"He's being buried this morning."

"This morning?"

Moments later a wagon rolled past drawn by two healthy mules with wet shining eyes, followed by a long line of people. The line, similar in length and number to the line of women that traveled to the fence whenever the mill whistle summoned them, differed in two significant ways: this line included men as well as women, and every person in this line was black. In the bed of the wagon was a coffin, simple in form and structure, but because it had been specially built to accommodate Kentucky Wonder's muscled girth and great height, it was impressive in its size. Every thirty or forty yards, the wagon driver, one of Kentucky Wonder's many brothers, hollered out and pulled the reins on the mules to halt them, while two or three women in the back of the line wailed and sang and shook like sheets hung out to dry on a windy day. It was a slow procession. The white people who curiously poked their heads out of shops when they heard the commotion became irritated, and a few men hollered invectives from their storefronts and wagons. But in this case, the black people intent on celebrating Kentucky Wonder's life and lamenting his premature death paid no mind. Their usual fear and rage had been temporarily replaced by sorrow, and as Klara was slowly discovering, sorrow was not nearly as manageable. The white folks would simply have to wait.

As the procession paused in front of his store, BenJo ushered the few remaining customers out the door, then led Klara onto the street and into the middle of the line. When the wagon began to move again, Klara moved along with it, looking around herself with wonder at how she came to be in this place but feeling as if it was where she belonged.

At the front of the line, stunning like a great blue heron in full plumage, was Kentucky Wonder's wife. She was tall, nearly equal in height to her dead husband, but thin and stately, with a perfect neck and straight back. Her hair, thick and long, gray mixed with black, was drawn away from her face and gathered in a braid that stretched to her waist. Anxious to have her husband's soul pass to heaven as quickly as possible, she wouldn't hear of delaying the funeral until all of his friends and family members, even those from distant towns to whom an envoy had been set the evening before carrying word of his demise, had visited him one last time. "If they haven't seen him enough in the past forty-five years, they'll have to wait to meet him in heaven. And if they haven't lived a life that will send them on to heaven so they can have a few more chats with 'tucky, they better get started real quick," she told one of her husband's brothers when he questioned her decision.

As they walked through town, Kentucky Wonder's wife sang her husband's body to the ground; at the graveyard, she sang his soul to heaven. Her voice, deep and rich, carried across the hills and into the valleys and somehow managed to tranquilize a bit of the pain carried on the backs of those who followed her; and the song itself, though mournful, was also full of hope. Klara had never heard such sadness expressed so precisely, except in her own heart, and though the song that had put an end to Jake's wake had been beautiful and everlasting, it paled in comparison to this. But comparing the two funerals, sacrilegious perhaps, would have been like comparing a peacock to a raven, an opera to a folk tune, a field of wildflowers to a single violet.

The graveyard where Kentucky Wonder was to be buried was tiny compared to that of the white people where Jake rested, just a small plot of land beneath a clump of oaks squared off by a handcrafted picket fence with a creaky gate. But at that midmorning hour, in the gray filtered light, Klara noticed that the snow had not yet been broken by footprints and that the grave markers, mostly river stones smoothed down by current, were covered by a shimmering sheath of ice. She wondered for a moment how a grave would be dug in ground hardened by the season, but realized after a moment of looking around that with brawn and determination on their side, Kentucky Wonder's brothers could and would accomplish what was necessary.

After the brothers carried Kentucky Wonder from the wagon to the graveyard and set him near the place where he would finally enter the ground, the people gathered around, some inside the fence, some outside the fence, and the reverend took his place on an overturned crate in the center. He was a short man with glasses who wore a deep purple robe that swished like a woman's skirt when he preached. As he began to talk about the glory of Kentucky Wonder's life, he saw Klara standing near the edge of the crowd, caught her eye, and stayed there for a long moment before moving on. For the next hour, in a booming, heart-rattling voice, he told stories of great faith and love. He raised his hands to heaven, shook his head, closed his eyes, and summoned the spirit of the Lord so powerfully and enigmatically that Klara felt her soul turn over with joy, a feeling that she wanted to grasp and carry home but couldn't.

It wasn't until many of the funeral goers had filed away, when Klara stood quietly over the clean swathe of upturned dirt that the brothers were making quick work of, that Kentucky Wonder's wife approached her. Though during the two hours prior her attention had been taken by her own loss, Beatrude Wonder had been aware of Klara's presence and of BenJo's encouragement of that presence. Now, standing next to her over Kentucky's grave, she wanted to holler at Klara, accuse her of intruding, spend some of her sorrow on this ragged white woman, but she didn't. Instead she simply watched and waited for Klara to speak first.

"I was there, you know," Klara began, still staring at the dirt. "I was in Nig. . . . I was in the balcony." Klara had called it Nigger Heaven for so long and heard it called that by those around her that for a moment she couldn't even find the simple word *balcony* in her mind, but she also couldn't say the word *nigger* to this woman. It felt as if someone had stuffed pinecones in her mouth and brain.

"I know you were," Beatrude said. "I saw you last night, and one of the boys told me that my husband carried you out of the fire."

Klara looked up and met her eyes. They were somewhere between green and brown, and although they'd been full of tears during the hours since Kentucky Wonder's death, they were dry now. The moment of joy Klara had experienced earlier during the reverend's preaching had flown, and she was full of shame and sadness, a shame that wouldn't be voiced or worked out in any significant way for at least two more generations of Bozic women and a sadness that would permeate the lineage forever.

"I'm grateful to your husband for my life," Klara finally said. "I'm here because of that."

Beatrude nodded, stood quietly for another moment, then turned and walked away. The long braid that hung down to her waist swung gently back and forth, and she held her head high. Beneath the odors of the mill just beyond and the crisp scent of winter clinging to the naked trees, Klara suddenly detected the fresh smell of river water. She looked to see that Kentucky Wonder's gravestone, marked simply with the year and his initials, was a smooth, round rock drawn from up-river that very morning. She watched as one of the brothers cleared a small space in the snow, dug a shallow grave in the frozen earth for the rock, and pressed it into place.

As she turned to go, Klara realized that she envied Beatrude Wonder. However much she'd loved her husband, however much she'd cherished the routine of their life together, however much she needed a father for her children, she was now free. Free to walk as she wished to walk, free to talk with whomever whenever however she pleased, free to wear her hair as she liked. To Klara, that was an enviable position.

Hearing that Klara had traveled in Kentucky's final procession, Katherine had covered her head with a bonnet and made her way to the graveyard. When Klara turned to see Katherine leaning on the post, her heart gave and she shed the first tears she had allowed herself since she'd sat on the floor of her kitchen surrounded by locks of her own hair.

"You know," Katherine said, as they turned to make their way home, "I've gathered a tale about the fold in BenJo's back, trying to figure truth from fairytale."

Klara smiled as a few snowflakes began to fall from the sky. Leave it to Katherine to find a proper way to distract her from sorrow. "Yeah?" she said. "What have you learned?"

"Well, I started with his name. Most womenfolk don't want to talk about it, being how it gets to intimate things and such, but Bonnie the seamstress told me that she'd heard that BenJo's mother had loved two men equally and being unable to figure which had planted the seed that resulted in her beloved son, had decided to pay tribute to both. Obviously there must have been a Benjamin and a Joe, but being how BenJo was raised far from Thirsty, few folks around here know anything about them. Bonnie says they must have been like most men, handsome with little interest in staying by too long." She laughed. "Bonnie said too that by the time BenJo was old enough to resemble one more strongly than the other around the eyes or along the jawline, both men were forever gone and his mother announced that it was much too late to accustom her son to a new name. To do so would have meant changing an identity that had already begun to take shape. His mother, wise in the ways of humankind, decided that protecting both men, or perhaps protecting BenJo, was her only interest. She never revealed the identity of either man to BenJo or anyone else for that matter. Least that's what Bonnie says. His momma simply closed her eyes and smiled when folks got overcurious."

Klara didn't know whether to believe such talk, but she prodded Katherine with her elbow, pushing her for more.

"Now as for BenJo's unique angle in life," Katherine said, "that's a whole other bucket of goods, one Bonnie didn't know anything about. But I've asked around, quiet like, and I've collected a good tale."

"Well, share it, friend," Klara said quietly. "I'm in a place with no walls today, and I need something to hold on to."

Katherine looped her arm through Klara's and began. "Well, rumor has it that while BenJo didn't have any memories of his own about the bend in his back until he came to Thirsty, he'd heard murmurings from the folks who'd changed his diapers and chased him across fields when he snuck away as a boy. They'd told him about an unquenchable thirst for water he suffered as a child when he was still upright like the rest of us and the long, frightening path his mother took to change it."

"What do you mean, unquenchable thirst for water? Are you saying BenJo didn't drink his momma's milk?"

"No, ma'am, and supposedly he'd been born that way, opening his mouth not for milk like all the babies we know, but for the clear cool refreshment of water. From the moment he was out of the womb, he refused to take to his mother's breasts, which then stayed full with milk for weeks on end and leaked whenever he was near. I imagine they eventually gave up and shrank back to their original size and offering, and the story goes that this must have eased things greatly for his mother because even the scent of milk sent BenJo into a screaming frenzy. He was an unusual child. In his first days of life, frightened by his refusal to suckle, his mother worried over his health. While he slept—peacefully, she thought, for a baby who refused to take milk—she would pace back and forth in front of his cradle, glancing down at him each time she turned to make sure that his small chest was rising and falling as expected. No other babies she'd ever seen had said no to milk. But then one morning, just a few days into his life, hoping to prevent him from drying up like a cornstalk in the summer sun, she offered him a bit of water in a bottle. To her great surprise, he drank the whole thing.

"From that day on, the story tells that BenJo drank eighteen to twenty bottles of water a day, and despite talk and speculation, he grew as radiantly as the other children born in the same month. His cheeks were ruddy. His limbs were plump. His belly was full and round. Most especially, he cooed and laughed whenever his mother came near. One man who says he knew BenJo as a child told me that a few of the older women, those who had experienced many oddities in life, talked amongst themselves, saying things like, 'If that boy don't start drinking milk soon, he ain't going to have no teeth to chew with' and 'Someday that boy's wife is going to be very disappointed 'cause without milk, that boy's yong-yong will stay limp as a blade of grass after a heavy rain.' Thankfully, time proved the old ladies wrong. BenJo's teeth grew in white and sturdy, and his numerous children and smiling wife now served as proof of the strength of his yong-yong."

Klara remembered the day she happened in to BenJo's store and found all eight of his little ones sitting on pickle barrels in the back room. They were laughing and telling tales just like their father.

"But you see," Katherine continued, "as BenJo grew, no matter how much water his mother offered, it seemed never to be enough. She watched her son crawl around the yard after a rainfall and slurp water from puddles and upturned leaves. He snuck into the bathhouse during bath day and drank from the tub whenever the room was empty and the water fresh. And when he was a mite older, he even took to collecting rainwater in sizable containers, barrels and such, which would have lasted a normal person half a season, but in his case, were drained in less than a day.

"Now the story gets good," Katherine said, sliding down the easy side of a hill on an icy spot. "Keep your ears up."

"As if I couldn't now," Klara answered.

"Of course, BenJo's mother wanted to figure out what was driving her son's thirst, so she visited as many specialists as time and money allowed. One Sunday after church when he was just a toddler, she rode thirteen miles on muleback to visit an herb doctor who lived in the woods. She was an old woman who looked to be at least a hundred years. She wasn't surprised by BenJo's thirst, and she told his mother that every once in a while a child of the water was born. With little ceremony, she passed on a few herbs to be added to his water by the spoonful and a paste that she said should be rubbed on his throat before bed. 'Other than that,' the old woman said, 'there's little I can do. Keep the boy near water. Without it, he will die.'

"Just like she was told, BenJo's mother added the foul-smelling herbs to her son's water and spread the paste on his throat before bed, and each morning she waited for him to push away a bottle of water or crawl past a delicious puddle without so much as a glance. It didn't happen, though. His thirst was mighty strong, and after a month or so, she threw both remedies to the dogs and rode off on muleback to a woman said to be the leader of a clan of witches. The visit scared the bejeebies out of BenJo's mother, but she did what she had to do. The witch woman was gnarled and hunched, wrinkled in every place on her body, including the skin on her nose and the lobes of her ears. She laughed when BenJo's mother explained his thirst and promised that it would not be cured except by tragedy. Unwilling to hear more, BenJo's mother mounted the mule, rode home as quickly as the stubborn animal allowed, and kept her son close by her side, trying her best to forget the words of the white-skinned witch-woman.

"In the end, though she didn't think he could cure even the slightest fever, BenJo's mother talked with the medical doctor who stopped by their community from time to time to offer advice and visit with extreme cases. After listening to BenJo's heart, which pounded rhythmically like most, and checking the spread of his toes, which seemed ridiculous, he prescribed a medicine that had to be given in the ear. This failed, too, and finally BenJo's mother simply decided to accept her son's great thirst."

Katherine paused to shake the cold from her limbs, but Klara nudged her again. "Well, don't stop now. What happened next?"

"Well, as you might guess, the tragedy warned about by the witch-woman came to pass on a summer day when BenJo was about four. Thirsty like always, he snuck away one morning when his mother turned her attention to a pot of dirty clothes and walked, following his nose, until he found a stream. The stream, straddled by a railroad trestle, could not be gotten to on the near side because of an endless line of sharp-thorned bushes, so he climbed to the trestle and, keeping his head bent so that he could see the water far below between the ties, he began to cross. Halfway to his destination, a train roared around the bend, and at the last minute, in an effort to escape harm, he lay across one of the rails with his legs hanging loose at a ninety-degree angle. The train came over him just like that, blasting its whistle and trying, though failing, to stop. Of course, according to the laws of nature, BenJo should have died. He should have been cut in two by the weight of the train and the heat of the wheels, but the laws of God must have saved him. From that moment on, the story goes, though unable to straighten himself from the ninety-degree angle, BenJo was cured of his magnificent thirst."

"Just like the witch-woman said?" Klara asked.

"Just like the witch-woman said. From then on, BenJo was forever folded at the waist, but he began drinking milk like the rest of us."

By the time Katherine reached this point in the telling, the women had arrived at the end of their street. Through the sheer curtain of falling snow, they could see their houses standing next to one another.

A chill traveled up Klara's spine, and she shook her head back and forth in protest. "That's not possible," she finally said. "BenJo would have died under the weight of a train. Anyone would."

"Yes," Katherine answered, "that's what makes sense. But that's the only story I could get from anyone."

"How could that be?"

"I don't know, Klara. But other than being blessed by God, how do you explain that BenJo is more accepted than other blacks by the white folks here in Thirsty. Doesn't it seem odd that he has a store and even a little respect by some?"

"Of course, but I attribute it to his graciousness and kind way."

"Ah, Klara, there are lots of nice black folks living around here, and they suffer tenfold against BenJo."

The women stood in front of Klara's house now, absorbed in story. After a few quiet moments, Katherine patted her friend on the shoulder and turned to go. Before she did, she laughed out loud and said, "Don't take this wrong, but you look mighty entertaining with that hairdo."

It was the first time they'd been able to see even the littlest bit of humor in the sprigs of hair sprouting from Klara's head. It felt good.

"Yes," Klara said, smiling, "but it's not as funny as a bald woman."

For many weeks after Kentucky Wonder's funeral, Klara and Drago did not speak, except to settle the necessities of life as they arose. As usual, she woke him for his shift at the mill, but instead of sharing a bit of conversation about the future or the past or the first bloom breaking through the winter's snow as they readied for the day, they moved around each other like boxers before a fight with heads bowed and bodies stiff. There was a scent about them, caught only by the keenest nose, a scent deeper than fire or dirt, one that clung like disease or pestilence. The anger had crawled away from both, but the chasm left by this particular battle was wider and deeper than any left before. Because she refused to have Lucy Giller organize her shorn hair into something presentable, Klara's hair grew back at different lengths so that it resembled a determined patch of weeds, blond at the ends and brown at the roots, and though Drago did not feel remorse for what he had done, he did not like to be reminded of the altercation. At first he insisted that she cover her head with a babushka when she left the house, but her refusal to obey was so quietly adamant that in some faraway place in his heart, he felt fear and decided to simply allow her to embarrass herself and her family as she wished. As far as Klara knew, Drago did not hear rumors of either her trip to the balcony at the show house on the night of the fire or her attendance at Kentucky Wonder's funeral, which served her well, because if confronted by her husband on these issues, she would not have known how to respond, and any response would have grown from instinct, not rational thought.

After the funeral, Klara found herself watching the simplest of things, aspects of life that she had rarely owned interest in before—birds in flight, melting snow, smoke separating from itself after leaving the smokestacks—but in the years that followed, she discovered the object of observation that proved to be most fascinating: Sky.

Though Sky had been fooling with men for more years than Klara would have wanted to know, the frequency of her sexual encounters had increased to the point where she was slipping away from the house for a rendezvous at least once a week. Her after-dark escape routine became so refined that she could slip from her bedroom window onto the porch roof, cross the roof, and shimmy down the wooden porch post onto firm ground. At first, when her feet struck the ground, the reverberations were loud, causing Sky to wait anxiously for her father to pound out of the house to confront her, but over time, she perfected the routine to such a degree that even in everyday life, she moved without sound. Once on the ground, she stayed close to the houses for a block or two, moving in and out of the shadows like a cat, glancing back toward her house with hope that her father's head or the nose of his rifle would not be jutting from the window. But then, seduced by the promise of love once again, she would wander onto the road and walk down its middle, daydreaming about the prince she was about to meet at the river's edge or in the alleyway behind a row of shops. If her father had caught her, Sky was sure he would have murdered her on the spot, but her hatred of him was so great by then that she nearly didn't care. Sometimes as she walked, her face and heart lit by the glow of the fires at the top of the smokestacks, she imagined how she might kill him the next time he struck her mother. She imagined lighting a fire beneath his bed while he slept, after a shift when his sleep was heavy and full, and watching through the window from the porch roof for the moment he woke and realized that every inch of his skin was alight with flame. She imagined adding a bit of poison to his morning coffee, a pinch each day, so that slowly he lost control of his muscles and his mind and his heart.

As Sky's lovemaking skills had greatly improved since the early days with Chuckie in the cow pasture, and as her reputation traveled by word of mouth through the mill—barrow to barrow, furnace to furnace, in much the same way word of Jake's death had traveled—it grew easier and easier to attract men to her lair. Though the men she met in the night were an odd lot—some older, some married, some widowed, some who had lost an arm or a leg in a mill accident, some with pockmarks or deep scars she could trace with her fingers, some with odd requests (such as tying her hands behind her back or placing a cloth sack over her head)—most were mill workers who were simply lonely and desperate in one way or another. Once or twice she discovered a man who took her fancy as well as her sex, but those men, knowing her reputation, had little interest in what she had to offer beyond her finely tuned skills. She was a temptress, and though men longed for her pleasuring ways, they did not desire her heart.

Some time after Kentucky Wonder's funeral, Klara began to follow her daughter in the night, slipping down the stairs and out the door after her, knowing full well that if Drago were asleep, movement of any kind would never wake him. Years had taught her that during these hours when he slumbered, she was safe. The first time she followed Sky, she stayed far behind, hiding behind trees and bushes and wagon beds, shielding herself with shadows. Twice she leapt behind the corner of a building when a horse whinnied at her presence, but Sky, who seemed not to take notice, simply continued on her path, arms swinging loosely at her sides and hips rocking back and forth.

The first time, Klara turned back halfway to Sky's destination, not wanting to know for sure what her only daughter was up to. The second time, she followed her all the way to the river and curiously watched her daughter dip bare toes into the sludge that gathered in oily pools and glance anxiously around her as if waiting for someone, but she slipped away before the mystery person arrived. It was the third time that Klara sat down on a rock and watched her daughter unbutton the trousers of a man twice her age and peel her own blouse from her back to give him access to her breasts. Unaware of her mother's presence, Sky bent and took the man's penis in her mouth, sucking and licking and moaning with his hands driving her head closer and closer until he reared back his own head and groaned. Though what she saw disturbed Klara in the way it would disturb most mothers, she was envious. She knelt behind the rock, hid her face, and tried to cover her ears, but Sky's pleasure was too great to block out completely. As quiet as Sky's step had become, walking there to here without sound, her lovemaking had become the opposite: clangorous, shrill, and powerful. She used this time and space to yell and holler, squeal and bark, not so much in response to the kissing and groping and grabbing, but in response to the enormous sadness that filled her.

After Klara crawled back to the road from behind the rock and made her way home, following the same path by which she had come—curiosity replaced by envy, confusion, and anger—Sky sucked off the man she'd met at the butcher shop that afternoon one more time, then slipped off her layers of skirt, one by one, until only the petticoat remained. She put his hands on her ass and begged him in deep throaty pleadings to bite her nipples, *harder,* she said. That redhot fire crawled up her thighs and spread through her pussy so hard and so fast that she nearly tipped over taking off the petticoat. Her eyes fluttered, and even before the man was sufficiently hard again, she climbed on top and pressed him into her. She suckled his neck, and he slapped her ass until he was firm and ready. Then she pumped up and down, eyes closed, forgetting who and where she was, until she exploded—all lights and tremors—and screamed so loud the man clamped a callused hand over her mouth and told her to hush up. But she didn't care what he said because she'd gotten what she'd come for. She climbed down, dressed herself, and turned for home.

1906

Klara didn't attend Sky's wedding, but her choice was a mandate, not a decision. Left to her own devices, she would have attended the ceremony whether Maxwell Plumter had been a Catholic, a Jew, or an atheist. After all, she was a mother, and she would have attended her only daughter's wedding even if she'd had to walk all the way to California, even if she'd had to swim all the way back to Croatia. But as it was, her own devices were all but gone, and Drago had promised, while pinning her to the wall by her throat, that if she so much as took a step toward city hall, that would be the end of her. He'd already surprised her with a black eye that morning, cold-cocked her just to make a point.

So on the morning the ceremony was to take place, Klara rose from her bed, said her usual prayers with an extra one for Sky, and lit a candle in her window. Then, after dressing and taking care of the morning's chores, she gathered her skirts in her hand and stepped outside. Of course, all of Thirsty knew that Sky was about to marry a well-off Methodist whose family had nothing to do with the Croatian tradition, so the stoops and streets were filled with overcurious townsfolk waiting to see if anyone from the Bozic family would attend. Seeing them there, milling from one side of the street to the other like a herd of dumb cattle, Klara wanted to holler, tell them to mind their business. As she stood on the stoop watching their anxious faces, she imagined walking through the crowd swinging an iron skillet, knocking anyone in the head who came too close. But instead, she looked at the ground and ran all the way to Katherine's kitchen, where it was warm and safe.

Katherine looked up as Klara came in the door. Her smooth, bald head shone in the morning sun like a wet rock in the garden. As she said good morning, she saw that Klara's left eye was red and swollen with the missing of her daughter's wedding and the right one was black and bloody with Drago's anger.

"Being courted by sorrow, I see," Katherine said, wiping her hands on a rag.

Klara sat in a chair and cried, while Katherine knelt beside her and shook her head at it all. At Drago's big fist held over their lives, at the townsfolk so tired of their own business they had to turn to the trouble of others for entertainment, at Klara, who couldn't or wouldn't take her own direction through things, and even at herself, for still missing Jake as much as ever and for knowing that had he lived, this never would have happened. When she felt Klara still, she squeezed her arm and said, "Let's bake bread." And they did. All morning they stirred, patted, kneaded, and studied over great balls of dough.

"Either of the boys going to the ceremony?" Katherine asked when she judged Klara deep enough into work to talk without tears.

"Drago watched them so close last night and this morning, they're lucky they got to use the outhouse. They'd be too scared to head out now, even if Sky tried to sneak them away. Besides, Drago walked both of them to the mill this morning, despite the fact he isn't scheduled to work until this afternoon. He said it'll do them good, learning a little something from their father."

Katherine laughed. "Like those two boys haven't learned enough from their father during the past ten years. He's insulting, even to himself."

But seeing how Klara's face softened to near melting at the mention of her two boys who grew up so hard, Katherine changed the subject, and they got through the morning and into the early afternoon talking about whatnot: the barge that got grounded near the tip of the point, suctioned in the mud like a lost boot until two sister barges combined their might to push her out; the new textile store opening next to BenJo's place; and most importantly, the strange rumor that Old Man Rupert had begun to fix up his house.

"Who said so?" Klara asked. She'd been so engrossed in her own turmoil over Sky's wedding she hadn't even heard.

"Not just one who," Katherine said, "all the who's. Everyone's talking about it. First I heard was three days ago. Folks say Old Man Rupert hasn't had a drink in two weeks now and you can hear him hammering before the crack of dawn. That man hasn't hammered anything but a bar table in thirty years. I can't believe he still knows how."

"Maybe it's all a story folks made up to keep themselves entertained," Klara said.

"I thought so too, but Maggie actually walked up there herself just to take a look. There are tools and stacks of wood lying all over the place. It's true, all right. She saw it with her own eyes."

"Praise the Lord," Klara said. "That house is too beautiful to die off."

"Amen to that. I hear he's starting from the bottom up. He's ripped the entire porch off the main level and he's rebuilding it from scratch. He's even hired a few of those boys he used to chase out of his fields to clear them."

"Clear the fields?"

"Yup."

"Anybody speculating about why all this is going on?"

"Some say he's got another wife coming in."

"Old Man Rupert? At his age? He's got to be past seventy!"

"Sixty or so, I'd say. Liquor has added some to him over the years."

"Well, sixty or seventy, what woman in her right mind is going to take him on?"

"I don't know, but I say that as soon as we get this mess cleaned up, we head up there ourselves."

"This might be the biggest news since the butterflies," Klara said, and then she was lost again in the dough, in her worries about Sky, and her concerns about Georgie and Ivo.

Klara and Katherine took the same walk they took the night of Sky's birth so many years before except they were older and slower and the spring day was fresh and warm with the great sun burning through the mill gases. At first, folks on the street assumed they were heading for the wedding, defying Drago's almighty word, so for the first mile, Klara and Katherine could feel footsteps behind them. But when the women turned up the hill instead of down, disappointment spread and the street emptied. On the way, the women chuckled together, remembering that night dressed in Angelo Costello's long johns. It seemed like forever ago, and each was thankful the other was still walking by her side.

When they finally reached the peak, they saw that no lies had been told. Old Man Rupert was tearing his house apart board by board. Ten or so local boys were strung up on platforms and scaffolding, pulling nails and pounding them in. And right in the midst of it all was Old Man Rupert himself, done up in a slinglike apparatus hung from a chimney on the east side of the house, barking orders and accomplishing equal work himself.

The women stood for a bit enjoying the process until the old man caught sight of them and unrigged himself quickly enough to greet them by the front gate. Though he couldn't yet reveal his plans for the house to anyone, his heart thumped with joy at the sight of Klara and Katherine in his front yard. He noticed Klara's black eye, hidden for the most part by the bow of her head and the scalloped edge of her bonnet, and he showed respect by not staring or calling attention to the deep bruise. Instead he met Katherine's eyes. "This sure is a pleasure," he said, "getting the two of you to visit my home on better terms."

"It's looking rather grand," Katherine said, eyeing the house and its pieces close up. Stacks of boards were piled ten feet high in the yard, and boxes of saws, hammers, and nails were scattered about. Three rusty wheelbarrows rested in the long grass, and a couple of ladders lay on top.

Old Man Rupert laughed. "Well, not grand just yet, Mrs. Z, but I plan on getting there. What comes down takes equal time to go up again, I suppose."

"I suppose," Katherine said. "But this surely seems a good start."

"Indeed," Klara echoed. All of this, including the conversation and kindness, was surprising and confusing. It was true that Old Man Rupert had been showing signs of improvement in his person for a number of years, ever since he started courting Sky and Klara as friends. But renovating this house was even bigger than a bouquet of flowers or a warm loaf of raisin bread. This house had the heart of the Rupert family built right into its structure, and to revive that heart just at the point where it had almost stopped beating for good was profound. Klara and Katherine instructed Mr. Rupert to return to his task, and after a few more minutes of wonder, they turned for home. A cool breeze caught their skirts as they walked.

"Crazy as it seems," Katherine said, "I think the old man's finished drinking for good. Not a whiff of whiskey on him."

Klara nodded. "It doesn't seem possible, does it? Especially after all that terrible business on the night of Sky's birth. But I suppose anything is possible in God's world." By the time they reached home, Klara was sure Sky's wedding ceremony had already ended.

It was the scent of peony blossoms that would always remind Sky of her marriage ceremony. Peony blossoms and lemon wax. An association that in the beginning might have made her smile, but that within a few weeks, made her nauseated and bitter. No one from either family approved of the marriage—the Bozics because Maxwell Plumter was a Methodist, and the Plumters because Sky was a working-class Catholic. So the two married without the benefit of their parents' blessings in the courtroom of the justice of the peace in the county building in downtown Pittsburgh, settling on a nondenominational ceremony to eliminate the struggle of their religious ties. It was a small, polished room outfitted in dark, gleaming wood, and Maxwell's closest friends, June and Riley, arrived to serve as witnesses and moral support. June brought a large bouquet of white peonies, and in the stark surroundings, Sky cast a beautiful shadow. In a green dress that showed off her long slim legs—a dress that in no way resembled the wedding gown she'd dreamed of as a young girl, long before Jake passed on—she stood off from the center of the room, tapping her foot. Her pale hair was trimmed into a curly cap and her lips were stained deep red. Although she smiled a little, her heart was lonely for her mother. A few feet away, across the gray-walled room, Maxwell stood with Riley near Justice O'Leary's desk. The law diplomas that hung behind glass in gilt frames reminded him of his own father, an attorney, who when told of Maxwell's impending marriage to Sky kept his voice quite even as he ordered his son out of the house for good.

As a boy, Maxwell had gone with his father on Sunday afternoons to the local cemetery, a small graveyard on a gently sloping hill where the headstones were lined in neat rows, ten across and thirty or so deep. In winter, the man and his son shoveled ice and snow from the winding path, and in summer, when the sun sank low and glowed a bitter orange, they trimmed belligerent tufts of onion grass from each plot, planted tulips at the entrance gate, and left a single red rose from Maxwell Sr.'s garden on each stone that honored the anniversary of a death on that particular day. Like his father, Maxwell was handsome. For the ceremony, he wore a dark gray suit with a white stiff-collared shirt and thick necktie. Although he had removed his gray felt hat as etiquette required, it would once again sit at a jaunty angle on his head when they left the building and returned to daily life. As always, his shoes were polished, and he stood erect, head high, square jaw jutting forward. He was smiling, dark brown eyes glittering with gold flecks. He was tall, over six feet, with a deep dimple in the cleft of his chin.

When the justice of the peace finally appeared, looking more like a bespectacled, stoop-shouldered pharmacist than a judge, the four friends gathered around his desk, and before Sky could count to twenty, Maxwell leaned in for a kiss and they were outside on the great granite steps that led down to the street, busy with end-of-day traffic, vendors calling their wares, a newsboy hawking his papers. There was no photograph to remember it by, just the scents that would always bring Sky to her knees.

When Sky met Maxwell, he was still living with his parents in a small moral town just north of Pittsburgh in the same magnificent house in which he'd grown up. From his window, over the tops of the leafy maples that lined the avenue, Maxwell could see the steeple of the massive Methodist church that stood across the street.

For Maxwell's father, Maxwell Sr., life was about hard work and money—who had it and who didn't—and he worked hard to pass this belief system on to his son. In fact, Maxwell told Sky during their first encounter, the story was that on the day his mother carried him home from the maternity ward at the hospital, Maxwell Sr. wrenched the pram from her grasp, wheeled it from the bedroom to the nursery, closed the door, and said, "Let the boy cry it out. He best learn young that sissy-sobbing gets you nowhere in this world."

Maxwell's toughest lesson began on his tenth birthday when, with the blessing of his father, Maxwell accepted his first job. As a newspaper delivery boy, he proudly carried the canvas sack that touted the name of the paper in gray scripted letters. Each morning, he woke before the church bells, hustled three blocks to the newsstand on the corner of Harrow and Willow streets, folded forty-seven papers into neat bundles, stuffed them into his sack, and began his daily trek. From his starting point at the newsstand, he walked along Harrow Street and each of its tributaries, all the way to the far end of Elm, where Mary Kay Waters lived. She was a thin girl with brown pigtails for whom he had felt a slight flurry during his primary school years. On winter mornings when it was still dark, Maxwell would often see the lamp in her bedroom flutter as she prepared for school. But by that year in his life, the flurry had long since passed, and his interest was no greater than the need for warmth and a cup of cocoa.

Two years from the day Maxwell began carrying the news, Mr. Blainey, the manager of the newsstand, asked if he would mind crossing over into Jacobsburg for a few extra stops along Schneider Road. "It would mean, of course, a few extra pennies in your pocket each week," he added, knowing how loudly money spoke to a boy of Maxwell's upbringing. Maxwell's first inclination, knowing how his father felt about the working-class folks in Jacobsburg, was to refuse—he'd learned over the years how best to protect his behind—but then, perhaps for the very same reason, he agreed.

It was here on Schneider Road that Maxwell met St. Peter, a tall man with a red beard so long it snagged the third button of his robe. Early each morning, St. Peter turned his apple crate upside down on a conspicuous corner in Jacobsburg, and at its base, placed a stack of hand-scrawled pamphlets touting the tenets of the Bible as he interpreted them. Like the twelve disciples of Jesus, St. Peter wore a belted robe and a pair of thong sandals constructed from discarded shoe leather and frayed rope. His fingernails, untrimmed during the last decade, were thick as bark, yellow as pus. When he raised his hands from the sleeves of the robe and lifted them heavenward, as he was apt to do during a morning's sermon, you could see that his fingernails wound around his digits and across his palms toward his elbows like sun-dried earthworms. He called himself St. Peter, but because each morning, when most of the townspeople preferred to be asleep, he stepped onto that upturned apple crate and preached about the sins of the people, their reservations in hell, and the possibility, with his guidance, of course, of Redemption, the townsfolk called him Rooster.

Twice, many years before, the lawmakers of Jacobsburg had attempted to put a stop to Rooster's early morning sermons. But when they discovered that even confinement could not prevent his voice from seeping through the jailhouse walls, floating across the open fields, and bleeding into their houses during the wee morning hours, permeating their dreams, they decided that perhaps he was in fact loosely affiliated with the Almighty himself and thus released him into the care of the community. From that time on, Rooster spent each evening at home with a different family. Each night he prayed at a different table, slept in a different bed, and washed in a different basin. He was passed from family to family like a worn, but valued, cloth, and in return for this care, he awakened them each morning at the same time with his sonorous prayers.

So on the day that Maxwell first crossed the train tracks into Jacobsburg and saw Rooster stretched high on his upturned apple crate, he was awestruck. Each morning thereafter, once he'd tossed the last paper onto the last porch on Schneider Road, Maxwell retraced his steps until he reached Rooster's corner. There he leaned against the trunk of a rotting pine and savored each gesture, motion, and inflection of voice, until Rooster stepped down from his platform, offered him a peach or plum from the deep pocket of his robe, and shared his apple crate as a bench. They became friends, and Rooster told him stories of the way things were before God decided to put man on earth. "You see, boy, back in those times, things didn't fall down. They fell up, toward the sky, which wasn't called the sky but the ocean. Fish flew on silver wings, landing in trees, and birds spoke English like you and me. Nothing was the same here on earth and nothing made a nugget of sense, not until God decided that man should and would right the wrongs, most of them anyhow. And he did. Scientists are always figuring out how things are supposed to work, and God lets people like me, his messengers, come down and deliver His word. Fish swim. Birds fly. Nothing speaks English but English-speaking folk." Rooster smiled and draped an arm around Maxwell's shoulders. "Aren't you glad you're living now, boy?" he always added.

It was two years before Maxwell Sr. became suspicious of his son's goings-on, but when he finally looked up from his desk and noticed that his son hadn't returned directly from his delivery route, he climbed into his buggy, made a few inquiries on the street, and crossed the border into Jacobsburg. He rode the team hard until he saw the canvas newspaper sack hung from the limb of a dilapidated pine tree at the end of Schneider Road and then he drew the horses to a halt. He stepped down and walked until he saw Rooster preaching to a gathering of shaggy devotees from his makeshift pulpit. His eyes wandered until they happened upon his only son, neatly folded beneath the tree, looking more relaxed and confident than he had ever seen him before. With his eyes, he divided the crowd, and when he got within range, he snatched up Maxwell Jr. by the scruff of the neck and hoisted him onto his feet. As he did, Rooster crowed, "God protects the boy you handle. Leave him and no harm will come to you."

Maxwell Sr. threw Rooster a look and laughed. "What do you know about God? God wouldn't waste his time out here with the likes of you." He swept his eyes across the crowd. "All of you! Out here filling my son's head with your nonsense. He won't be back. Get on with your lives."

When they were halfway home, just over the railroad tracks, Maxwell Jr. remembered his newspaper sack still hanging from a branch of the pine tree a mile or so back, but when he turned to say so to his father, Maxwell Sr. said, "You won't be needing that sack any longer. You've quit the newspaper business. It's time you tried something new."

"But I like delivering the paper."

"Mr. Blainey should never have asked you to cross into country where the people are not proper. That was his error."

"Don't blame Mr. Blainey," Maxwell said. "It isn't . . ."

"Your error, son," Maxwell Sr. continued, "was in accepting such an offer."

As they drove the rest of the way in silence, Maxwell Jr. swelled with hate and measured with his eyes the breadth of his own hand against his thigh with that of his father's gripped tightly on the reins. He first wondered when the two would be equal in size and strength and then when his own would be able to cover his father's and crush it.

1914

Instead Maxwell crushed Sky. And when she appeared on Klara's porch for the first time in eight years with two daughters—Lizzy and Petunia—in tow, she didn't knock or call out. She just stood there, waiting, like a patient dog, until Klara happened to spy them through the window, three bundled figures standing quietly with sacks piled at their feet. It wasn't until Klara opened the door that Sky even moved, and then it was only to turn her face away. When she looked back, Klara recognized her and gasped, but instead of moving onto the porch to embrace her daughter, she left the door open, keeping them standing on the stoop in the first slice of winter wind, and returned to the kitchen. There it was warm and familiar, safe, and to keep from crying out, Klara sat down at the table and buried her face in her hands. Sky was overwhelming. In just eight years, she had become ugly, hideous really. Just a rack of bones now, without any meat to hold her together. Her hair hung dull and ragged around her face; black rings encircled her eyes; her jaw and neck were bruised and swollen. Like an old whore who'd been put out to pasture, she slumped at the shoulders and was bent funny in the hips, because, Klara would later learn, Maxwell had sent her down a flight of stairs one too many times.

While Klara sat gathering courage and strength, Sky and the girls waited quietly. The wind tunneled down the hallway and whistled softly as it escaped through the cracks around the back window. A pot rattled on the stove. For a while, it seemed that the day might pass like this, until Klara remembered Drago. His shift in the mill that day was nearly over, and in just a few hours, he would be coming through the door. Without another thought, Klara stood, shook herself, and moved into action.

"Come along," she said, shuffling the girls into the house by the shoulders. "Your grandfather will be home soon, and we need to get you settled long before that so he can't make you leave."

Obediently, the girls disrobed and settled on the floor in front of the fire with bowls of soup. And after carrying the sacks of clothes and toys upstairs, Klara settled Sky nearby.

"The little one is Tunia," Sky said quietly. "Petunia, really, for the flower."

Klara nodded and studied the girl. She was light, ethereal, and pale, with Sky's light hair and narrow shoulders. She was the kind of girl who could talk to angels.

"And the older one is Lizzy," Sky added.

At the sound of her name, Lizzy looked up and smiled a little. She was dark, like Maxwell, with firm features and a sturdy confidence. She seemed relieved to be there, but she kept a cautious eye on her mother, just as Sky had always kept an eye on Klara. This one is Sky's protector, Klara thought.

For a long time, there were no words. Sky leaned back into the rocking chair, stared into the fire, and sipped a cup of tea. Klara sewed, and when the girls fell asleep, she covered them with blankets.

An hour later, when the front door opened, both Klara and Sky jumped to their feet. They thought Drago was returning early from his shift, and neither was prepared yet for that battle. But thankfully, it was Katherine's slow, deliberate footsteps they heard in the hallway, and when she reached the kitchen, surveyed the scene, and finally recognized Sky beneath bruises and hair and bone, she crossed the room, pulled Sky into her arms, and rocked her. It was that easy. "Just like your mother," she said quietly into Sky's hair. "Just like your mother."

"No," Sky answered, "not really. I finally found the courage to leave."

When Drago did return home a few hours later, Katherine met him at the door and held him on the porch with a threat. Klara never learned exactly what she'd said or promised, but whatever it was, Drago never said a word about the presence of Sky or the girls in the house. He also, never once, met their eyes or spoke to them. To him, they were simply dead.

When Christmas arrived a few weeks later, no one was surprised that Maxwell showed up without an invitation. Busybodies who'd seen him lurking about town made a point of stopping by the Bozic house for a look at Sky and an opportunity to share their observations. One by one they'd arrived at the door, some carrying offerings of cake or pie, others empty-handed. "He looks like the devil," one woman proclaimed. "I saw him getting sick in an alleyway, heaving in a way no human ever could." Katherine rolled her eyes at such tales and tried throughout the weeks before Christmas to shield Sky, and especially the girls, from them. But though she and the Bozic women steeled themselves for a Christmas visit from Maxwell, none of them was truly prepared, except maybe Sky, for the scene that would unfold.

He did, of course, enter without knocking. And after greeting Klara with a low growl, Maxwell moved into the kitchen. He stood with Drago, Janko, and the rest of the men, nestled a beer bottle close to his chest, and for the next couple of hours, passed shots of slivovitz from man to man as if he belonged. Twice Drago told him to leave, not for Sky's sake, but because the thought of having this particular Methodist in his home was nearly as bad as having a Jew or a nigger at his table. But Maxwell was already drunk and already angry, and he had no intention of going anywhere until he saw his wife.

It was midnight before Sky returned from an extra-long shift at the valley home where she'd taken a cleaning job. By the time she slunk through the door, she was so tired and full of sadness that not even the sight of her girls clumped together in a knot on the stairs made her smile. The whites of her eyes were red and bloodshot, and though the swelling of her jaw was nearly gone, the bruises were still yellow. When she moved to the hallway to slip out of her coat, keeping on the brown sweater she always wore to warm her bones, Klara leaned close. "Maxwell is here," she whispered.

Sky stopped, turned, and looked at the kitchen door. "Georgie and Ivo?" she asked.

Klara shook her head. "They're out at friends' houses." She paused. "Maxwell is very drunk," she added.

"He usually is," Sky said.

A moment later, when Sky pushed into the kitchen, the Bozic house closed in and shrank. Cousin Natasa, Uncle Janko, his family, and the remaining guests who may have been enjoying themselves before she arrived snuck past Drago, then Maxwell, and out the back door.

"I thought you'd be too ashamed to show your face here," Sky said when she finally stood facing her husband. "This isn't your home, Maxwell. You don't have a home anymore." Then she walked out of the room. Klara followed.

"Sky," she said, "how can we get him out of here?"

"Out of here?" Sky said, looking at the Christmas tree. "Oh, Mum, don't even try. Max isn't going anywhere until he's finished, and he's nowhere near finished."

For a few moments, Klara and Sky stood at the tree, each praying or wishing or pleading that the night would end, but when Maxwell moved into the room and said, "Sky, you'll be sorry you said all those terrible things when you see the gift I've brought you," both knew Sky's prediction was right.

Sky turned. She looked at her mother and Katherine. Drago was standing behind them, but she knew better than to meet his eye or to look to him for help. "Gift?" she said.

"It's under the tree," Maxwell answered. He dropped into the overstuffed chair next to the tree.

At any other time, the front room would have seemed beautiful and comfortable. All lamps were extinguished except the tall Christmas candle in the blue glass that cast a blue glow over them, and there was a sweet smell of fruitcake and butter cookies. In the dim light, Klara saw a box under the tree that hadn't been there before. She didn't know when Maxwell had slipped it in; she hadn't seen him arrive with anything. Although she was tempted to ask Drago for help, the bemused, curious look on his face as he leaned against the doorframe, as if he couldn't wait to see how his daughter's fate would unfold, stopped her.

Sky, shrouded in a soft blue fog, knelt over the gift. She fingered its corners, slid the flat of her hand along its edges, head bowed.

"Hurry up," Maxwell grunted. "I want to see what you think of it."

Sky swung a look at him. "I told you. I don't want anything from you," she said. "Besides, you can't afford your own dinner, let alone a gift for me."

"Shut up," Maxwell said.

Sky pried a corner of the wrapping loose. Drago leaned in closer.

"There's no goddamn money for gifts—not for the girls and especially not for me," Sky said.

Maxwell pushed to the edge of the chair, rested his arms on his knees, and clenched his hands into fists. Sky clawed the wrapping free. Then she lifted the lid of the box, folded back the tissue paper, and pulled from it a full-length silk gown. It was red with creamy flowers embroidered on the collar. Maxwell preened.

"Lordy!" Drago said, shaking his head. "That's a hell of a dress."

"Maxwell!" Klara cried.

But it was Sky's response that sent Maxwell into action. "You're a goddamn bastard!" she yelled, and then Maxwell pounced. He pinned her shoulders against the floor with his fists and jammed one knee into her chest over and over again. She grunted at every blow. He straddled her waist, leaned back, raised a flat hand high in the air, and walloped her across the face. His biceps flexed and bulged under his shirtsleeves. Drago took a step forward as if he might step in to help, but then rethought his position and instead moved into the hallway, put on his coat, and walked out the door, past his granddaughters. As he did, Lizzy looked up at him and cried out for help. "I'm going to the saloon," he said to her, "if your grandmother asks."

In the front room, Sky broke free and crab-walked backward, away from her husband. Klara leapt onto his back and buried her fingernails in his cheeks, but he stood and threw her against the wall. "Stop it, Maxwell!" she screamed, but he shoved her out of the way. Sky jumped up and grabbed a dish from the table. She and Maxwell faced each other like angry dogs. Blood streamed down Sky's chin onto her cleaning uniform. "Why are you ruining our lives?" she screamed, holding the dish in front of her. "Leave us alone!"

Sky raised the dish with both hands, and using it like a baseball bat, swung and cracked it sideways to Maxwell's head. He groaned, teetered, and crouched. Klara prayed that he would fall over and pass out, but instead he tackled Sky at the knees and knocked the Christmas candle to the floor. It flashed for a moment and then went out. The room was pitch dark except for the light of flames from the mill.

One of the girls lit a lamp, and Klara screamed, "Maxwell, stop it! That's enough!" Maxwell gripped Sky's arms from behind, but she peeled out of her sweater, leaving him holding the empty sleeves. Then she slammed the door open. "He's going to kill me!" she screamed. He was out the door after her. Klara sobbed, hiccupped, then saw Lizzy and Tunia on the stairs. "They're going to come, girls. The police are going to come. Katherine's gone to fetch them!"

A few minutes later, at the window opposite the bed, Lizzy knelt, resting her chin on the cold wooden sill. "Stay in bed," she ordered Tunia, who slid across the sheets toward her. She lifted the pane, reached out, and scraped her fingertips across the rough, snowy shingles of the porch roof. The porch lamp bathed the snowdrifts in a golden blaze. Sky was curled in a ball beneath the buckeye tree, protecting herself like a turtle in its shell. Maxwell boxed around her, trampling a deep path in the snow, pummeling her in the head, bellowing "Bitch!" over and over. A few doors up at the Mandic house, a yellow lamp was lit. Old Mr. M's round silhouette shuffled across the porch. Tears soaked the neck of Lizzy's nightgown. She squeezed her eyes shut. When she opened them, the cold wind shuffled the white sheers around her like a ghost, grazing her arms. She shivered. Tunia whimpered behind her. Then the officers were there. Like magic. And Lizzy saw Katherine standing on a snowdrift wrapped in scarves and a woolen hat. Before Maxwell could strike again, one officer wrestled him to the ground and buried his face in the snow. Finally it was quiet. "Don't hurt him," Lizzy whispered. Her chest heaved as she watched her mother sob. "All this because I bought you a goddamn present," she heard her father say as he stumbled back into the house between the officers. When she heard their footsteps on the stairs, she leapt under the covers, wrapped an arm around her shivering sister, and yanked the quilt to their chins. It was satiny, cool.

"Wish your daughters a merry Christmas," one officer muttered to Maxwell, shoving him into the girls' room. They'd brought him upstairs to say good night. Maxwell flung himself across the bed and sobbed, his head buried in their knees, the quaking of his shoulders ramming the headboard against the wall, banging like it did on other nights when Lizzy and Tunia tickled each other and giggled too hard until Klara knocked from her side of the wall for them to quiet down and get to sleep. But on that night, Tunia and Lizzy didn't giggle; their throats burned raw from all the screaming. They didn't move in the dark, just held hands under the yellow quilt so tightly that in the morning each would discover a series of pink fingernail half-moons cut into her palm. They listened with closed eyes to their father's mucousy moans and *I'm sorry*'s all strung together. It was always like that. Then from the hallway Klara leaned into the room; she was backlit by the single lamp hung from the hallway ceiling. All Lizzy could see was her outline—the rounded cap of hair, the straight hem of her skirt, and though Lizzy very much wanted to see the details of her face—nose, cheeks, eyes, and wrinkled forehead—Klara's face was just a black oval. "Maxwell," she said, "it's time." The two big-faced officers stepped out of the shadows, pulled him off the bed, cuffed Maxwell's blood-knuckled hands behind his back, and shoved him out the door. Klara's padded footsteps followed. Lizzy stepped out of bed and into her slippers, then squatted once again at the window.

When the wagon with Maxwell in it drove away, Mr. M's porch lamp flickered and died. Snowflakes drifted down from thick clouds. Klara stood next to Sky under the bare-limbed buckeye tree, caressing her head, smoothing back her hair. Her voice floated up to Lizzy. "It's all right, Sky. He's gone now." Sky finally stood, stooped and crying, and before Lizzy could duck her head below the sill, Klara called up, "Go to sleep, now, Liz. Your mum's okay." After a long moment, Lizzy pushed the window shut, eased away, crawled onto the big double bed, and slipped under the quilt next to Tunia.

That night, Klara dreamt of a long, marble banquet table with strands of morning glory vines looping down from chandeliers. At the head of the table, Uncle Janko chewed on scallions, the ends poking from between his lips like a row of frayed, green cigarettes. Cousin Natasa's raucous laughter barreled down the table to greet Klara at the other end, and she quivered as she caught it in cupped hands. Tunia smiled at the crowd and fluttered her eyelashes. Then, gripping Drago's callused hand, Lizzy stepped onto the table. "A beautiful specimen," Cousin Natasa whispered as Lizzy tiptoed along the table toward the center. Sky and Klara and Katherine marched in carrying a huge silver platter between them; on it was a giant steamed cabbage leaf, pale green, curled up slightly at the edges. "Coming through!" Sky whistled brightly. They set it on the table, and with Drago's guiding hand, Lizzy lay down on the leaf, flat-backed, straight-legged, stiff. On her left, from shoulder to ankle, Klara spooned ground pork; on her right, her mother spooned ground ham. Drago topped it off with a few handfuls of rice and a sprinkling of salt and pepper. "Eggs! Eggs!" someone called, and Cousin Natasa did the honors, cracking a single egg over Lizzy's middle.

"Bravo! Bravo!" Drago shouted, then rolled Lizzy, the ham, the pork, the egg, and the rice tightly into the cabbage leaf and carried her in his arms to the kitchen. Without a word, he lowered her onto a bed of sauerkraut in a huge pot that simmered over a fire. A warm, golden glow swallowed her, and just as the lid was snapped into place, Klara said, "Don't anyone stir the stuffed cabbage!"

On the morning after the dream, Klara and Sky awakened and rose to the same sun, and together, with few words, they left the house that was darkened with their spirits.

"Watch the girls," Sky called to Katherine as they passed the house.

Katherine nodded. "They'll be fine," she said, and from her kitchen window, she watched Klara and Sky move down the road. For once, neither was hollering, swinging, or crying—though both were crooked in the back from battling their husbands' blows for so many years. And though she knew better than to hope for change that would astonish the world, she knew enough to pray for minute changes that would bring peace to her friends' lives. She closed her eyes and said her words out loud, knowing that there was no one in the house to hear but God.

As they walked, Klara noted that the mill still rose from the valley like a dragon whipping its jagged tail and spewing forth its flame, that Mrs. Hravic was sweeping bits of snow from her front stoop for the first of a thousand times this day, and that the same small birds with a pale, nearly imperceptible yellow tinge to the underside of their wings, whose name Klara could never remember despite the number of times BenJo told her, gathered in great flocks in the bare bushes that lined the road as they did every morning, chirping and chattering. The world looked the same as it ever had, yet Klara could feel something had shifted. It was as if a small bone or muscle deep within her being had tightened, or maybe loosened, a mere one-thousandth of an inch. It was as if she had received forgiveness or light. Though she didn't know how or whether the shift would manifest itself in her day-to-day life, she did know that whatever it was, it felt good. For the first time in a long time, she felt strong enough to hold up her head.

Together the Bozic women tromped through the snowy streets of Thirsty. They walked past Lucy Giller's High-Style Salon and waved to the women gathered inside whose hair was wrapped in rollers or done up in rags, and though both were tempted, neither mentioned the catastrophe that had followed Klara's final visit to the salon. They stopped to greet BenJo, who was shelving canned beets. He smiled when he saw them walking together toward him, shoulders touching, and as they neared, he handed each a hard candy as a token of his pleasure. They passed the butcher shop without bending to the stench of blood and guts, and the five-and-dime and hat shop without even pausing to look in the windows. As they crossed the railroad tracks, Klara told Sky about the dream she had had so many years before about driving the camels through the desert. Their pace quickened and slowed with their thoughts and dreams. When they reached the hill that rose to Old Man Rupert's home, they didn't stop to discuss whether or not they should continue. They simply chose the road presented to them and began to climb.

It was on the steepest hills that Klara knew she was beginning to grow old, when that sour odor built up under her armpits and the muscles in her legs tired more quickly than she remembered. She watched her daughter from the corner of her eye, daring to hope for the first time that life might someday be something other than that which lay below them. She had a long way to go in forgiveness, but this was a beginning.

It was hard to believe Old Man Rupert was still alive—folks used to bet on his death as often as they bet on the horses—but ever since he had given up the bottle and begun to rebuild his home and replenish his land, he seemed to grow younger each year. While the rest of Thirsty became crippled and bent, Old Man Rupert straightened and strengthened. His hair, which during his drinking years had been matted and filthy, had grown thick and richly white. His broken body filled out and firmed. Most surprisingly, he had put away his guns and found his heart.

Though during Sky's eight-year absence the old man had continued to visit Klara, always bringing some small offering of friendship, Klara hadn't returned to visit his home since the day of Sky's marriage to Maxwell. Sky had never been there at all. Rumors of a stunning transformation that would send them reeling backward into the river had made their way down the hill, and now, as they rounded the final bend in the road that opened to the land and the Rupert house, they saw that the rumors were true.

"Is this possible?" Klara said. She shook her head, believing her eyes had deceived her.

"It's beautiful," Sky said.

"It's blue," Klara said.

"Not just blue," Sky answered. "It's the most beautiful blue I've ever seen."

They were stunned, as had been promised by the busybodies who did such a thorough job keeping track of other people's business. The house was plumb, its porches and widow's walk were straight, its windows gleamed with a fresh shine, and the chimneys, which had been little more than fallen stacks of stones on the ground, reached high into the sky.

Klara dropped her head. "We should have come. He's been so kind to us, to you especially, and we didn't come."

Sky put her hand on her mother's arm. "We're here now."

They stood for a bit looking at the white, snowy fields that highlighted the blue house.

As they stood, reverent, Sky spotted Old Man Rupert near a shed and waved.

"Come on," she said.

"I can't," Klara said. "I don't know what to say. We should have come."

"Say that," Sky said, and she led her mother to the shed where Old Man Rupert waited.

Klara wanted to run away, to run down the hill and hide behind a sturdy pile of slag, but instead she walked right up to Old Man Rupert, took his hand in hers, and repeated her words. "We should have come."

But despite her trepidation and apologies, Old Man Rupert was delighted to see them. He loved Sky and Klara equally, worried over them in that dark, stinking house down the hill.

"Welcome, Bozic women," he said, smiling. "What do you think?"

1918

The mill ate Georgie the same year the war took Ivo, and in the end, Klara was left with one daughter, two granddaughters, and a heart so tight with ache it dried and shriveled. By then, the whistle had fallen into disrepair, so John, whose job was still to carry the news of mill deaths to the womenfolk, journeyed to their homes instead. But if the women had expected this to be a better solution, in fact it proved worse than going to the fence themselves. Once he crossed the doorstep into their homes, the memory of him lingered in their living rooms and kitchens, like the odor of burnt pie crust embedded in cracks in the ceiling and crevices in the floorboards, those hidden, hard-to-reach places that couldn't be scrubbed clean with an easy rag.

On a gray autumn day, with a layer of cloud cover so dense most of the yellowed mill sky was all but shrouded, John was unable to set aside the agony of delivering Klara her news. He was heavy now, swollen from neck to kneecap from too many pots of sausages and pints of beer, bald on top and with a thick gray mustache tangled on his upper lip. It was late afternoon when he was first spotted by the folks in Thirsty. He walked head down and panted from the climb; sweat dripped from the tip of his nose and a letter on official mill paper was tucked into the front pocket of his vest. Like a mule drawing an overloaded cart, he trudged slowly up the road, dragging his feet through dirt and soot. As word of his arrival traveled, women peered from behind curtains and window frames, afraid to open doors, lest it be their stoop on which he settled. Children gasped and scooted home, folded into the safety of their mothers' skirts, until the streets were nearly empty, except for Katherine, still bald and smooth, who was coming from town with two brown-paper packages neatly tucked under her arm. She met him three houses in and, believing she suffered no immediate risk, no husband or son or father to lose, fell into step beside him.

"Mrs. Zupanovic." He was short of breath and hunched over at the middle.

"Mr. John."

"How are you doing today, ma'am?"

"Fine," she paused, "until now." She slowed their pace until it felt as if they weren't moving forward at all.

"Sorry for that."

"Heard you're getting married."

"Yes, ma'am."

"A girl from out of town?"

"Yes, ma'am."

"Where?"

"Excuse me?"

"Where is she from? What town?"

"Over home."

"Ah." Katherine paused. "How many little ones you still got coming up?"

"All are grown and on their own now, except my oldest girl who can't seem to leave her father's house, knowing I've got no one to care for me."

"That's going to change."

"Yes, I'm hoping she'll find herself a husband now."

"I expect she will."

Their exchange was polite, measured, and each time Katherine and John passed a house without pausing or turning into the walk, it was as if the house itself breathed a sigh of relief. Once they passed, the woman of that house collected her courage, opened her door, and moved onto her porch, letting out a sigh as well. After crossing herself and reciting a short prayer of thanks, she moved onto the street and gathered with the other women to watch for John's final destination. Children, released from the grip of their mothers' eyes, followed at a safe distance.

"Does she know what you do for a living?" Katherine asked.

"Ma'am?"

"The woman you're bringing here to marry, does she know what kind of goods you deliver?"

"She knows I work for the mill."

"Going to surprise her with that, huh, Mr. John?"

"She's a good woman."

"She'll have to be. She's not going to have many friends up this way. No fault of her own, though."

"She's got a sister close by."

"Mmm. Good thing."

They were coming close to the end of Katherine's street, and when John didn't take the left fork down Rib, Katherine stopped, shifted her packages, and looked sideways at him.

"Mr. John," she said, tasting her words like bitters, "exactly where are you heading right now?"

His eyes went to the Bozic house before his mouth did. She followed them, stared, and then dropped both packages. Drago? She teetered for a moment, in danger of falling like a felled tree, until John reached out and held her arm. "Drago?" she finally said, not knowing whether to laugh or cry. For a long moment, Katherine imagined how life could be for Klara without the hand of her husband held over her. She had never dared to dream such glory. But John's silence spoke more loudly. She regained her balance and noticed he was still looking at the Bozic house. It was a cleaner white than any of the others in the row, almost milky under Klara's diligent scouring. In the silence, John looked from the house to his feet, then up to Katherine's prodding eyes.

"Mrs. Zupanovic, it's not Drago I'm visiting about."

"What are you saying?"

"Drago's not on at the mill today."

There was another long pause as Katherine rolled the only other possibility over in her mind. "Don't tell me it's her boy," she finally said.

"Mrs. Zupanovic . . ."

"Nah, John, don't tell me that. Don't you tell me it's her boy."

"It's Georgie, Mrs. Zupanovic."

"No, it's not. It can't be. You and them crazies down at that mill must be mistaken. You must have misread the body somehow. Georgie isn't more than a baby."

"George. Yes, George Bozic."

"But he hasn't even taken a wife yet."

"It's George, Mrs. Zupanovic. There's no mistake."

"Nah, you can't take the boy," Katherine begged. She shook her head.

"It got him, Mrs. Z. It got him good."

Another long pause.

"Does Drago know yet?"

"No, ma'am. I'm hoping to find him at home."

Katherine straightened her skirt. She forgot all about the packages lying on the ground. "I'm going with you."

John turned toward the house. "I'd appreciate that, Mrs. Zupanovic. It will be easier on Mrs. Bozic."

Katherine fell into step beside him again, thinking back to that first night without Jake after his funeral. She'd sat in the dark living room, trying not to wait for him to open the door, but waiting anyway, thinking maybe he wasn't in that casket at all, maybe they'd mistaken him for someone else. He'd been burned up so bad, it could have happened. She didn't even have a face to bid good-bye to, just a pile of bones they'd promised was her husband. She'd had to believe them, trust in a bunch of men who had never stood in her kitchen in the mornings listening to the scrape of Jake's razor across his cheek or the rumble of his throat when he sang during his bath. She'd had to put her faith in a bunch of men who had never sat at her dining table watching him take three helpings of potatoes before he was even near full, then delicately wiping his mouth with the corner of a napkin like he was eating in some fancy restaurant. These men hadn't known a thing except that a pile of bones was something she had to let go of, and even though she'd have preferred to keep them with her, she'd given in and let them bury him. Ten years passed before she stopped looking at the doorway every time the wind knocked.

Klara was in the cellar reorganizing the canning shelves. Lost in thought, she didn't hear the knock or the holler or even the footsteps on the staircase until both John and Katherine were standing in the cellar with her, and never could she have guessed she could burn so hot inside as she did from the sight of those two at the bottom of her stairs. A white piece of paper stuck up from the pocket of John's vest, and he gripped so tightly to the railing, it looked as if he might turn and run if he dared to let go. She knew she should greet them, nod, say hello, but instead she stood still with a jar of stewed plums in each hand, listening to the water bubbling on the fire upstairs and the squawk of a bird outside the house that she imagined had to be one of those black crows carrying death on his wings, lighting on a branch in the pine tree. More than anything, she wanted to push past her visitors, rush outside, and shoo the bird off with a swish of the broom. After all that, she wanted to walk back down to her cellar and continue her work. But she stood still while that bird cawed and cawed.

After John and Katherine had stood there a good long minute, not saying a word, just looking at her, Klara shook a jar of plums at them and turned away. "Go back upstairs, back the way you came," she said over her shoulder, setting the jars of plums down with a crack sharp enough to shatter them. "I'm busy down here, and it looks like you two don't know what busy is, walking all over the hill during working hours like there isn't anything better to be done."

"Klara, you've got to come with me," Katherine said, and she moved a few steps across the room. But Klara held up her hand.

"I don't have to go anywhere I don't want to go," she said and pointed a finger at Katherine, "and I do not want to go with you. I've got fourteen shelves of goods that haven't been organized all season. Lizzy's been running them down here and shelving them without so much as looking at the labels. Thought I taught the girl better than that. Look here. See this?" She held up a jar. "I got peaches next to pickles, tomatoes mixed with rhubarb, and a few I never even got around to labeling so now I have to guess the dates. All of this going on, and you're telling me I have to go with you? You two are the only ones who've got to go. Leave me to my business."

"Klara, John's here. You know John. He's come to see you. Got some business he's got to share."

Klara glared at Katherine, then glanced at John. "Yes, I recognize John. Yes, I do. I know all about John." His name tasted like poison in her mouth. "I know all about his business, too. Walking around town like Father Death himself, doing the devil's work. Well, not in my house. You hear me? Not in my house. The devil isn't coming to the Bozic house. I've been fighting his work for years, struggling with the rest of this town to keep his footprints off my porch, and I've done good. There isn't any way he's coming in here now, just when I'm growing to be an old lady."

As if he'd been summoned, John let go of the railing and stepped forward. When he did, Klara felt a surge of heat in her chest and leapt backward. She crashed into the cupboard and toppled a few jars. John backed up until he struck the wall. He shook his head. When Klara was steady again, she looked up and crossed herself. "You keep your distance, Mister Devil. I can smell you all the way over here. The stink of you slicing through my sweet plums, stink of that mill, stink of death. I want nothing from you. Nothing you're offering pleases me. If Drago comes downstairs and finds you here, he'll toss you out faster than I can spit. So you best go on while two legs still carry you. I wouldn't want you crawling back down the road you came on."

"Klara," Katherine said. "It's me. Katy. Listen to me."

"I am not listening to anyone. What? You've got no memory of the last time this man crossed into our lives? Just because he doesn't have a fence protecting him now doesn't mean he hasn't got the power to maim. You can't remember that far back? Huh, Katy? I've got memory, memory of you in my bones, and I am not getting maimed. I need my legs and arms, my heart. I can't keep living without them. So you just encourage him to leave my limbs as they are and get on with himself."

"Klara, we've got to talk. John came with some news that is best delivered upstairs in the sitting room."

"You gone deaf as well as bald, Katherine? Do you hear what I'm saying? I am not going anywhere. So, Devil, if you've got something to say to me, you'd better get it out now before I turn my back on you. This is the last time you'll be looking in my eyes."

John stepped forward again. This time Klara held her ground. "Well, Mrs. Bozic, . . ." His eyes were on the ceiling.

"You got something to say to me," Klara interrupted, "look at me straight."

John took a breath, cleared his throat, and looked her in the eye. "Mrs. Bozic, George is gone. He got swallowed up in a stream of hot metal when a crew jiggered a ladle loose too quick."

Klara closed her eyes. "Don't you be telling tales in my house, Devil. Get on out of here," she said. She turned her back and began shelving jars.

John sighed and glanced at Katherine. He removed the letter from his pocket and held it out to Klara.

"It's the truth, Mrs. Bozic. I'm sorry. I have the letter here."

Klara didn't turn. She was thinking about how hard it had been to keep the house in order back when all the children were young and how easy it had become, since they'd grown, to keep nose smudges from the windows and shoes stored in the closet where they belonged. How many times had she hollered at the boys not to slam the door on their way out, not to pick their noses, not to walk the railroad tracks down by the mill no matter how thick the blackberries grew around there, but there they'd come, mouths stained purple from so much eating and enough berries in a bucket to make three pies. But now she had those girls. Better than the boys, she thought, but still making messes wherever they went.

Katherine nodded to John and took the letter from his hand. "Klara, look here." She held up the letter.

Klara glanced over her shoulder. "That's nice, real nice."

"It's an official letter from the mill, Klara. You've got to read it."

Through the silence, they heard the slap of Drago's slippers on the floor above. Then his voice came down the stairs. "Klara, what's all the noise down there? Who you got down there? I'm trying to rest."

"Drago, it's me," Katherine said.

"Oh, should have guessed. Can't you two birds keep quiet in your business?"

"Drago, I'm not the only one here."

There was a short pause, then the sound of Drago's slippers on the stairs. When he reached the bottom, John stepped forward with his hand outstretched. Drago took it.

"What business have you got all the way in Thirsty, John?" Drago said.

"I'm not going to spend your time, Drago," John said. It was always easier delivering news to a man, though it didn't happen often. "It's your son George. He got lost as the ladle was being tapped, and it spilled. He died instantly. He's gone. They recovered his body not long after. It was quick. Real quick. He couldn't have felt any pain. Too much heat to feel it. You know that. His body has been taken to the funeral home, and they've got his belongings. I was home when the accident happened, but they sent for me, knowing how long you and I have been acquainted."

Drago glanced at his wife. She'd picked up a cloth and was wiping each jar clean before setting it on the shelf. "George, you say? Our George. You sure about that?"

"Yes, sir, no doubt."

Drago didn't know anything about taking a son's death so he shook John's hand again, thanked him, and then stepped out of the way so John could move back up the stairs. As he did, John nodded. "I'm sorry, Drago," he said.

When he was gone, Drago crossed to the middle of the cellar and turned in a full circle twice. "Klara?" he said.

"Mm?" Klara murmured.

"You going to keep working down here?"

"Mm."

He turned to Katherine. "Are you going to care for my wife?"

"Where are you going?" she asked.

"To the funeral home to see about arrangements."

"Sure you aren't going straight to the bar?"

He squeezed his hands into fists and opened them again. "Even I can't bury a son at the bar, Katherine," he said.

He moved slowly up the stairs and out the door, still wearing his slippers, not feeling the chill in the air or even noticing the gaggle of women take note and separate as he moved down the road.

When they were alone, Katherine stepped across the cellar into the damp corner where Klara stood. The corner was dark and cold.

"Klara," she said, "no wonder that cupboard of yours is out of sorts. Can't see a thing back here. Wouldn't know a jar of cherries from a leg of lamb." She began clearing jars from the top shelf, setting them on the ground until it was empty. "Let's start with the cherries, since that's what you've got the most of. Even got a few jars from last year, so we'll put them in front. When Lizzy comes to gather them, these will come natural."

Klara handed Katherine the jars according to the dates and for a while kept silent, then she began talking through her tears.

"He's my oldest boy, Katy. What am I to do without my oldest boy?"

"I know, I know."

"He hasn't even had time to find a wife. He hasn't even had time to grow a proper beard. How can the mill take a boy like that? A boy. My boy."

"Oh, but what a life he had. Think of that."

"Nobody even called him a man yet. Still calling him a boy. How does the mill get to take a life if it can't even call him a man? How can that be?"

Katherine waited for the anguish and wonder to turn to rage, and when Klara drew back and pitched the first jar of cherry jam across the cellar, she was ready. She didn't even flinch. The jar shattered and spilled. Katherine stood back as Klara followed with the peaches and plums and tomatoes, hurling each jar across the cellar until the cupboard was empty except for a few jars near the back of the bottom shelf that she'd overlooked. The floor was a mess of shattered glass and preserves. Then Katherine took Klara's hand, and slowly they moved upstairs into the twilight-filled living room and settled close on the couch to wait for Drago. Like a dutiful sentry, the crow held his place in the pine tree, but fell quiet soon after dusk, becoming just a dark shadow among many.

The second death came before the throb of the first subsided. A uniformed soldier appeared at the door, not heeding the black wreath or drawn curtains. He knocked anyway, and Klara, in her mourning clothes, black shoes clomping against the floorboards like horses' hooves, opened the door wide. She thought it might be Katherine coming to share a mug of coffee, but immediately knew, even before the young man opened his mouth, what was going to come out. And with that knowing, she shoved the door open so hard it cracked the boy in the chest and sent him reeling backward. Unable to keep his balance, despite a grab for Drago's finely carved porch post, the soldier tripped on the stairs and ended up on his ass in a pile of cinders. And the soldier, his perfectly pressed uniform now soiled, swore out loud although it was sacrilegious, especially on such an occasion, but asked forgiveness almost as soon as the curse left his mouth. *But who is this woman?* he thought, as Klara looked down at him with sprigs of hair poking out from the bun on the crown of her head. She had the sudden strength of an ox and she didn't nod, bow her head, take the letter he offered, and then gently shut the door to him to howl out her agony in private like most of the mothers he'd visited. No, this woman threw him her pain, so much so that he, there on the ground looking up, suddenly wanted to be her boy, returning home on leave for a surprise visit, rather than the soldier who had to tell her that her boy, her boy, was never coming home at all. He didn't want to be the soldier to tell her that her son had been shot so many times his chest had opened from collarbone to stomach like a cave in a stone wall, hollowed out by bullets, shards of bone and metal, strings of flesh, decorating its interior.

Standing there, hands clawing at the waistband of her black skirt, Klara looked down at the soldier and wondered how old she would have to be before all of this nonsense about sons dying before their mother would end. But as she realized that this was the last time, the last son, she dropped her hands to her sides so they hung limp. The knowledge that there couldn't even be a next time was somehow more damaging than the two deaths themselves, and when she closed her eyes, the soldier climbed to his feet, took off his hat, and bowed his head. But before he could gather enough spit to speak, Klara snapped her eyes open and silenced him with, "Don't tell me out loud, boy! Hand me that letter if you must, but don't you dare tell me out loud!" Those were the last words she would speak for a long time, lost words to a boy who looked nothing like her own but whose boy-smell was familiar enough for her to want to pull him close and bury her head in his neck. He nodded, swallowed the words that had almost escaped, and straightened his back. Without meeting her eye, he retrieved the letter from a secret interior pocket, then held it out to her at arm's length. And though he knew that the exchange was almost over, he didn't know for sure if she would strike at him again, and he thought, strangely enough, that this time she might actually kill him.

The boy heard a shuffle and turned his head. He saw an old woman run out of the house next door, barefoot and surprisingly bald. Despite her age, she crossed her porch and the spot of grass and dirt that separated them so quickly she might have been flying. She stopped a few feet away, shaking her head, and he heard her moan so softly it might have been part of his own thoughts. Then, suddenly remembering his duty in this place, he snapped to attention and saluted Klara. But she just stared at him, her large green eyes reminding him of a turtle's shell he'd found in the woods as a child. She held the letter in both hands against her chest, but didn't open it or ask the questions mothers often asked. She didn't ask if her son had been warm and fed in the place that took his life, if he'd been liked by his comrades, if he'd died honorably for his country, if she could be proud and cry his worth to friends and family in order to comfort herself with his memory. So after a few minutes of silence, the soldier saluted a second time and then backed down the path, his arms feeling the air behind him. He stepped into the street and for a time walked backward, watching the two women frozen in the yard. He didn't turn to walk forward until he was well past the fence post that marked the end of Tiny's property, crooked again by this time, then slowed his pace so much it seemed as if there were a string hitched between him and Klara that he couldn't loosen or untie. He would feel this way for many years to come.

By the time Katherine reached her, Klara had fallen into silence. She was kneeling on the ground with one hand resting on the spot of cinders where the soldier had fallen and the other resting on her belly. The letter lay unopened beside her. Later, after she'd risen from this place, she would place it in the top drawer of her bureau under a swatch of her mother's wedding dress with the letter from the mill announcing Georgie's death, both still sealed.

Katherine knelt beside her and set her hand on the back of her neck. "I know this isn't fair, Klara, but you can get through this. You can take anything the Lord gives you to carry. He gives it to you because you're strong." She continued to talk, about strength and Sky and the girls and those days so long ago when the butterflies reigned over Thirsty, but Klara didn't hear her. She was busy remembering all the times with her boys. How often Ivo slammed the front door, never heeding her warnings about the devil coming into a house where doors never shut gently, and Georgie, who never shut a door at all, just left it hanging open on its hinges whenever he came in or out, even in the dead of winter. And now the devil had walked right in, twice, the devil himself, and as she knelt there in the dirt, she tried to remember if she had ever been the one to slam the door or leave it ajar, because she knew it wasn't the boys who were consigned to hell.

By the time the sun rose on the morning after the soldier's visit, all of the townspeople in Thirsty, and many in the surrounding towns as well, knew Klara Bozic had stopped speaking. By noon, as the rhythm and pitch of the usual blend of noises dipped and bowed without her significant contribution, it had become the mission of the town to alter her mute condition. She was sitting in the brown overstuffed chair in an unlit corner of the living room when Widow Cane arrived. Katherine, who had sat all night by Klara's side looking into the dark beyond the window for her friend's voice and guarding what little remained, warned Widow Cane of the insistence of the silence. Drago, who had moved in and out of the house every few hours since arriving home to a cold kitchen and news of another dead son, hung his head and grumbled. Sky, frightened by her mother's weakness, had tucked her tail and disappeared with the girls. Widow Cane, her face as ashen as the mourning cape draped around her shoulders, cradled a freshly cooked leg of lamb against her chest like a nursing baby. It was wrapped in brown butcher paper and tied so intricately with stretches of twine, it looked as if no one would ever be able to unravel the knots in order to enjoy the meat.

A willowy woman with a sizable hump on her back, Widow Cane stood for a moment in the doorway, letting her eyes adjust to the dim light. When she finally spotted Klara in the shadows, she dismissed Katherine with a wave of her hand and crossed the room in a stiff staccato shuffle. Never before had she witnessed a woman so dispossessed of her dignity. Klara's hair, pulled from its bun, resembled a bed of thistles left to its own on a hillside, and a sweetish-sour odor, so strong it forced Widow Cane three steps back, rose from the folds of her skirt. From a good distance, she tossed the package onto Klara's lap, expecting her to reach out and catch it, but along with the loss of her voice, Klara's reactions had slowed. The package landed with a hard thump against her belly. Widow Cane waited. After a long moment, Klara reached for the package, picked it up, smoothed the brown paper with both hands, fingered the knots, and even pressed her nose to a crease and breathed in the rich scent. But then, just as Widow Cane was certain words would come, and she had straightened her back at the thought of the admiration she would enjoy from the townspeople, already taking credit for Klara's rediscovered voice, certain now that a "thank you" or an "it smells delicious" was going to spill from the hard line of Klara's mouth, Klara leaned back and resumed staring at the same pale spot on the wall at which she'd been staring for nearly twenty-four hours. It was a small, insignificant spot shaped like a wildflower, a long thin stem with a ragged splotch at its end. In all the years she had scrubbed soot and grime from the walls, she had never noticed it, and for some reason, in her silence, it seemed suddenly important.

"I heard the news," Widow Cane said when she realized Klara wasn't going to be the first to speak. "I'm sorry for your son. The lamb will make you better. Let me fix a plate."

She lifted the package from Klara's lap and moved into the kitchen past Katherine and Drago, who crouched behind the coatrack with their ears cocked, listening for the rasp of Klara's voice.

"Did she speak?" Katherine asked.

"No, but she will," Widow Cane said. "I saw the words forming in her throat. Small twitches. One bite of this lamb, and she'll be singing at the funeral."

Katherine glanced at her sharply.

"Well, maybe not singing," Widow Cane corrected, lowering her head, "but praying. She'll be praying."

After slicing through the paper and twine with a swift blade, she fixed a generous helping of lamb on a plate, set it with a fork and a cup of tea, then carried it into the living room where Klara was still sitting in the same place staring at the same spot on the wall. Her face and neck, usually quite pale, had, in the hours since the news of Ivo's death, blossomed to an alarming shade of red. And when the plate was set in her lap, she ate as if she hadn't eaten in years. She ignored the fork and picked up the long wet pieces of lamb with her fingers, pushing them into her mouth before she had swallowed what was already there. Soon, bits of meat and fat clung to her lips and chin. Widow Cane stepped back again, shaking her head. She glanced over her shoulder to check for Katherine, suddenly not wishing to be alone with Klara.

"There's more to be had," she said quietly. "Take your time." But Klara continued to ravage the plate until it was empty. Then she drank the cup of tea in one great swallow, set the plate and the cup on the floor, leaned back, and resumed her position.

"Good, eh?" Widow Cane said, more to herself now than Klara, and with shoulders slumped, she disappeared out the front door with nothing more than a curt nod to Katherine and Drago.

With a damp rag, Katherine kneeled next to Klara and wiped the remnants of lamb from her face. She rubbed hard, believing a bit of pain might cause Klara to cry out or holler at her for her insensitivity. But even when she scraped the cloth against the raw edge of Klara's nose, where the effects of mourning tears and mucous were most evident, Klara did not utter a sound. She sat perfectly silent.

"I'm finishing the lamb," Drago said, and he disappeared into the kitchen.

As Katherine watched him go, she leaned close to Klara's ear and whispered, "Who wants to talk to that old codger anyway?"

The next morning, early, at the short-lived moment in each day when you can peer through a window and not know whether to say "It's still dark" or "It's just now becoming light," Stella Jevic tapped on the back door of the Bozic house. She had spent the night in her kitchen crying sorrow for the loss of Ivo into a great roll of pie dough, as she did for all who passed in Thirsty. Her favorite pink apron, tinged with tears and scalloped at the edges, was still tied around her sizable waist. Stella was a round woman with heavy pockets of skin hanging from her arms and eyes and chin, and the layers of fat between her thighs were so thick that she rocked rather than walked. Because of this complication, it took her a good eight times as long as most to travel from one place to another, a problem most obvious on Sundays when she left her home at six in the morning in order to arrive at St. Jude's, a fifteen-minute stroll for many, in time for the eight o'clock mass. Worn out from the effort when she did finally arrive, she usually slept in the second-to-last pew with the hymnal folded over her face until the close of Father Tom's sermon, at which time she would shake out her limbs, straighten her spine, and listen to the remaining minutes of mass with great intensity.

Like any respectable baker, she had allowed the Bozics' pie ample time to cool and set, and then, at an hour when she hoped to avoid the burgeoning crowd her pies usually summoned, she covered the pie with a checkered cloth, went out her door, and slowly rocked her way through the streets until she reached the Bozic home.

When Katherine opened the door, the scent of strawberry rhubarb filled her nostrils, and her eyes, which had begun to close after two days of keeping watch over Klara, popped wide. The pie was large, a mound of fruit and sugar topped with a delicate lattice crust so thin and tender-brown she knew it would surely dissolve on her tongue like the first snowflake of winter. Despite her sorrow, her mouth began to water, and when she looked past Stella, out to the street, she saw the townspeople already gathering, straddling the boundary between the street and the Bozics' property, longing looks decorating their faces, waiting for word of the return of Klara's voice or for an extra slice of pie.

"Get on out of here!" Drago hollered out the door as he got behind Stella in order to shove both her and her pie through it. It was a tight fit that required him to plant both feet and push hard enough on her back and buttocks to fell a well-rooted tree. It took four tries, and when she was through, his brow was coated with sweat and his breath was ragged. It was only because he was ravenous again that he didn't mind that the neighbors saw his blue-and-red striped pajamas, worn at the knees and elbows, and the pair of gray slippers Klara had crocheted for him a few Christmases before, now with holes in the toes. "Go on!" he yelled, shaking his fist in the air. "Go home! There's nothing here for you!" He had enjoyed many of Stella's pies in the past, the most recent being the apple cinnamon delicacy she'd brought after word of Georgie's death reached her kitchen, and he knew if anything could make his mute wife speak and resume her household duties, it would be one savoring bite of Miss Stella Jevic's strawberry rhubarb pie.

"Pie," Katherine said, rubbing the expanse of Stella's back with her hand. "Stella, that's a good idea, bringing that pie."

Stella smiled as she rocked along the short hallway toward the kitchen. "Strawberry rhubarb. It's her favorite. Fix her up one every year on her birthday. Thought it might loosen her jaw, get the juices flowing again."

Drago followed them and once in the kitchen, he sat at the table near the pie holding his head in his hands.

"Drago," Stella said, "you okay? Keeping your back straight?"

"Mind your business," he answered.

"You mind your woman," she said. "She lost her boys."

"You heard what I said."

"You don't mind Klara, I'll take this pie and walk out that door the way I come."

"Hmph," Drago said, but he sat back in the chair and nodded.

The knife moved through the pie as easily as it might through soft butter. Stella set a large piece on a plate, dressed it with a fork, and carried it to the living room. Sometime during the night Klara had moved from the brown overstuffed chair to a hardwood straight-back chair. She sat like a statue with both feet planted flat on the ground and her hands folded in her lap. Through the open window, soot had washed in and cloaked her in a blackish sheath. It was built up around her mouth like a beard and wrapped around her neck like a scarf. Stella ignored the sight, which might have disturbed a woman with a weaker constitution, set the plate in Klara's lap, and watched as she dismissed the fork and devoured the slice of pie by burying her face in it. She then licked the plate clean and handed the plate to Stella, then resumed her position. She ate each slice Stella brought to her in the same manner until the entire pie was gone, and while Stella continually anticipated sound, accustomed to Klara's usual cacophony of praise on each birthday as she dove into the first slice, a symphony of *mmm*'s and *ooh*'s, Klara didn't utter a word. Not even a low pleasurable moan. And the absence of such a show made Stella feel downright ugly. She vowed to go home and whip up a pie so rich and sweet that upon merely setting her nose to it, Klara would burst into speech.

"Maybe the speaking tools she's got in there aren't working anymore," she told Katherine on her way out of the house, carrying the empty pie plate in her hands. "Might be worth calling Doc Slater to give her a checkup," she said after Drago had successfully squeezed her back through the door onto the porch. "Sorrow's a funny thing. Doesn't have a lot of rules to accompany it."

Doc Slater arrived that evening with his bag and a concerned look on his face. "The woman hasn't said a word in how long?" he asked. He was a brusque man with wide shoulders, meat shanks for hands, and a voice that sounded much like a load of slag being dumped from a railroad car. Katherine suspected that if nothing else, he might frighten Klara into speech.

"No," she said, "not a sound since she spoke to the soldier who gave her the news."

Doc Slater followed Katherine into the living room. A few lamps lit the room. "Is she eating?" he asked.

"Oh, yes. Anything we set on her lap."

"Hm."

Klara turned her head toward them as they spoke, then turned back to the window. Doc Slater bent over her and jumped back. The smell hit him hard.

"She won't let me bathe her," Katherine explained.

He nodded, took a deep breath, held it, and tried again. He lifted her right arm into the air, then let it drop into her lap. After doing the same to the left, he said, "Dead weight."

"Oh, don't let her fool you," Katherine said. "She devoured an entire pie just this morning."

"A Stella Jevic pie?"

"Mmmm."

"What kind?"

"Strawberry rhubarb."

Doc Slater closed his eyes and groaned, and for a moment Katherine thought she'd lost him to his reverie. "Doc?" she said.

He smiled and opened his eyes. "Just remembering." His voice had fallen to a quiet rumble.

"She blinks," he said, continuing his examination.

"Pretty often."

He tapped her knee with a small rubber mallet and her leg kicked out just as it was supposed to.

"Reactions are good."

He pulled his stethoscope from his black bag, put it on, and listened to her heart. She sat still and let him listen.

"It's beating."

"I was fairly sure of that," Katherine said. She was losing confidence.

Doc Slater packed his tools into his bag, then stood and shook his head. "Nothing physically wrong with this woman as far as I can tell. She is not feverish or devoid of life. There are no knocks or pings where there shouldn't be." He moved toward the door.

"What should we do?" Katherine asked.

"I would have to say nothing. Just keep feeding her, whatever she'll eat. When she's ready, I imagine she'll speak."

"Or she won't?" Katherine said.

"Or she won't."

"Doc," Katherine said, "we have to bury Ivo, but I don't think we should until all this is over. Klara needs to bury her boy herself."

"Ah," Doc Slater said, "it's not going to matter when you bury the boy. There's not much left to bury. It will be a closed coffin whether it happens tomorrow or six months from now."

Katherine looked at the floor and nodded.

Each morning for the next few weeks, after the ten o'clock bells at St. Jude's broke the air, a neighbor or friend, and sometimes even a stranger, arrived on the doorstep with some offering of food and a solemn promise that this would be the dish that would draw words from the silent woman's mouth. This, with its precise blend of pepper and garlic, slide of butter . . . or this, with its silky texture, stirred with white sugar, you know . . . or this, yes this, with its tart but palatable blessing from God. It wasn't much different from the time Jake suffered the hiccups—everyone wanting to help and no one being able. Katherine would once again listen to each visitor, her hope raised a pig's hair less each morning, then nod and tell him or her to wait right there—she had grown tired of sweeping soot from so many footsteps. Then, like one of the wise men carrying gifts to the Baby Jesus, she would carry the offering to Klara, who would devour it as voraciously as she had devoured Widow Cane's leg of lamb and Stella Jevic's strawberry rhubarb pie. Ever dutiful, Katherine would watch to see if the moment before she swallowed would indeed be the final moment of silence, but it wasn't. Even her swallowing was silent. As soon as she had set the dish on the floor, Klara would resume her stoic position. So each morning, after wrestling her own disappointment in the steps between the living room and the front door, Katherine would return to the porch saying *thank you,* but shaking her head. And the friend or neighbor, or even the stranger whose stake in the process should have been but wasn't a little less vital, would shuffle off the porch rich with dejection and sadness and sometimes even a touch of anger that Klara had not recognized the power of her particular gift.

In the first days of silence, Katherine worked hard to reassure all who came that Klara's silence had not yet been broken by anyone else, so they had nothing for which to feel ashamed. But as the weeks passed, and she fell into a routine of keeping watch over Klara at night and caring for her needs in the day, sleeping just a few hours in between when Sky hesitantly took over, she realized that she had only so much energy. It was then that her reassurances to friends and neighbors who failed in their intentions were reduced to a heartfelt thank you and a shaking of the head.

Klara herself settled into an easy routine. She moved between the brown overstuffed chair and the straight-back chair when she thought no one was looking, sometimes bending at the knees a few times to shake out the creaks.

It was on the twenty-fourth day of silence that BenJo knocked on the Bozics' door carrying a cage as big as a doghouse. It was such a curious offering—flat on the bottom, rounded at the top, and draped with a blue silk cloth—that the townspeople had followed him all the way from his shop and were lining themselves like spectators in front of the Bozic house.

The cloth itself had been passed down in BenJo's wife's family, a wrap for teacups of great fragility, and whatever was under the cloth in the cage was so heavy that by the time Drago opened the door and witnessed BenJo's bent black body leaning against his porch railing, beads of sweat were bleeding from the tip of BenJo's famous nose, saturating the silk cloth.

Incensed that a black man, any black man, would dare to step onto his porch, Drago threw open the door, stomped outside, and opened his mouth to holler. He grew angrier still when the thought crossed his mind that this black man had befriended his wife and handled his dinner vegetables. He cocked his arm to throw a punch. BenJo would have taken it, too. He stood fast, looking Drago in the eye and rolling his lips together, his eyebrows raised expectantly, but before Drago could put his weight behind the punch, Katherine grabbed his elbow from behind.

"This is not the time or the place for any of your non-sense, Drago Bozic!" she whispered. "Klara is sitting in that house taking herself farther and farther away from us each day, and you can bet your life my Jake is watching from above. I can't get my husband back from the dead, and God knows I'd sell my soul if I got an offer, but if this man can help pull Klara back to us, get her up and around, talking again, you are not going to stop him."

Drago let her words run through his mind. Though he was certain he wanted to send BenJo soaring through the air on the end of his fist, he was equally certain that he wanted his wife back, if for no other reason than to cook and clean and take care of domestic business. He was also sure he wanted Katherine Zupanovic out of his house for good. He stood for a moment, his arm still drawn behind him, but loose now, then he shook his head, cursed under his breath, and stepped back. "I am not sitting here for this business," he said and walked away. He turned when he got to the street. "What the hell is in there anyway?" he said, gesturing to the cage.

The crowd stiffened with anticipation. They'd been hoping for a quick end to the altercation so they could discover for themselves what was hidden under the blue silk cloth.

BenJo smiled. "A gift, Mr. Bozic, for Mrs. Bozic. I heard she was under the weather."

"Under the weather, hmm? What kind of present is that? Looks too big to eat. Everybody in town has been bringing things to eat because my wife hasn't been cooking since we got the news about our son."

"No," BenJo said. "Not supposed to eat this one."

"What is it?"

The crowd moved a little closer to the porch. Katherine waved them off.

"You'll see when Mrs. Bozic opens it."

"Go on, Drago," Katherine said. "I'll take care of this. It'll be here when you get back."

"Don't you let that jigaboo in my house," Drago warned as he walked away. "Don't you dare. There are not going to be any nigger footsteps in my house. You hear me, lady?"

"I hear you, man!" Katherine hollered back. "Now get on." Then he was gone around the bend. She turned to BenJo. "I am sorry. Drago Bozic has never been right. It's not the town secret, that's for sure."

"That's okay, Mrs. Z. I'm used to him. Lots like him in this world. May I see Mrs. Bozic now? I'll wait right here."

"BenJo, she hasn't left the house since the soldier's visit. She hasn't often left the living room."

"Just ask her."

"What?"

"Go on in, tell her I'm here, and ask her if she'll come out. Please."

"I'll take the gift to her, save me the steps."

The crowd pressed in.

BenJo gripped the cage. "It's something I need to give her myself. Please, Mrs. Zupanovic, tell her I need to speak with her." He swung the cage back and forth.

"All right, all right, I'll tell her. Guess it can't hurt anything. Maybe she'll talk and things can get back to somewhat normal around here."

BenJo moved back a step. When he stopped abruptly, something in the cage moved and made a small indiscernible noise. The crowd of onlookers murmured and glanced at one another with big eyes.

A moment later, Klara was standing on the porch. It was a bright day, and her eyes, unaccustomed to the light, squeezed shut. BenJo waited patiently until she could open them again. Her hair, mostly gray, was loose around her shoulders, and a few spots of grease or chicken fat decorated the front of her brown dress. It was the first sight many of the townspeople had had of her in weeks, and when they saw her disheveled state, a collective gasp spread down the street like a sheet of rain. Finally Klara opened her eyes. BenJo leaned close and looked into them. They were still green, a good sign. "Mrs. Bozic," he said, "are you doing all right?"

She looked back at him, even leaned down a little, mimicking his gesture, but she didn't answer. He lowered his eyes and watched her throat for tiny movements, words building in the voice box, but nothing moved.

He set the cage on the porch, then reached into his pocket and pulled out an orange. Klara smiled a little, reached out, and grabbed it from his hands.

As she peeled it, he said, "I got you something else, something special. From down at the carnival. You know the carnival's here, don't you?"

Klara glanced from the orange to BenJo. The bright peelings collected around her feet.

"Well," he said, "I know the carnival man pretty well, and I was down there playing cards after hours and sooner than he counted on—because he believes he's king of the table—the carnival man ran out of money. He wanted to keep playing, said he had a little bird he could offer in its place. I said okay, playing more for the game and the company than the winnings themselves, though those aren't so bad on a thin Sunday. I knew a few times I'd run low and threw in a crate of cucumbers or a few heads of new lettuce to make up the difference.

"So this man, the carnival owner, he went out somewhere in the dark to get this little bird he was going to toss in the pot, and me and a few others just sat around waiting for him, talking about this and that. The tall man, he was there, and even sitting down he's at least five times as high as my head. And one of the clowns was there, but he didn't have any makeup on and he looked as normal as you or me, except for the yellow pants and red suspenders. Nice men there. So a couple of minutes later my friend comes back and he's carrying this cage."

BenJo paused and patted the top of the cage. "And a few hands later, I was carrying this thing out of the tent wondering what I was going to do with it. If I brought a bird into my house, my wife would send me out so fast I would have missed the step." He laughed. The crowd, growing more anxious over the fact that they couldn't hear what was being said, pressed in even closer. "So see here, Mrs. Bozic, I thought this little bird would be just the thing to bring a little cheer back into you. He's a beauty."

Klara popped the last wedge of orange into her mouth and smacked her lips. BenJo hoisted the cage over his shoulder, stood on an old crate sitting in the corner, and hooked the top of the cage over a nail in the cross-post under the roof of the porch. It hung nicely. The crowd was tight around the house now.

"You go on, Mrs. Bozic. Pull off the wrap."

Klara reached up and fingered the blue silk cloth. It was cool and smooth under her fingertips.

"That cloth is a gift from my wife," BenJo said. "She sends her sympathies."

Klara looked at BenJo, then at the cage, and pulled one corner of the cloth. It slipped off like water in her hands. Underneath was a bird as large as two loaves of sweet bread pressed together, with a teal-blue head and a slate-blue beak. His back was brilliant green with red feathers around his neck like a collar. His belly and chest were pale yellow. His feet were black.

The crowd sucked in its breath. Klara smiled fully. Katherine, who'd been peeking through the window, ran from the house. "Oh, my goodness!" she cried. "Is he real?"

The bird, as if offended by such a question and happy to be free of the cloth and its implications, spread his wings so wide that their tips poked out of either side of the cage and shook them. The crowd jumped back, but Klara reached up again and touched one wing. The bird cocked its head and looked at her. It had black markings around its eyes.

"Hello," it said.

Klara did not respond but smiled again. She stepped closer to the cage.

"He talks, too," BenJo explained.

The townspeople had never seen a talking bird.

"What else does it say?" someone yelled.

"Where did you get him?" someone else called.

"We could get good money for a talking bird."

Klara looked at BenJo.

"I figure," he said quietly, "until you're ready to open up and tell us all what's on your mind, the bird can do some talking for you. But don't you worry none about talking, Mrs. Bozic. You do the Mrs. Bozic thing." He paused. "Now I best get on out of here before that husband of yours loses his good feeling and comes back looking for me. Keep in mind, we're all praying for you and your boys. Just remember, they never leave your heart."

Klara nodded and bowed her head.

No one knew where the bird picked up its language skills, whether Klara whispered words to it when no one was listening or whether it was just another mysterious member of a troupe that traveled to the ends of the earth and back, collecting odd bits of knowledge, colorful toys, fearless acrobats, and thick sumptuous odors no one could put a finger on. Either way, it proved to be a linguistic virtuoso, and before evening fell, the bird was speaking at a rate and in a style matched only by the swiftest and most practiced orators. Come dark, Klara decided for the first time since Ivo's death to climb the stairs to sleep in her own bed. She rose from her worn place on the straight-backed chair and covered the birdcage in the living room with the blue silk cloth. When she walked away, toward the stairs, the bird flew into a frenzy, shaking its wings and hollering something awful.

"Don't go! Don't go!" it hollered again and again, presumably in four or five languages though Klara recognized only two—Croatian and English. It hollered and shouted until Drago, three hours from his next shift, yelled down the stairs to shut that goddamn bird up or he'd skin it and fry it for breakfast. So Klara removed the silk cloth, folded it neatly on the dining table, opened the cage, and allowed the now quiet bird to hop onto her shoulder. Awed by its size, she expected to feel off balance with its weight unevenly distributed on one shoulder, but instead it felt just fine, comfortable even. Its feet gripped her cotton nightrobe, and just like that, the bird rode upstairs with her, nibbling her earlobe as they went. That night, and for many nights after, the bird kept watch over Klara from the bedpost, perched like a sentry, alert and ready.

The next morning, much to Katherine and Drago's surprise, Klara decided that if the carnival had such offerings as talking birds, she should see for herself what other goods were there for the taking. So twenty-five days after she stopped speaking, still silent but active now, Klara dressed in the mourning skirt and blouse she seemed to have been wearing for years and then walked out the door. Though she had been on an emotional hiatus for the last twenty-four days, this was the first time in over thirty years she had consciously refused to cook Drago his breakfast or make his lunch. As she walked out the door, Drago moved as if to grab her and pull her back, but Katherine stepped between them and held him off.

With the bird perched on her shoulder, Klara made her way to the carnival grounds set up in an untilled field on the other side of town. It was a warm day with a thick cloud of pale yellow smog. The wind roared as she walked, and quiet from the inside out, she listened to the grind and slip of cinders and gravel under the shiny worn soles of her shoes. She likened it to a type of music she had heard as a girl back home in Croatia, though in truth it was nothing like that at all. She pushed past the blend of mill noise and listened to the walnuts disengage from the limbs of great trees and drop to the ground with delicate intent. She believed she heard color itself: the green of snap beans like a blouse being slung through a basin of boiling water during the wash; the purple smudge of blackberries like the soft press of a hand to a ball of dough; the red of a cardinal's wing like the easy thump necessary when shaking roots free of precious earth. And other sounds: the gray of the buckeye tree stretching itself in growth like the patter of slow rain on the rooftop; the movement of her own eyeballs turning in their sockets similar to the rusty creak a jar lid makes as it is twisted into place. As she walked along the rutted, sloppy road, she listened to all this and more, sounds she'd never been able to distinguish from those of the mill. Her feet lifting bits of mud. Pebbles kicked clear by the toes of her shoes. She passed Mrs. Livingstone, who nodded, said hello, and paused as if to chat. But Klara kept her eyes averted and walked by as if she hadn't seen her at all. On the railroad track, slick with rain, she slipped and fell to her knees. Though Mr. Ragoni raced to her side, she caught herself and shook off his hand. Her palms were bloody with bits of rock and cinder embedded in the broken skin, and the front of her skirt was soiled, but throughout the turmoil the bird never left her shoulder. It held on without so much as an extra pinch, patient until she had righted herself. She looked down without feeling the sting and wiped her hands on the folds of her skirt. In the days since Ivo's death, her hair had turned gray and gotten tangled into lumpy knots. As she passed the salon where she'd gotten her hair bleached so many years before, Lucy rose from the rocking chair, moved to the edge of the porch, and called, "Miss Klara, come on in here. Let me fix you up good. Straighten up them locks. Come on. Got a hot pot of coffee brewing on the stove." She stood with her hands on her ever-widening hips and shook her head when Klara walked past without so much as a smile.

Then Klara took the back way, one she never would have taken before the deaths of her two sons, just a path tucked behind the rows of leaning houses that skirted the woods like a hem. Because fewer people traveled this path, she could walk without hearing voices clanging like broken bells. On the main road, everyone had something to offer as they passed: *I'm so sorry, Mrs. Bozic. God is watching. We're praying for you.* All that clang-clanging was getting in the way. She needed silence, or as close to it as she could get. After all, this was the first time in her life that all thoughts to which she'd never had words shone shiny and bright, and she wanted them as clear as the crystal vase in the center of Mrs. Stoughton's dining table.

Once it was quiet, there they were, all shrouded thoughts unveiled. *I am unhappy. I despise my husband. I settled in ways I'd never planned. I am not honest. All my life I've shared in lies. I lied to my children, told them this world was good and kind despite their father's cruelty.*

From time to time, between thoughts, the bird leaned in and nibbled Klara's ear, and she, in turn, reached up and scratched its chest or rounded head.

Halfway to the carnival, she coughed. Her mouth was dry, parched, and her tongue was swollen where she'd bitten it when she tumbled. It throbbed and ached but she walked on, satiating her thirst with the promise of a long sip of water from the well at the base of the steepest hill when she returned.

The carnival met Klara's ears before her eyes, sounds from around the bend, through a copse of oaks—a medley of delighted notes, the whicker of a horse, a long, thin whistle. The cacophony lifted her in ways similar to those the butterflies had so many years before, and a fluttering of excitement blended with a calm, easy warmth. Coming around the bend, she saw three tents, once bright orange, now speckled like the rest of her world to a dull sooty gray. She wondered for a moment if the mill would always smother everything in its path, if it would ever sit back on its mammoth haunches and rest, but she knew in her heart that such imaginings were futile and believed as others did that the mills had come before the land and the people, and that in the end, they would outlast them all.

The day was still young, and few people had arrived, but Klara continued on until she reached the first tent where a man not more than three feet tall, no taller than BenJo bent at the waist, stood brushing a small pony. He turned as she passed, smiled. But Klara walked by him as she had so many others, knowing that she was looking for something specific, though she didn't know what. The flap of the second tent was tied open, and a full smell of horse manure rushed at her; when she peeked in, she saw four clowns sitting around a low table, their faces bright but sad. She went on. Finally, just inside the third tent, she saw the birdman. He was hefty, boxy, solid, with the sleeves of his coarse blue shirt rolled to the elbows, exposing neatly muscled forearms and the tattoo of a lizard on the outside of his left wrist. His skin was the color of olives, somewhere between brown and a rich earthy green. His hair was long, pulled back with a leather strap, and he smelled like an ancient spice.

Until now, Klara had slept with only one man. One when there were so many to choose from. When there were so many willing. After all, she was probably the only woman in Thirsty who hadn't bedded the button man at least once.

How many times she had stood at the well listening to others talk about that place between his legs, so full and satisfying, especially for a short man, as if they had many with which they could compare. Whenever he passed the house, waving a hand to Klara, hoping for business, she stared and wondered, but never once did she invite him for a cup of coffee or a slice of hot bread. She always let him pass.

Now she faced the birdman with the claws of his beautiful green and blue bird gripping her shoulder. He didn't smile or ask her to speak. He didn't offer prayers or an explanation for God's plan. He simply recognized the longing in her eyes and led her gently by the elbow to a small cot in a tent far away from the hubbub. The bird moved naturally to its old, wooden perch while the birdman peeled off Klara's clothes layer by layer. Then his own. When they were naked, he lay on his back on the cot, and she mounted him.

"Thank you," she whispered, not surprised at all to hear her own voice.

Later that day when Klara gathered herself and left the tent, the carnival buzzed with activity. Children raced from spectacle to spectacle, carrying sticks thick with cotton candy, and barkers called out their wares. Klara moved through the crowd quietly, careful not to touch the elephant as it trod past, enjoying the scent of the birdman on her hands and neck and between her legs. She walked home the way she'd come, the bird perched on her shoulder as it would be until her death many years from that day, and at the base of the steepest hill, she kept her promise to herself and stopped at the well for a long draught of water.

At Ivo's funeral, Klara walked hand in hand with Beatrude Wonder. Two women, one white and one black, married in sorrow, led the funeral procession through Thirsty to Ivo's grave. Behind them moved Katherine and Sky, heads bowed in prayer and fret, and behind them, confused by their required attendance at yet another funeral, Tunia and Lizzy. BenJo and many of the men who had watched Klara with curiosity that night in the balcony of the theater made a large dark clot in the road, matching their pace to that of those who led them. Neighbors and friends followed as well, enticed not only by their obligation to certify Ivo's passing, but also by their curiosity about the uninvited attendees, the group of Negroes, *niggers* they whispered, who appeared like a thundercloud in the Bozic yard early that morning before even the wagon showed up. Old Man Rupert walked on the outskirts of the party, holding his hat over his heart. Drago—ashamed of his wife's choice of company and angry at her continued silence and withdrawal from wifely duties—walked somewhere near the tail of the procession. He shuffled his feet and moved two steps sideways for each step he took forward, as if he might be drunk or somnambulant. For the first time in Thirsty's memory, his shoulders slumped and his back was bowed.

The mule-drawn wagon carrying Ivo's hollowed-out shell was driven by one of Kentucky Wonder's brothers, and every few feet, the man nearly as large as Kentucky Wonder himself drew in the reins and pulled the mules to a halt so that Beatrude and her women friends could sing Ivo's body to the grave and his soul to heaven. They wailed and hollered, shook and shied, their words and rhythm reaching over the mountains and down into the valleys so that nearly everyone who resided in the meeting of the three rivers felt their anguish and their love. And though Klara moved in time with their music, closing her eyes and shaking her head, she did not utter a sound, just gripped Beatrude's hand and let the music flow through her. At those moments when Beatrude felt Klara slipping away, out of her grip and into the dry earth, she squeezed her hand, pulled her up, leaned to her ear, and whispered, "God is great."

Klara was so close to death herself, so near to giving up, she saw the mill bobbing in the distance as if the river, the great Monongahela, had risen over its banks and carried it to sea.

Despite Drago's grumbling disappointment, Klara had rejected the suggestion of a military burial. When pressed, she had vetoed all accoutrements of such, except for the draping of an American flag over the casket. A handful of soldiers who had served with Ivo and been sent home after injuries—those who might have witnessed his final moments, who might have been able to share a story or two of Ivo's bravery in the field—were relegated to the end of the procession. They were denied any access to Klara. But despite their confusion over this particular mother's sadness and because they were accustomed to following orders, they took their place behind Drago and marched accordingly in full dress uniform despite the heat of the Indian summer. Someday, many years down the road, Klara would wonder what those soldiers might have said about her boy, but by then it would be too late.

Each night after Ivo's burial, the devil snuck into Klara's dreams. He moved in with a quiet hum, and she heard him there, in her restless sleep, knocking like any good neighbor might, waiting for her to open the door to his havoc. Since the deaths of her boys, she'd felt as if she'd been climbing one of those steep Thirsty hills, not daring to look back to see how far she'd come and too frightened to look up to see how far she had to go. In life and dreams, she was growing weary. In her belly she wanted to resist the devil's summons, but he offered patience as his calling card, and eventually she gave in.

In the dream, she always killed Drago first, waited until the moon took pity on the pathetic little house and rose high and bright in the window. She always waited until Drago was sprawled on his back, snoring, rattling the house, the rafters, the windowpanes, the bird on the bedpost, his snores blending with the rumble of the mill, shaking Klara so deep, she could not lie still a moment longer. She would crawl from the bed, cross the floor on hands and knees, then stand and move through the dark in her long white nightgown, barefoot, careful not to tread on the swatches of moonlight carved into the floorboards. In the kitchen, after choosing the blade the rag man had sharpened that very morning, a thick-bladed butcher's knife that could make easy work of a lamb shank or a side of beef, she would go back the way she had come, through the living room, up the staircase, along the short hallway, and into the bedroom she shared with her husband. At this moment she always felt as if she'd reached the peak of that Thirsty hill and even passed on to the other side, the downward slope, where breath returned and the heart slowed. Despite the solid wall that separated them, she would see Sky, asleep in the room next door, and she would watch as her only daughter half woke to a small noise, a bump or rattle, but instead of waking to stop her, to stop the devil's work, Sky would simply bury her face in the pillow and pull the quilt over her head.

Klara never took any time at all to study her husband, to make sure this was the path she wanted to take. She just leaned over him, so close that had he woken he could have kissed her, then slid the blade into place, pulled it across his throat, and buried it so deep that in the end his head was left hanging by just a few threads of flesh. In the dream she imagined that folks would say it wasn't possible that she acted alone, that no woman alive possessed enough strength to render such damage, but Klara would say, and Katherine would agree, that these folks, like many in the world, underestimated most things about women. Drago always flinched at the first cut, raised his hands halfway to his throat, and then dropped them, as if his brain could no longer comply. And while he lay there, watching his wife through open slits of eye, her hair disheveled and loose about her shoulders, he always remembered the wish he'd made then forgotten when Jake fireballed from the third-story tar roof so many years before. He'd wished to be gone from this place and realized now that this one wish had finally come true.

Midway through her work, Klara's blade always pulled as if slicing through a cut of tough meat, hitting a trail of gristle, spine, and while her hands, now sleek and red with blood, nearly slipped off the handle, she never let go, just gripped tighter, bent her knees into the effort, and pulled. And then Drago, resigned to his destiny, would shake all over, limbs flopping against the mattress, head bobbing. And after she'd pulled the blade clean through, Klara never thought to straighten the mess, never even waited for Drago's convulsions stop, just moved into Sky's room to continue her work.

Her daughter was easy, the peach-white throat flushed with freckles, still so thin and girl-like, no gristle at all to drag the blade. But the girls were not so easy, and before she cut Lizzy, she had to remind herself that loving them dead would always be easier than loving them alive and waiting for them to die. In the midst of the cutting, Tunia always woke into that twilight place of sleep for just a moment, a flutter of thin-blue lids that almost stopped Klara but didn't. She heard the devil knocking.

By morning, the four bodies, emptied of fluid and life, would be stiff and raw with stench that cut through the walls, drawing the townspeople close enough to wonder what had happened behind that door, behind those windows, why there wasn't smoke drifting from the chimney, and why Sky or Lizzy hadn't been seen at the well. So much blood would have emptied onto the floor, seeped into the floorboards, then dripped through the ceiling into the rooms below, leaving pools of dark stain on the finely sanded grain of the kitchen table and soaking into the thin cushion of the chair, that by the time Katherine entered, climbed the stairs, and peered into the first room and by the time Klara looked up from her place next to Drago in the bed and said, "Couldn't wait for God is Great to take them one by one," there was nothing to do but forgive.

Each morning when Klara woke from this dream, she was covered in sweat that at first she took to be blood. Her heart throbbed with the knowing as she raced from her room to Sky's, from Sky's to the girls'. Once satisfied that it was still just a dream, she settled at the window, the bird perched on her shoulder, and waited for the devil to come.

1919

The first day of spring cracked open like a freshly laid egg. It was full and round and warm, bright yellow and so full of promise that even the worms deep in the ground sensed that winter had once again been exiled from Thirsty and that the frigid winds and icy snowfalls that had sent them burrowing months before had taken to other lands. As the sun warmed the earth, the worms began their annual pilgrimage to the surface, gnawing their way through dirt and leaves, dog shit, rotten fruit, and last year's peelings of carrot and potato and onion. The moment from winter to spring was one of those dramatic transformations when in the small space of twenty-four hours what was once brown turned green, what was once closed, opened. Vines threaded along fence posts, withered and pale, now pulsed with life, like hot green veins. Buds on oaks, sugar maples, and cherry trees popped and unfolded like small hands. Snowdrops and crocuses and daffodils sprang from the ground, handfuls of delight under trees, beside outhouses, and below kitchen windows. Robins, blue jays, and cardinals squawked and squabbled. The change was profound, and when Klara woke to the sun tapping on the window, she climbed from bed, opened the sash, and let the balmy breeze blow in, bringing the curtains to a full curtsy. Inspired, she stirred up a batch of breakfast muffins that with a slab of butter surely would melt away any lingering memory of winter's icy grip and sent Sky and the girls into the garden to knead the dirt and get it ready for planting.

"Not so different from the year Sky was born," Katherine said to Klara as they made their way to the well. And although Klara nodded, neither looked into the tangle of milkweed where a bloom of iridescent blue butterflies slowly flapped their fragile wings, fresh from their chrysalides.

But perhaps the greatest transformation occurred high on the hill at Old Man Rupert's house, where so much change had occurred already. Like the rest of Thirsty, the old man woke to the breeze and the sun and a sense of marvel, but instead of settling himself comfortably in its embrace, easing onto the porch for a long day of watching, he thought of the Bozic women and of Drago and of darkness. At the end of his thoughts, he decided he could no longer wait to make his offer. *It's time*, he said to himself as he rose from his bed and saluted the sun that pierced the wall opposite his window. *Today is the day*. He washed, ate, placed his cap on his head and shoes on his feet, and then marched down the hill in the direction of the Bozic house, carrying his question, his invitation, his offer, over one shoulder like most men carry an axe or a hoe, the weighty head of it behind him. Though he hadn't visited St. Jude's in two decades' time, and though age and wisdom had long ago taught him that marriage was not his own destiny, Old Man Rupert was dressed as if he were heading to Sunday Mass or a cousin's wedding. His shirt was pressed, without holes or stains; his pants were creased; and his fancy buckle shoes— still stiff with the buying—creaked with each step he took and gleamed in the morning sunlight.

As he walked, he reflected that enough time had passed between then and now, between the boys' deaths and this first day of spring, between the fire at the theater and Klara's shorn hair and this new day, between Sky's birth and too many hours Klara had spent on the floor at the mercy of Drago's boot. Enough time, he calculated, for Klara's sadness to settle into rage, and if she weren't taken far from that husband of hers, whose sympathy for his wife's losses was possibly extinct, rage would soon move to action. After all the years he'd spent chewing on his own anger, Old Man Rupert knew it stayed quiet for only so long. Soon enough it wanted to get out, breathe, punch, battle, and he couldn't let that happen to Klara, not when he had a way of changing it.

Just before making the final turn toward Klara's house, he stooped and picked a handful of purple buds. He tied them in a bouquet with a length of grass, then wiped the dust and soot from his shoes, straightened his back, and walked on. Before he knew it, Old Man Rupert was standing on Klara's porch, the flowers just beginning to droop in the morning's warmth. Since he was too old for nerves, he bowed his head and knocked.

Just inside, Klara sat at the kitchen table spooning sorrow and sugar into muffin tins. The batter moved nicely off her spoon, and the small task allowed her the space and time she needed to recover from her dream. She sat, reliving it as she did each morning until she had the faces of her loved ones settled safe and smiling. Drago she always left lying in the bed, dead and stiff. When she heard the knock, she stretched her neck to judge the visitor. From her chair, she saw Old Man Rupert standing at the door holding the flowers, and she thought for a moment that someone else had passed on, that he was there to share news of another friend gone by. She clutched her chest.

Ready and resigned, she stood, picked up a tea towel, wiped her hands, and walked down the hallway. By the time she reached the door, Old Man Rupert was smiling in a quiet way, and her fear left her.

"Well, bless the Lord," she said, "at least you're not wearing the smile of death."

"No, ma'am," Old Man Rupert said. "Nothing but goodness today."

From Klara's shoulder, the bird announced Old Man Rupert, as he was apt to do whenever visitors arrived. "Old Man Rupert," he squawked, tugging Klara's ear as if she hadn't noticed. "Old Man Rupert."

Klara opened the door and stepped onto the porch. In the spring air, it seemed more appropriate to step out than to invite the old man in.

"Good morning, Mr. Rupert," she said.

"Good morning, Mrs. Bozic," he said.

"Fine day," she said.

"Indeed it is," he answered. Old Man Rupert had lived most of his long life alone, and though there had been times when he'd wondered why God had even kept him around, now, feeling blisters blossoming on his heels, he knew God had a strong purpose in that choice.

The two might have continued with the pleasantries for quite some time had Sky and the girls not come around the house to settle on the stoop and eavesdrop.

"What can I do for you so early in the morning?" Klara asked.

"It's not what you can do for me," Old Man Rupert replied, handing her the small bouquet of flowers. "No, you and the girls have done much for me over the years, taking me in as a friend when very few thought that a good decision." He took his hat off and held it at his belt buckle in both hands. He bowed his head. "Now it's what I would like to do for you."

Klara looked at Sky and felt something strange and hopeful roar through her.

"You see, Mrs. Bozic," Old Man Rupert began, "you're familiar with the fact that I've remade the house my great-grandfather built. You've visited and seen the results of my toil."

"I am indeed aware of the changes on your hill, and the house is more than lovely. You've done your duty to your great-grandfather."

"Well, perhaps, but I didn't do it out of duty. In fact, Mrs. Bozic, I didn't do it for my father or my grandfather or my great-grandfather. Of course, I'm sure they're happy looking down from heaven, especially after the mess I made of things early on in life, but still, I didn't do it for them."

"No?"

"No, ma'am." Old Man Rupert took a deep breath. "I did it for you and for Sky and for the girls."

No one said anything for a long moment. Klara didn't know what the old man was talking about; she thought perhaps he'd taken to the bottle once again.

"Excuse me," she said. "I don't understand."

Old Man Rupert didn't quite know how to explain his reasoning to Klara and her girls without looking like a fool or a crazy man. Over the years he'd practiced telling them about the tiny click he'd heard in his head and felt in his heart on the night of Sky's birth, how he had looked at the place between Klara's legs where Sky lay, like a bundle of potatoes or a warm loaf of bread, her limbs reaching and stretching, her tiny nose crinkled and blue. He'd practiced telling them about the tiny click that changed everything, how until that moment the world had always seemed slightly out of focus, but how afterward it was as clear as creek water. In that moment, he had become a different man. Some time later, a sober man. And eventually, a kind man.

"Mrs. Bozic, I built the house up for you," he said. "I want you and Sky and the girls to leave this house," and he waved his hand, "to leave behind Drago and any pain you've got. I want you to spend the rest of your lives peaceful and happy on the hill, Rupert's hill, in my house that will be your house."

Klara was so accustomed to visitors bearing bad news she didn't know what to make of Old Man Rupert and his offer. Her knees trembled, and the blood rushed from her face, leaving her as white as a freshly laundered sheet. Old Man Rupert grasped her elbow and eased her into a chair.

"Now though I don't see any sense in putting off a decision, I can give you a few days to get used to the idea if you like," he said.

Klara nodded, but Sky, thankful for the goodness God was offering, stood, climbed the stairs, and took Old Man Rupert's hand. She smiled. "Mr. Rupert," Sky said, "my mother would never accept such generosity on her own. If she had been here alone this morning, she would likely have sent you packing. If you give her a few days' thinking time, she'll discover too many reasons to say no and we'll be sitting with the list until doomsday. Right now she thinks she'd rather live out her days in suffering, but I have greater hopes for her. And for my girls. We don't need time for further discussion or for getting used to the idea. We accept your offer."

Klara looked up. For a moment she wanted to intercede and tell Mr. Rupert that Sky was insolent and disrespectful, stepping in like that and taking over. She was tempted to stand, face Sky, and slap her in the face good for such behavior. But then she heard a familiar sound—the drumfire of beating wings—and a blizzard of butterflies rounded the house. Fat reds. Slender greens. Shiny blues. Brilliant yellows. The butterflies dropped low and engulfed the group on the porch, swallowed them into a fizzy, sizzling frenzy, then flew off toward Tiny's property. When it was all over, Klara tossed back her head and laughed. Then she looked from her daughter to Old Man Rupert. This kind old man was offering what she'd dreamed of since setting sail from Croatia. A beautiful home on a beautiful plot of land with flowers and vegetables and fruits growing all around. He was offering safety and peace. That wasn't something to say no to, was it? That was God's word.

Though deciding to leave Drago after all these years wasn't easy—she worried over him despite things—, she knew that it was the right thing, that it would be better than living out her devil dream one night when sadness overflowed. Perhaps it was because she had somewhere to go or perhaps because she had nowhere else to go that she nodded again without further consideration.

"Yes, Mr. Rupert," she said, "we accept."

When word reached Drago down at the mill, he swelled up with anger faster than a hungry tick on a hound's rump, but Klara didn't care. To her, the world felt huge and lovely.

Old Man Rupert's house rose up like a great blue wave on the horizon. As Klara climbed the hill, keeping the smokestacks at her back, following the mule and wagon that carried the last of her belongings, she remembered the large, white sea birds she had watched during the journey from Croatia to America. Gulls, the shipmen had called them. Seagulls. They had made a sound unlike that of any bird she had ever heard, before or since, and they scavenged for scraps like hungry men. Seeing the house like that reminded her of that journey, and she wondered how it could have ended here.

All those years in Drago's house, and it had taken only three days to pack their belongings. She and Sky and the girls left almost everything behind, taking nothing more than their clothes and a few personal items. Sky had the dress she married Maxwell in, which she believed would always remind her what path not to take through life. Lizzy and Tunia brought along some books, a few games, and some favorite old dolls. Klara debated whether to take the carvings Drago had given her back in Croatia at the beginning of their time together. She still thought them beautiful, but the sentiment with which they had been given had faded long ago. In the end, she left them behind. Of course, Drago protested his wife's departure, but for the first time in forever, he did not lift a hand against her. Perhaps Jake's spirit moved into the house and set a hand on Drago's heart, letting him know he had no more rights to Klara, or perhaps it was simply the threat of Kentucky Wonder's mammoth brothers standing guard on the stoop.

On that first night in the new home, the women gathered together on the porch. Katherine climbed the hill for company as she would on most evenings until she sold her house a few years down the road and moved into a small room on the third floor. Beatrude Wonder combed Tunia's hair and sang a funny song about turtles. They drank tea, gossiped about Stella Jevic's new hairdo, and watched the flames rise from the smokestacks in the valley below. The warm spring wind had made itself comfortable in Thirsty, and night settled in around the women like a well-worn blanket. It was quieter here and fearless.

Earlier, Old Man Rupert had moved into the small visitor's cabin in the back that he'd fixed up during the past months, readying for the arrival of the Bozic women. "An old man doesn't need much," he told them, "just a bed and a soft chair and a reading lamp." His happiness he carried with him. Within a few weeks, he began to join them for most meals, always leaving his hat on the rack in the hallway beforehand and always dressing the table with a vase of fresh flowers. Every night before going to sleep, Klara said her prayers and then looked out the window at the warm glow of Mr. Rupert's cabin after dark. God's word, she said right before climbing into bed. God's word.